T0297435

A PLUME BOOK

THE LONG ROAD

SPARKPIX

G. MICHAEL HOPF is the bestselling author of *The End: A Post-apocalyptic Novel*. He spent two decades living a life of adventure before settling down to pursue his passion for writing. He is a former combat veteran of the U.S. Marine Corps and former bodyguard. He lives with his family in San Diego, California.

G. MICHAEL HOPF

THE
LONG ROAD

A Postapocalyptic Novel

• • •

BOOK 2 OF THE NEW WORLD SERIES

A PLUME BOOK

PLUME
Published by the Penguin Group
Penguin Group (USA) LLC
375 Hudson Street
New York, New York 10014

USA | Canada | UK | Ireland | Australia
New Zealand | India | South Africa | China
penguin.com
A Penguin Random House Company

First published by Plume, a member of Penguin Group (USA) LLC, 2013
Previously published in digital and print formats by the author.

℗ REGISTERED TRADEMARK—MARCA REGISTRADA

LIBRARY OF CONGRESS CATALOGING-IN-PUBLICATION DATA IS AVAILABLE
ISBN 978-0-14-218150-8

Set in Minion Pro
Designed by Eve Kirch

To my daughters

Acknowledgments

The friend in my adversity I shall always cherish most. I can better trust those who helped to relieve the gloom of my dark hours than those who are so ready to enjoy with me the sunshine of my prosperity.

—Ulysses S. Grant

In my books, I use quotes from people who are wiser and more knowledgeable than I am. Sometimes when I'm at a loss for words, my feelings can be best represented by a simple quote.

We all have had times in our lives when things are bad or things just don't seem to work out. It's called the "Human Condition." It is in those times of struggle that you discover who you are and who are your true friends. I believe that all challenges in life can be lessons. I for one have learned many lessons. As my dear father would say, "They build character."

I want to acknowledge two special people who came to my family's aid when we needed someone.

Thank you, Rock and Misty.

THE LONG ROAD

OCTOBER 15, 2066

· · ·

Olympia, Washington, Republic of Cascadia

aley rubbed her thumb repeatedly across the smooth surface of the compass. Touching it soothed her. She needed it after having just spent almost an hour talking about her parents and life in San Diego after the lights went out. The compass brought her such comfort and gave her a connection to her now-distant family.

She knew John was not a fool and had picked up on her not answering his direct question about Hunter earlier. She was hesitant to go back into the living room; she didn't want to face the question, she didn't want to have to relive that time on the road. Even though she'd told him she wanted to talk about it, she now regretted her decision. The road to Idaho had been tough and had become one of those moments her father told her occurs in a life where your course changes.

Deciding she had stalled long enough, she put the compass back in the box on the shelf and walked into the hallway. She could hear John and the camera crew laughing. Their laughter echoed off of the bare wood floors and the walls of the sparsely furnished home. She thought that these men knew nothing of true hardship. To her, their laughter displayed an innocence and ignorance of years before. She didn't blame them; it wasn't their fault when they were born. However, she did hold a grudge in some ways against those many who now enjoyed the fruits of her and her family's labor but disregarded the cost.

The Great Civil War was not unlike many civil wars in history. It was brutal and hard. It did have one distinction that separated it from those before it: The rules that governed war were gone. The divisions that had been fostered over the most recent generations in America became more pronounced and deadly. Once the last bits of fabric that had held the country together vanished in that instant fifty-two years ago, it took only days for Americans to rip and tear at other Americans.

Haley was only five years old when it happened; she never got to enjoy the typical twentieth-century invention of a child's life. Gone were the birthday parties with abundant cakes and ice cream. Gone were the Christmases with dozens of beautifully wrapped toys. Gone was the innocence. She was forced to grow up quickly and act like an adult. Even though her father did all he could to protect her from the horrors while they were living at Rancho Valentino, he could not shield her from the depravity of life once they made their way to Idaho.

She walked into the living room and just stood there looking at the men. None of them noticed her; they were absorbed in the typical conversations that young single men have.

After clearing her throat loudly, she said, "I'm ready if you are."

"Great!" John said, jumping up. He was surprised to see her. He felt a bit foolish, as he hadn't known how long she had been there, and the topic the men had been enjoying was not entirely appropriate.

Haley walked back to her chair and sat down. She smoothed out the creases in her skirt and sat pensively waiting.

John shuffled around and quickly grabbed the pad he had been taking notes on. Taking the seat across from her, he said, "Sorry, one second."

"Take your time," Haley responded.

"I'd like to start with the trip to Idaho. From the sounds of it, a lot happened on the way there, and I think that's a good starting point."

"Very well," Haley answered. She clasped her hands tightly to keep them from nervously fiddling with her skirt or sleeve.

"There is one item I'd like to ask before, though."

"Go ahead."

"Before today I never knew you had a brother. I apologize if I didn't do my research, but like your father and mother, you have been very reserved in sharing details of your past life," John stated, twirling his pen.

"The thing is, my brother is all around us. How many places in Olympia are named Hunter?" Haley asked.

After pausing to think, John blurted out, "You're right; I never thought anything about it before. So what happened to him, your brother?"

"My brother was not unlike my father in his passion to protect his family. He took it quite seriously." Haley stopped talking and looked down. The pitch of her voice changed. She unclasped her hands and again started to pat down the creases in her skirt.

John, noticing her discomfort, chose to move on to something else. "Haley, if you want, let's talk about the trip to Idaho."

"He was a good boy," Haley said just above a whisper. She was still looking down, fidgeting with her clothes.

"What's that?" John asked, leaning in toward Haley.

"Nothing, sorry, nothing," she said loudly, looking up.

"Okay, so let's begin with the trip to Idaho."

"Sure, let's do that. So as to not bore you, let's start on our third day into the drive. That day revisits me in my thoughts often. Let's begin there."

JANUARY 8, 2014

· · ·

We must travel in the direction of our fear.

—John Berryman

Barstow, California

"Run, Haley, run!" Gordon screamed.

Haley stood frozen in fear. She had never seen a person burn to death before, and now she was watching flames dance off of Candace Pomeroy's back as she slowly crawled away from her car.

"Hunter, grab your sister and run over there!" Gordon yelled out, pointing to a dropoff in the road that led to a culvert large enough only to provide protection for the kids.

Hunter ran over to Haley and grabbed her with force, causing her to drop the small teddy bear she held.

"No, my bear!" she yelled out.

"No, Haley, we gotta run!" Hunter screamed.

Gunfire was raining down on the vehicles from a few covered positions up the road. There wasn't much cover for Gordon and his convoy. To either side of the road lay flat, open desert dotted with creosote plants. Even their vehicles didn't provide the protection needed, as was the case with the Pomeroys' car. The initial rain of bullets had hit their fuel tank just right, causing their car to explode into a ball of flames.

Hunter pulled Haley to the small culvert. Gordon and Nelson had hidden behind Gordon's truck. The banging of bullets rattled the truck and their ears. Gordon attempted to look over the truck but was met by a hail of gunfire.

"Fuck!" he screamed in frustration. He looked for Samantha but didn't see her.

"What do we do, Gordo?" Nelson asked. Each bullet that struck the truck caused him to flinch.

The Pomeroys' burning car was draping them in thick black smoke. Sensing an advantage, Gordon ran for the jeep. Holloway had been driving it but was nowhere to be seen. He jumped in the back and grabbed the handles of the .50-caliber machine gun mounted there. Not wasting any more time, he pressed the butterfly trigger and started to fire on the positions the gunfire was coming from. Dirt and debris were flying in the air as the .50 did its work. He transitioned from one position to the next. He remembered seeing three areas from which they were taking fire. Gordon was in a rage as he screamed out while firing the heavy gun. It took only moments on each position to destroy whomever had ambushed them, but he kept firing until the gun ran out of ammunition. Looking over the top of the smoking barrel, Gordon could not see anyone up ahead, but he needed to be sure. He jumped into the driver's seat and put the jeep in gear. As he began to pull away, Holloway came running toward him.

"Where the fuck were you?" Gordon asked, clearly angered.

"I went to my family and made sure they were okay," Holloway answered directly, not intimidated by Gordon's gruffness.

"Jump in, we need to make sure these fuckers are dead," Gordon said.

Holloway jumped in, and both men proceeded cautiously. When they came upon the first position, Holloway jumped out and ran over to discover two dead men; both had been ripped apart by the machine gun. He continued on by foot and discovered a similar scene at the second, but at the third one a man was alive.

"We've got a live one here!" Holloway yelled.

Gordon drove the jeep over to Holloway's position and got out. He stepped over to the wounded man, pulled his handgun out, and put it to the wounded man's head.

"Are there any more of you?"

The man didn't respond but coughed up blood.

"Answer me, you piece of shit!" Gordon screamed, pressing the barrel against the man's sweaty forehead.

Gordon began to slowly squeeze the trigger but stopped when screaming rang out from behind him. He stood and looked; the screams gave way to gunfire. He could tell people were moving, but the dark smoke was making it impossible to see what was really happening. He took a step, then remembered the wounded man. He turned, took aim, and shot the man.

• • •

"I'm scared. Where's Mommy? Where's Daddy?" Haley cried.

Not answering his little sister, Hunter could see a few men marching toward them and the convoy from the eastern desert.

Haley began to cry loudly.

"Ssshh! Haley, be quiet!" Hunter commanded.

"I can't, I can't, I'm scared!" Haley whimpered, her body trembling uncontrollably.

"Mommy and Daddy will come soon, I promise."

"What if they're dead, what if Mommy and Daddy are dead?"

"Haley, you have to be quiet."

More gunfire rang out from the men approaching. Haley screamed.

Hunter reached over and put his hand on top of her mouth. She attempted to pull away, but he forced his hand with pressure equal to her resistance. "Stop, just stop!" Hunter demanded.

Looking into her brother's eyes, she calmed down, but tears were still flowing and she was having a hard time controlling her breathing.

He could no longer see the men in the distance, but he could hear gunfire coming from them and from the convoy. He wanted to know where the men were, so he pulled away from Haley and started to crawl toward the entrance of the culvert.

"No, stop, where are you going?" Haley cried out.

"I'm checking to see where those guys went."

"Stop, don't leave me."

"I'm just going to poke my head out."

Haley began to cry loudly, making Hunter stop and go back to her. He held her close and told her things would be okay. Reaching into his pocket, he pulled out a silver compass and gave it to her.

"Here, take this. Dad gave it to me. He said it would keep me safe, and if I give it to you, it will keep you safe."

Taking the compass in her trembling hands, she looked up at her brother.

He smiled and said, "I'll be right back." Hunter crawled away to the opening of the culvert and peered out. He looked left and then right. Seeing one of the men not two feet away, he attempted to duck back inside, but the man grabbed him and pulled him out. Hunter kicked, but he wasn't a match for the man, who punched him once in the face, knocking him out.

Haley began to scream, knowing that something bad had happened to her brother.

The man peered into the culvert and said, "Come here, little girl."

USS *Makin Island* off the coast of Southern California

Sebastian's patience was at its breaking point. As each day passed without notice of his departure from the cold gray walls of his cell, he grew more agitated and restless. Knowing that his brother's house was only twenty miles away made the wait worse. After having traveled thousands of miles and enduring hardships, not to be able to just leave was unbearable. Since Gunny had taken him topside three days before, he hadn't seen the light of day. His treatment was fair, but this now was feeling like torture. One advantage the wait gave him was the ability to establish a plan. Gunny had allowed him to have a map, paper, and a pencil. He mapped several routes and identified waypoints. Knowing that traveling the highways could be bad, he plotted surface streets and natural trails to lead him to Carmel Valley.

It had been six weeks since the attacks, and the last intelligence he had on San Diego was days old. In a nutshell, the city had collapsed into chaos. The Villista Army was now occupying large parts of the city. Some Marine squads who had gone ashore to gather family had encountered them. Barone had no intention of securing San Diego but at the same time was not about to allow an organized mob to harass his Marines. He had attacked many of the Villista strongholds and encampments, destroying resources and killing many of their people. Sebastian supported this approach and appreciated anything Barone did that would increase his chances for survival.

The welcome sound of keys unlocking his door echoed off the walls of cell.

Sebastian stopped what he was doing and stared at the door; he knew it was too early for chow, so someone was coming to pay a visit.

The large metal door opened, and Gunny stepped inside.

Sebastian stood up, excited to see Gunny because his appearance might portend his release.

"Van Zandt, how ya holdin' up?"

"Good, Gunny."

"I have some good news and some bad news. What ya want first?" Gunny said, standing tall with his arms crossed.

Sebastian's eyes widened with anticipation. He was nervous about what the bad news was, but he wanted to save the good news for last.

"Bad news."

"Well, Corporal, San Diego is a total clusterfuck. It's worse than Fallujah back in '04."

"I kinda figured it would be bad," Sebastian answered.

"Not sure if this is good news based upon the bad news, but we're leaving early and so are you. The colonel wants all the prisoners dropped off by sixteen hundred hours. So, you finally get what you want, Corporal. Your precious California awaits. Now grab your shit, you're coming with me."

"Ah, now!" Sebastian exclaimed, not quite prepared. Just moments before he'd been grumbling to himself about the wait; now the reality of navigating in the chaos of what was San Diego took him off guard.

"Yes, Corporal. Get your trash, a bird is waiting for you and the other scumbags," Gunny barked.

Nervously grabbing what few items he had been allowed, Sebastian followed Gunny out of the cell and down the narrow passageways toward the flight deck.

"Are you giving me everything you mentioned before?" Sebastian asked.

"Don't worry, Corporal, we're not cruel. We will give you enough to get by."

"Thank you."

Stepping out on the flight deck, Sebastian thought that he'd never see this ship or Gunny again. He had a flash of nostalgia. He really wished that things had gone differently, but the path Barone was on was not one he could follow. Gunny escorted him to the ramp and patted him on the back.

"This is it, Van Zandt. I brought you up first; there's another handful of Marines joining you on this one-way trip. I wanted you to get first dibs on the gear on board," Gunny said, pointing inside the helicopter.

"Thank you, Gunny," Sebastian said, putting out his hand.

Gunny looked at his hand, hesitated, then grabbed it firmly, "God damn you, Van Zandt, I really wanted you to come with us; but no, you had to go renegade. Listen, I couldn't let you go without some goodies and a surprise. Grab the pack with the black strap tied on the top."

"Roger that," Sebastian said; he still had Gunny's hand.

"If you find your brother, and I hope you do, tell him Smitty says hello, okay?"

"Will do, Gunny."

They stared at each other for another brief moment before Sebastian turned and walked onto the helicopter. Packs with rifles were lined up on the webbing on both sides of the chopper. By a rough count, he totaled a dozen. This gave Sebastian some encouragement; he hoped he could convince some of them to come with him. He located the pack Gunny had mentioned and sat down next to it. Picking it up was not easy; the pack had to weigh sixty pounds. He wanted to see what surprise Gunny had for him, so he opened the pack up and started digging around. Inside he found the familiar tools of the Marine trade. MREs, a tent, can opener, matches, tarp, poncho, extra bootlaces, extra set of clothes, rope, compass, two flashlights with spare batteries, a Ka-Bar knife, extra boxes of 5.56-mm ammunition, two boxes of 9-mm ammo, and four grenades, two high explosive and two smoke. He just assumed that the grenades were the surprise, but then he felt something in the bottom of the pack. He pulled it out and knew that these would come in handy: night-vision goggles with spare batteries. Hearing others coming on board, Sebastian repacked everything and sat back. He checked his rifle and put on his shoulder holster for the 9-mm while the others boarded.

As each one boarded and sat down, he tried to see if he recognized them. No luck, he didn't know any of these men; not that it mattered, he just wanted in some strange way to have a familiar face with him. Once everyone was aboard, the crew chief came on and raised the ramp. As the turbines of CH-53 chopper began to spin, Sebastian thought back to his time in the Marines. He loved the Corps, and the way he was leaving it made him sad. When the chopper lifted off the flight deck, he said his typical prayer, this time with meaning. Finishing, he looked over his shoulder at the ship below. He wished the best for the Marines of his battalion and hoped that wherever they ended up they could find peace. Settling into his seat for the short ride, he thought about what he might encounter on the ground in San Diego. He couldn't lie to himself; he was anxious, but knowing he'd be able to complete his long journey gave him solace. He just hoped that Gordon and his family were still alive.

Cheyenne Mountain, Colorado

"Nothing? Nothing is not an answer! It's an excuse! It's a cop-out!" Julia screamed at Cruz and Dylan.

"Mrs. Conner, please understand that until we can get some more intelligence, there's nothing we can do," Cruz tried to explain with a cautious tone.

"You listen here, Andrew, you're my husband's best friend and his vice president. You need to have men out there every second of the day looking for him,"

"We don't even know if he's alive, Julia; you have to understand," Cruz said, defending himself.

"All you have are excuses. I want results!"

"Mrs. Conner, if you would just listen to the vice president," Dylan attempted to interject.

Waving a finger, Julia scolded him. "Don't even tell me what I should do. I've listened long enough. It's been three days and nothing has been done. You all just sit here and talk. This is exactly what Brad hated about this group. You just sit around and talk all the time."

"Julia, we have limited manpower, we can't have them going door to door," Cruz said.

"Yes, you could. I'm not asking for you to search every building from here to where he went missing, but you should have teams going door to door there."

"We tried, but we were repelled by a superior force," Cruz exclaimed. "We even sent two-man teams; neither team has come back."

"Don't we have any resources here to do something? Are we that helpless?" Julia asked. She was getting increasingly frustrated by this back-and-forth.

"We have more men coming soon, and when they arrive, we will have a plan."

Julia looked tired and frustrated. She finally sat down at the table. The waiting was wearing on her physically and emotionally. It had been three days since Conner had disappeared. Cruz had sent a team to find him, but when they attempted to conduct a search, they were fired upon by the locals. Cruz had requested support from the handful of military installations that still had operations. But with only two aircraft, it would take some time before they could have those men on the ground.

"Julia, believe me when I say that if I could go get Brad I would, but we are vulnerable now. I'm making my decisions based upon what I think Brad would do," Cruz said. He sat down next to her.

Lifting her weary head, Julia responded, "Thank you for saying that; you're right. Brad would look at the big picture, and if searching for someone would jeopardize the greater good, he would not do it." She reached over and touched his hand. Cruz responded by placing his hand on top of hers.

Gripping her hand a bit tighter, he said, "I will not rest until we find him. Please trust me; I will find him."

Barstow, California

Haley screamed; she didn't move but was stiff with fear. Each swipe and lunge the man made caused her to scream even more.

"Come here," the man barked again.

When his hand touched her shoes, she finally reacted by kicking at him. She looked into his dark eyes; his unshaven face was smeared with grease and dirt. Sweat poured off of his brow, and the smell of the many weeks he'd gone unwashed wafted over her. Knowing he was only inches away, he forced himself farther into the small opening.

"Come here, damn it!" the man ordered. His voice echoed off the walls of the culvert.

Haley continued to kick and moved away from his grasp. The man stuffed himself farther into the culvert and made another lunge for her; this time he was successful. He grabbed her ankle and pulled her toward him. Haley fought back by kicking him, but his grip was too firm. Tears of utter fear ran down her face as she drew closer and closer to him.

Suddenly his grip loosened, and without notice he was forcibly pulled out of the culvert. The absence of his hulking body allowed the sunlight to cascade across Haley. She scurried away from the opening and watched as Nelson plunged his knife into the man's chest.

Nelson stabbed the man over and over. As he pulled the knife out and swung his arm up, blood sprayed over the man and Nelson. He thrust the blade again and again.

"Die, you son of a bitch!" Nelson screamed.

Haley just stared at Nelson, clearly in shock. Her trembling had become uncontrollable.

Someone then appeared at the entrance of the culvert. Haley couldn't make out who it was. Her eyes were trying to adjust when the sound of a familiar and comforting voice bounced off the sides of the culvert.

"Come here, baby. It's Mommy; come here, honey."

Haley hesitated briefly, then crawled toward Samantha, who grabbed her and yanked her out and into her warm arms.

Samantha held her tight and whispered, "It's okay now, honey, it's okay."

Haley buried her face in Samantha's shoulder and cried. She lifted her head for a second to see Eric hovering over Hunter, who was still unconscious. Then another welcoming and secure voice bellowed over everyone else's.

"Hunter, Haley!" Gordon yelled.

"Here!" Samantha responded.

Gordon tore over to them in a sprint and hugged them both. Then he saw Hunter lying motionless on the ground. He pulled away from Samantha and Haley and went to his son's side.

"How is he?" Gordon asked Eric.

"I'm not sure. We just got here and he was lying there."

Gordon bent over and placed his ear against his son's mouth. The faint warmth of his breath tickled his cheek. He then looked over Hunter, first noticing a dark bruise on his forehead. From there he examined his arms and chest. He couldn't find anything. When Gordon carefully rolled him onto his side to look at his back, Hunter moved.

"Son," Gordon said.

Hunter's eyes flickered, then opened. "Dad," he said in a groggy voice.

"Yes, I'm here. You okay?"

"My head hurts," Hunter said, raising his hand to where the bruise was.

"Anywhere else?"

"No." Hunter paused then continued. "Haley, where's Haley?"

"She okay, she's fine," Gordon reassured him.

"I tried to protect her, but the guy was too strong. I'm sorry."

"Son, no, don't say that; it's my fault. I should have been here," Gordon said, cradling Hunter in his arms and lifting him off the ground.

Samantha and Gordon walked their shocked and injured children to the trailer. Gordon had tried to protect his children from the horrors of this new world, but without notice it had been thrust upon them. He vowed that he would never allow Hunter to go unprotected again; this was a lesson for him. Now was time to treat Hunter like the young man he was becoming.

Tijuana, Mexico

Pablo Juarez sat in the cushioned leather chair in his father's beautifully decorated office. He leaned back and looked up at the coffered ceiling. His eyes followed the hand-hewn beams until they intersected with the ornately decorated upholstered walls. If you took away the security cameras, computers, and other signs of technology, you would think you were in a room in Versailles. His father, Alfredo, loved the finer things and without regard for money ensured he had the best in furniture and decorations. Being one of the largest drug lords in Mexico helped Alfredo adorn his homes from wall to wall with the best.

Pablo did not have his father's taste for these things. What he wanted more than anything was power. His father had summoned him back from San Diego to discuss his son's long-term goals. He allowed Pablo to do whatever he wanted, but now he wanted his son to know who was really in charge.

Pablo looked at his watch; his father was thirty minutes late. Growing impatient, he stood up and walked to the window. He couldn't make anything out through the thick bulletproof glass, just distorted shades of green and blue.

"This is bullshit," Pablo said after looking at his watch again. He exhaled deeply and started for the door.

When he reached for the golden brass handle, the door opened. He stepped back to see his father there.

"Ah, Pablo, my son," Alfredo said, putting his arms in the air, then leaning in to hug him.

"Good to see you, Father," Pablo responded, returning the hug.

"Where were you going? We have a meeting, right?" Alfredo asked, looking at Pablo. He then nodded and walked past him toward his desk.

"You were over thirty minutes late, and I have to get back to San Diego," Pablo answered, his tone showing a tinge of frustration.

"No, I wasn't late, you were early, I said three-thirty, didn't I?"

"No, Father, you said, three p.m.," Pablo snapped.

Alfredo grinned and sat down in his chair. "Whatever. I am here now. Please, please sit down," he said, motioning to the chair Pablo had been sitting in earlier.

Looking agitated but understanding the hierarchy, Pablo sat back down.

Alfredo leaned forward, opened a humidor on his desk, and pulled out a large cigar. As he prepped the cigar for smoking he asked, "Son, tell me, what are your plans up north?"

Pablo watched his father precisely cut the butt off the cigar. Alfredo was very meticulous about his cigars and how he smoked them.

"Sorry, do you want one?" Alfredo asked.

"No thank you."

Taking his butane lighter, Alfredo lit the cigar, carefully spinning it in the blue flame. He puffed and puffed, the orange flames of the tobacco dancing with each puff. He exhaled, took another puff, then blew the smoke on the lit end of his cigar. Pablo knew not to start talking to his father until his full attention was on him, hence his hesitation in answering the question.

Leaning back in his chair, Alfredo asked again, "Son, what are your plans up north?"

"We have a chance to do something we never could before. We have a chance to have real power and control. We can now take back what was once ours."

"Whose?"

Looking at his father oddly, Pablo answered, "Mexico's."

"Really, you're doing what you're doing for Mexico? Since when were you a patriot?"

"Father, we have a real chance now to expand outside of drugs to have real power," Pablo said, the tempo of his speech increasing.

"So you are playing around up north with hopes of glory for Mexico?" Alfredo said with a chuckle.

"Why am I here? Why did you call for me?"

Leaning forward and placing his elbows on his desk, Alfredo exhaled a large cloud in Pablo's direction. "Son, I called you here to see exactly what your plans are, and you tell me for the greater glory of Mexico!"

"The glory can be ours too."

"Pablo, my boy, we have everything we need. What we should be doing is getting as many things as possible to make our lives easier. If you were here it wouldn't have taken me four weeks to get everything back up and running. Your place is here, not up north causing trouble. You're starting something you can't win, a war. I heard what happened. I heard that you lost many men and supplies when the Marines landed. We even had some losses here because they traced your origins back to us. I don't like that. I think you're in over your head, and I can't support this reckless behavior anymore."

"Father, listen, please,"

"No, you listen, Pablo. I need you here helping us get what supplies we need to outlast this. Do you honestly think you can fight the U.S. Army and win?"

"Father, please, we have a real chance here," Pablo pleaded.

"I sent you to the best universities, you had the best tutors since you were a little boy. You're a smart kid, but what you're doing now is stupid. It ends now!"

"Please, Father, just listen!"

Slamming his fist down on his desk, Alfredo barked, "No, you listen, Pablo! It's over! Your Villista game is over! Now leave me, go see your cousin José over at the distillery, and don't forget to see your mother, she misses you."

Pablo's face had turned ashen, and thoughts filled his mind. He wanted to press his father about the urgency of his crusade, but he knew the old man well enough to know he'd do a better job talking to the wall.

"Yes, Father," Pablo said, then quickly stood up and left. The short walk from the chair to the door seemed to take forever. His inner self kept telling him to stand up to his father; then his more pragmatic side would keep him quiet. He knew he was right; he knew what he was doing could grow into something large. He knew that, if left to his own devices, he could be bigger and more powerful than his father. If given the chance, he could be something much larger than a leader of a drug cartel; he could be the leader of a new empire.

San Diego, California

Grabbing their packs, the Marines stood up and slowly walked off the chopper. The drop-off point was the main beach in Oceanside. Sebastian was familiar with where he was and calculated that it would take him a few days on foot to get to Gordon's house. When he reached the back of the chopper, the crew chief stopped him.

"Stay here!" the chief yelled in his ear. The noise of the chopper blades and engine made it difficult to hear.

"Why? What's up?" Sebastian asked, looking confused. He saw the others were already heading off in their own directions. Sebastian hadn't gotten a chance to talk to any of them to see if they could join up on a trek to the south. "Listen, I need to go, I need to talk to those guys."

"Sit down, over there," the crew chief said, pointing to the webbing just behind Sebastian.

Unsure of himself, he decided to listen to the crew chief and took a seat. Within moments of the ramp rising, the chopper slowly lifted.

Reaching over and tugging on the crew chief's sleeve, Sebastian asked, "Where are you taking me?"

The crew chief held up his index finger to indicate that he needed a second.

Sebastian looked over his shoulder and noticed they had banked and now were heading south. The crew chief finished what he was doing and approached him. To Sebastian's surprise, he handed him a headset. Sebastian took it and put it on.

"This is Corporal Van Zandt," Sebastian said into mic.

"Hello, Corporal. This is First Lieutenant Wasserman. Gunny Smith asked us to give you a ride to wherever you needed to go."

Sebastian's eyes opened wide at what Gunny had done for him. He just looked at the crew chief with astonishment.

"Corporal, you there?" Wasserman asked.

"Ah, yes, sir. Um . . . keep heading south. Do you know where Carmel Valley is?"

"Yes, I do."

"Sir, the best route to where I need to go is take the coast till you can see Highway 56, then head east."

"Roger that, Corporal. I'll ask for further directions once we start heading east," Wasserman said.

The headset went silent. Sebastian took it off and just held it. "What do ya know?" he said to himself with a grin on his face. Too excited to relax, he turned around so he could see out the small window. He looked down on the houses that dotted the shoreline. One thing he noticed was the absence of people. Even though it was starting to get dark, there was enough light out for those runners or walkers who liked to take to the beach just after work or those who wanted to glimpse the setting sun. They passed familiar landmarks along the beach until he recognized one that meant he was close to heading east: the long strand called San Elijo State Beach. He put the headset back on and said, "Lieutenant Wasserman, I think we can head east sooner. I can guide us to where you need to go."

"Roger that, Corporal, let me know where," Wasserman replied.

"When we get to the end of the long beach, bank east-southeast."

"Roger that."

Sebastian was getting a bit concerned because the sun was now below the horizon and soon it would be dark. The pilot was on mark and banked the chopper east-southeast. Sebastian walked over to the other side of the chopper so he could see the landmarks. He saw the road he was looking for. Lomas Santa Fe would lead him east enough. Then all he had to do was turn south and he'd be right on top of Gordon's neighborhood. Wasserman had lowered the chopper enough that Sebastian could see a small group of people clearly in a cul-de-sac; looking more intently, he thought they had rifles. Really focusing on them, he noticed two of them had the rifles on their shoulders.

"Oh, shit; go higher, go higher!" Sebastian yelled into the mic.

No response came from Wasserman. A few streaking flashes confirmed that they were being shot at.

"Lieutenant Wasserman, we're being shot at, go higher!" Sebastian yelled again.

No response again, but Wasserman did what Sebastian said. Still looking down, Sebastian could see what appeared to be more men and more flashes, followed by loud panging on the upper fuselage. They kept going higher and higher until the chopper shuddered and dropped, causing a feeling of weightlessness. Sebastian was pushed into the ceiling and hit his head. The chopper regained power and stopped its fall for only a moment before he heard the engine winding down.

Lying on his back, Sebastian had an uneasy feeling, which grew worse when black smoke entered the chopper from outside. He got to his knees but was thrown down again when the chopper banked hard to the left. He rolled across the floor and slammed into the webbing. He reached out and grabbed it to hold himself; the chopper was now on its side and falling out of the sky. He could see the ground through the open window.

More shuddering and the engine fired up again; he could hear the blades start to spin. The chopper stabilized but was not far off the ground. He crawled up onto the webbing and looked out the window. They couldn't be more than two hundred feet from the ground. Fear had gripped Sebastian. He thought that after all the fighting to get home, this was how he would die, and only a few miles from Gordon's house. He looked outside but did not know where they were.

"Sir, what's our game plan?" Sebastian asked.

"No time to chat, Corporal. We need to try to get this bird back to the *Makin Island*."

"What about me?"

"Sorry, Corporal. I need to get back if I can."

Just then the chopper banked to the left and started to head north.

Sebastian tore the headset off and tossed it in anger. He lay back against the wall and yelled, "Damn it!"

They hadn't flown for two minutes before the same violent shuddering returned. Again, black smoke poured in and the props stopped. Gravity took over, and the chopper dropped. Sebastian held on to his seat and looked at the crew chief, who was busily strapping himself down. Sebastian knew the ground was coming fast, and the anticipation of impact was intense. He wondered how it would feel. He wondered if he would die. *Of course,* he thought. *How many people fall out of the sky in a huge helicopter and walk away?*

The first impact stopped his thoughts. Whatever they hit forced the chopper to turn 120 degrees and jarred Sebastian. He lost his grip and flew to the other side of the chopper. The second impact tipped the rear end up. Sebastian slid across the deck and slammed into the front wall. All he could think was they were hitting was large trees; that meant the ground and final impact were close. Dazed, he scrambled to find something stable to hold on to, but his search was futile. The helicopter slammed nose-first into the ground, tipping over onto its back before settling on its side. Remarkably, the chopper was almost intact; the propellers had been sheared off and the fuselage crushed, but it didn't break in two despite the multiple collisions.

• • •

Sebastian awoke to an unfamiliar face. His vision was blurry, so making out clearly who it was was impossible. A sharp pain shot up from his left leg. He knew he was not okay, but at least he was alive. He blinked repeatedly in the hope that his vision would clear, but it didn't work.

"This one is alive!" the person yelled.

Sebastian tried to speak but couldn't. He then attempted to move but was met with severe pain. He winced and stopped his attempts at talking and moving.

"Over here, he needs help, now!" the person said, squatting down next to him.

Opening his eyes again, Sebastian noticed it was a young woman, her light blond hair pulled back into a long ponytail. He reached toward her face, but she grabbed his hand and brought it back down.

"Just rest, we'll take care of you," she reassured him.

Sebastian felt safe, but then again, there wasn't much he could do. He closed his eyes and passed out.

Barstow, California

"You can't be the one who always runs off and does everything! We needed you here. Hunter and Haley needed you!" Samantha screamed at Gordon.

They were in their trailer; the kids were both lying in bed resting from the earlier ordeal. Gordon had led the convoy farther up the road, then headed across the desert away from the town of Barstow. Adhering to their plan, they circled the vehicles at night. Moving under the cover of darkness might be beneficial, but Gordon felt it was too risky. Even though the attack today had been conducted during daylight hours, traveling during the day allowed them at least the chance to see an ambush or questionable situation. The darkness provided too much cover for those who wished to do harm.

"Sam, we were being shot at. I saw the machine gun and did what needed to be done. We needed to confirm they were dead."

"I understand. But this time, we needed you and you weren't there. Plus, why did you have them hide in the culvert? Why not take shelter in the trailer with me?"

"The trailer didn't provide real protection. In case you didn't notice, they were showering bullets down on us. I felt the culvert was safe. I obviously didn't know this group had people hiding in the desert to our right," Gordon said defensively.

"All I am saying is that you don't always have to be the one. What if one of them was killed?"

"You're being ridiculous, Sam. If I didn't do something, more of us might have died. We lost an entire family today, burned alive in their car. I'll tell you this, I won't let Hunter go unprotected again," Gordon said, pacing the short distance in the trailer.

"What does that mean?"

"It means from now on he will have the tools necessary to defend himself and whoever."

"He's a boy, Gordon!"

"Not anymore! That is a twentieth-century invention. He's now a young man and needs to step up!"

Putting her hand up in a motion to indicate she was done hearing from Gordon, Samantha opened the door and left.

Gordon just watched her as she slammed the door. He shook his head and tossed the water bottle he had in his hand.

"Dada?" Haley whispered from her bed.

Hearing her sweet little voice brought Gordon back from his thoughts. He quickly walked to the rear of trailer and sat on the edge of the bed. Haley sat up, rubbed her eyes, and hugged him.

"Hi, honey," he said softly, kissing the top of her head.

"Can you cuddle me, Dada?"

"Sure, sweetie" He looked over at Hunter, who was still sleeping. Gordon lay next to Haley and cradled her small body. He kissed her head and rubbed her arms till he could hear the heavier breathing indicating she had fallen back asleep. He then thought about the events of the day. He replayed them over and over. It haunted him that the kids had been directly attacked. He tried to convince himself that he was right, but Samantha's voice kept echoing in his head. Maybe she was right, he thought. Then again, maybe she was being too impractical. One thing he didn't want to do was ponder what to do when the shit was hitting the fan. His instincts had gotten them this far. Many conflicting thoughts battled in his mind, but one was constant and nagged him more than anything . . . the thought that he alone couldn't keep his children safe anymore.

JANUARY 9, 2014

· · ·

**Out of suffering have emerged the strongest
souls; the most massive characters are seared
with scars.**

—Kahlil Gibran

San Diego, California

The slight breeze felt good on Sebastian's face. The noise of the
wood blinds banging against the windowsill had awakened
him. His vision was blurry, so he blinked repeatedly in an attempt
to focus. He gazed around the quaintly decorated room. Little
tchotchkes adorned the small shelves and tops of all the furniture.
Reproductions of well-known oil paintings hung on all the walls.
In the air was a faint smell of lavender. When he adjusted himself
in the bed, a sharp pain emanated from his left leg. He tossed off
the blanket and looked at a tight bandage. He ran his hands across
the textured fabric until he found the center of the pain. Exhaling
deeply, he tried to recall how he had arrived where he was. He
remembered the chopper crash but not much after. An image of a
young woman came to him, then flashes of blood, lots of blood.
He must have blacked out again after that, because he couldn't
remember anything else. He glanced around the room looking for
his clothes but saw nothing. The shorts he had on were not his,

and by the way his wound had been treated and the condition of the room, he assumed those who had rescued him were good people.

The door opening startled him. He adjusted himself, preparing to meet whoever had rescued him. The door had slowly creaked open not more than nine inches when a child's head appeared from around it. The boy saw Sebastian awake and staring at him. Shyly, he tucked his head back. Sebastian could hear unintelligible whispering followed by a woman's voice.

"You two close that door this minute and get back to your chores."

The children listened to the unseen woman and scurried away without closing the door.

Sebastian sat farther up in the bed and said, "Hello?"

The door opened fully to reveal the woman; he recognized her face. She was the young blond woman he remembered from the crash site. Now able to see her clearly, he was drawn in by her beauty. She was average height, he guessed around five feet five inches, and slender. Her facial features had a cuteness that he was attracted to. Her long, straight hair was pulled back in a ponytail, revealing her full cheeks, small nose, and pouty lips.

She stepped into the room and said, "You're awake. How are you feeling?"

"Good, good," he replied. He felt nervous for a reason he could only assume was his attraction to her.

"Are you hungry?" she asked. She stood at the foot of the bed. She was dressed plainly; a buttoned-up white shirt was tucked into faded jeans.

"Actually, I am."

"Good, I'll go get some food," she said, then turned around.

"Wait, don't go just yet. I have questions, a lot of questions."

"Let's answer your questions after you get fed, okay?"

"Sure, that's fine."

Before she left, she approached the bed, put out her hand, and said, "I'm Annaliese."

Sebastian took her hand and shook it. "I'm—"

"Corporal Sebastian Van Zandt. I know," she answered confidently.

He looked at her oddly, not knowing how she knew his name.

Pointing at his chest, she said, "Your dog tags."

"Of course."

"Unless you need something else besides your questions answered, I'll go and get your food."

He found her abundance of confidence and maturity attractive. She didn't look as if she could be any older than twenty-five, but he could tell by their minimal conversation that she was wiser than her peers.

As she stepped toward the door he said, "I know you'll answer my questions later, but where am I?"

"You're in Bishop Sorenson's house."

"Who's Bishop Sorenson?"

"He's my father, and you'll meet him very soon."

40 miles east of Barstow, California

"Here, take this," Gordon said to Hunter, handing him a small .38-caliber revolver.

Hunter looked stunned. He hadn't expected this when his father pulled him aside to talk.

Gordon and the group had awakened early to start their journey east toward Las Vegas. He strove to stay far away from major cities, but the best improved route took them very close to Vegas. While they were deciding the route, Gordon had spotted Fort Irwin on the map. Thinking they might find something worth value if the base was accessible, he planned to recon it. Nelson disagreed with this approach, thinking they needed to keep heading toward Idaho. Nelson argued that they had plenty of food, water, ammunition, and weapons to make the trip. But Gordon had an ally in Holloway, who helped him outvote Nelson. Making it a point never to leave anything behind of value, he had gone back and stripped his attackers from yesterday.

The handgun he was giving Hunter came from one of those men.

Hunter looked at the gun he was now holding. Even though it was a compact model, it appeared large in his hands. He flipped the gun back and forth, looking nervous. He knew how strict his dad was about gun handling.

"It's a revolver, so all you have to do is point and squeeze the trigger. If for some reason it doesn't shoot, squeeze the trigger again," Gordon instructed him.

"I want a gun like yours," Hunter said, pointing at Gordon's holstered handgun.

"Later, once you have more training. Revolvers are simple. If you had to troubleshoot a malfunction with a semiauto, you could get into trouble. For right now, this will do," Gordon said, tussling Hunter's hair.

"Thanks, Dad," Hunter said. He then pointed the gun toward the open desert and closed his left eye. He took aim at an abandoned car and pretended to shoot it.

"Hunter, having this is a big responsibility. Do you understand?"

Nodding, Hunter replied, "Yes."

Gordon squatted down so he could look his son in the eyes. He grabbed both shoulders and said, "Things are different now; this isn't the world of seven weeks ago. In this world we can't play games anymore. You're now a man, and you need to act like one. I need you to truly understand this."

"I do, Dad."

"Listen, Son, you need to always look after your little sister. I don't know what the future holds, but if something happens to me, you become the man of the family. The toys need to be put away. I will be giving you responsibilities within our group, okay?"

"I understand, and I'll make you proud of me."

Gordon looked into his son's eyes. He could remember the day he was born. Hunter was always so alert, even at birth. He wasn't seconds old and Gordon remembered him looking out of his swaddling clothes with fascination in his eyes. Of course, this was how Gordon remembered it, and a parent's love for his children always makes them seem more than they might actually be. Gordon brought him in closer and hugged him tightly.

"I love you, Hunter."

"I love you too, Dad."

Cheyenne Mountain, Colorado

Cruz placed the receiver down on the phone's base and stared at it. Thoughts were pulsating so rapidly through his mind that he didn't move except for the blinking of his eyes and the throbbing of his temple. He was alone in the command post briefing room.

Like Conner before him, he hadn't asked for this job; it was thrust upon him. The events that had led him to this once-coveted position now grew darker and more complex.

All decisions have consequences, and the decisions that Conner had made as president were coming back to haunt him. Conner's nuclear strikes across the globe had finally come home to roost. First, they were starting to register environmental issues. Higher levels of radiation had been showing up in the rains that fell across the country. The estimates from some were that the blasts from D.C., New York, and now the more than a dozen large nuclear strikes would make global temperatures drop by two degrees centigrade. This could be enough to cause further degradation to any crops that the survivors would be planting. They had stopped global warming with a small nuclear winter.

The second issue Cruz was facing was abandonment by all nations that had previously pledged their support. The last to drop its support was Australia. He had resorted to begging the prime minister, but nothing would work. The overall consensus from the nations not affected by the EMPs was to pull all support to the United States. As if scripted, they all expressed dismay that Conner would unilaterally attack all of those countries with massive nuclear strikes without regard for civilians. Conner had briefed all leaders of state but only after the weapons had reached their targets. He felt he couldn't trust anyone after New York had been struck.

Cruz's feelings were mixed; he'd supported Conner's decision then, especially after the incident with Griswald, but had reservations he hadn't shared with his old friend. Cruz only now appreciated the pressure that Conner had been under. It's easy to judge and second-guess those in charge, but when the ball stops with you, the responsibility can become overwhelming. The situation the country found itself in now was hard for him to get his arms around. He didn't know where to start. Conner was gone, most likely dead, but a body hadn't been found. The limited number of troops they had made a search for him impossible. Cruz believed that Conner had been right about setting up a new capital to show the American people that the country was rebuilding, but he couldn't decide if he should do it now or wait to find out the true fate of the president.

Everything was a mess, but he had found good counsel in the new secretary of defense, General Samuel Baxter, the commanding officer of Cheyenne Mountain. Baxter was the typical career officer. He was a graduate of the Air Force Academy, smart, quick-witted, and honest in his assessments. This honesty had cost him some positions. The command of Cheyenne Mountain was actually considered a demotion for him. Since the end of the Cold War, Cheyenne Mountain had been considered a relic that still received funding only because some of the "old dogs" in Washington insisted. Now it was the de facto capital of the United States and sanctuary for what was left of the centralized command and control.

Picking up the phone again, Cruz dialed and sat patiently waiting for the person on the other end to answer.

"General, I need you and the rest of the staff to report to the briefing room ASAP."

Cruz relaxed into the leather chair and looked at the walls. He spun around and faced a map of the United States, staring at the red lines drawn around parts of the country. These lines represented areas now considered contaminated. The red lines on the right side of the map connected and overlapped. From east of the Mississippi, many regions fell into contaminated areas. With the two nuclear strikes and dozens of meltdowns from Florida to New Hampshire, this part of the country was now being considered a total loss.

To the right of the map hung a large dry-erase board. On it were more than fifty evenly spaced columns, each with a total at the bottom. The number Cruz could not tear his gaze from was the one circled on the far right bottom: 13,152,891. That number was too impossible to believe. After almost seven weeks, they estimated that more than 13 million Americans were dead. The initial day had killed hundreds of thousands, then those in need of urgent medical care had followed in the tens of thousands over the next few days. Civil unrest took thousands more in the first days. Starvation began to take those weak, young, and old by more tens of thousands. If they didn't have the SIPRNet, they wouldn't have been able to communicate with anyone outside Cheyenne Mountain.

The news was sobering, but information was critical. With each relay from those outside, the picture came to seem insurmountable. There were large riots, murders, mass executions, starvation, rapes, and total chaos in the bigger cities. If that wasn't enough, the nuclear plants began to melt down, causing mass radiation sickness. This was followed by the nuclear strike on New York, which killed millions. They truly didn't know how many were dead; the numbers were just good guesses. But judging by what they saw on some of their patrols and from reports across the country, they were probably right.

Some of the latest troubling news concerned the sighting of mass migrations out of the East. Hundreds of thousands were heading west. Some word must have spread that the government planned to focus the recovery efforts in the West first. The densely populated Eastern Seaboard had turned into a bloody grinder. Streets were covered by starving bands of people fighting for what few scraps of food they could find. Murder was now commonplace. Strewn along with the trash were bodies of those who had either been killed or had starved to death. The stench on many streets in the big cities was unbearable. Even if no one had told them to leave, many knew the cities were now death traps and if they had a chance for survival it was not to be found there. Many saw the West as wide open and rich with natural resources.

Cruz knew these mass migrations were going to cause problems for his government. With no support coming now from their former allies, he needed to make a plan for their survival.

The door opened and General Baxter stepped in with purpose. He was a man who always walked around looking like he had somewhere to go. He had a stack of binders tucked under his arm. The other staff, including Dylan, followed.

"Good morning, General, everyone," Cruz said after turning around and facing the front of the room. He motioned for Baxter to take a seat next to him.

"Thank you, sir," Baxter said, sitting down and spreading the binders in front of him.

"I called you because I just got off the phone with the Australian prime minister and the news isn't good."

"Okay," Baxter said, anxiously awaiting the news.

Everyone else suspected what Cruz would say, but they were just as anxious as the general.

"They have dropped all support for us, citing the Christmas strikes."

"I think we kinda saw that coming, didn't we?" Baxter replied.

"Yes, we did. So we need to lay out a plan for reconstruction that doesn't include support from anyone. Let's go over everything. I need to get it all straight in my head," Cruz said, looking exhausted.

Baxter opened up the first binder and said, "Sir, there isn't much we can do in the East. I think we need to pull our assets out. My recommendations are to have both groups get as many troops as possible from those bases there and then set sail for the West Coast. There we can start to redeploy those assets to our new capital."

"You have my attention; go ahead," Cruz said, sitting back in his chair.

"I know we touched on this briefly yesterday; but we need to just abandon any efforts back east. Look at the map behind you, sir. It's a loss. With everything that has happened back there and with what limited assets we have, we really can't do anything for those people. We need to set up a new capital, work on repairing our relations with our allies, and then after we get our own infrastructure back up, we can start to think about anything back east."

"That's it, just abandon it? General, you sound like that rogue colonel," Cruz said sarcastically.

"Mr. Vice President, when you asked me to be the secretary of defense, you told me to be honest, and sir, I'm being honest. I don't agree with the colonel; however, I can't help it if we share some beliefs. In the end it is your decision. If you want us to stay back east and continue to salvage what we can, then I'm with you. If you don't, then I'm with you. I'm a loyal soldier," Baxter said defensively.

"Sorry, General, it's just that what you're suggesting is unthinkable in some ways."

"But necessary, sir. If we are to help them, anyone, we must help ourselves first. Especially with the loss of resupply and equipment from our allies, it's just impossible. We need to target and focus what we do have to make sure we have a government."

Cruz looked at all present and asked for a yea or nay on the topic of abandoning the East Coast.

Remembering the incident with Griswald, many looked around the room for affirmation before they answered. One by one, each person agreed with Baxter. Taking this all in, Cruz came to a decision.

"General, give our troops back east the command to evacuate all bases and to coordinate with the command elements of both groups. Let's get those men and women to the West Coast."

Baxter just nodded his acknowledgment of the new order. He then stood and approached the map. Taking a green marker, he started to draw a line down the map. Beginning on the border of North Dakota and Minnesota, he moved down South Dakota to Nebraska; he then cut off the eastern part of Nebraska and went straight down to the border of Oklahoma and Texas, then took his marker west all the way to Nevada, then north along the Nevada-California border to Oregon and back west to the ocean. Then he turned and said, "Mr. Vice President, the area I just outlined is the area we need to secure, protect, and consider the new United States."

Some cross talk began after Baxter made his declaration. Cruz hushed the group and said to the general, "I see the red areas, so I know why you're marking this territory."

"The contamination from all the meltdowns is too much for us to deal with. It would be an impossible task if we had everything at our disposal. It's just too much to overcome. These are the new boundaries that I propose we defend. We need to contact the gov-

ernors of these states to inform them that we aim to take care of
them. We need them to put what assets they can along their bor-
ders to stop others from migrating into their states. Not all of the
migrants will make it, but a majority will, and the sheer numbers
will overwhelm them." Baxter spoke while pointing at the states
that bordered the red-outlined states to the east.

Others at the table began to whisper to each other. Cruz sat
looking at the map. He stared for what seemed like minutes; then
he spoke.

"Okay, General, I agree with you on what boundaries we
need to defend. However, I will not abandon Americans who seek
sanctuary. This is their country, and we will do what we can for
them. Inform the governors to establish tent cities, if they can, of
course, and to supply what they can as far as food or water for
these areas. What we will need to do is get those two naval groups
to the West Coast as soon as possible. When they arrive we will
set up a tight perimeter around Portland. We then will start building up the new capital, but we will have to make it secure, so we
will limit access. That is as far as I will go in restricting Americans' free access. Understood?"

"Yes, sir," Baxter replied.

"What is the update on reinforcements?"

"Arriving late today, sir."

"Good, get them here, fed and outfitted. We need to send
several teams back out to look for Conner," Cruz said as he
stood.

"Sir, we have made several attempts and you know the results,"
Baxter reminded Cruz.

"I'm quite aware of the difficulties. Until we know for sure the
president's fate, I will assume he's alive."

"Yes, sir," Baxter answered; he knew debating with Cruz was hopeless. If Conner was still alive and they could bring him back, that would give people hope.

Cruz rose and walked to the map. He stood looking at the line that created a new border for his country.

"I noticed you bypassed Texas and California," Cruz stated.

"Yes, sir. The Texas legislature was able to get a quorum, and their decision was to exercise what they believe is their right to leave the union. I spoke with the Texas governor early this morning, and they overwhelmingly decided to break away. They acknowledged this might cause some issues with us but felt they could handle the situation themselves. They will work on a draft agreement that formalizes a treaty with the U.S. and get it to me soon,"

"Unbelievable. That quickly they decided to jump ship," Cruz said.

"You know those Texans. They've always had an independent streak in them," Baxter joked.

"As far as California goes, I disagree with you; we can't let her go. California is rich in natural resources. I see the red lines designating the hot spots, but the state is big. I want California under our wing. Anything new from Sacramento?"

"Nothing new since we talked with the governor two days ago. The legislature there is in disarray. The civil unrest has been crippling for them at the capital and all around the state. They are having issues with the militarization of the drug cartels in the southern part of the state. That group called the Villistas has secured many strategic parts of San Diego County and shows no signs of stopping. Our rogue colonel helped us a bit out there."

"How's that?" Cruz said, sitting back down and looking interested. He hadn't heard about Colonel Barone in a while.

"It appears his ARG attacked many of the Villistas' positions throughout the county. While this set them back, the cartel is a threat we will eventually have to deal with."

"Well, bravo, Colonel. As far as he goes, though, we can't deal with him right now. We have bigger fish to fry. Fortunately for us, most of our armed forces have stuck with us."

"Agreed, sir, we need to allocate our resources to getting our infrastructure back up."

Raising his hand, Dylan asked, "Excuse me, Mr. Vice President, but can we go back to the map?"

"Sure, what's on your mind?" Cruz asked.

"Sir, I agree, we need to 'allocate,' in the word the general used, to areas where we have to get our infrastructure back up, but I don't think we should be announcing any type of abandonment of the East, at least formally. We should put a happy face on everything and do what we can when we can back there. While I agree the East has troubles, it still has many things we can use. I suggest we don't signal our hand to the world that we're giving up."

Dylan's statement was heartfelt and prudent, and all in the room were quiet. Cruz sat and looked at his adviser. He rocked back in his chair a few times before directly answering him. "You know, Dylan, you're right. We can't go on record as having 'abandoned' the East. What we should do is inform those governors in the border states that they need to be prepared for many refugees from the other states and that we'll support them in those efforts. If we make a formal announcement, it will cause more problems for those states than they can handle. We will go back and start rebuilding later, but for now let's just focus on Portland and build out from there."

Baxter nodded his approval of Cruz's comments.

"Now, let's cover a time line for Portland," Cruz said, looking at Baxter.

The general opened another binder, but just before he could begin talking about the contents, a knock on the door disturbed them.

The door opened, and a young officer stepped in and walked to Baxter. He bent over and whispered into his ear. The look on Baxter's face told everyone that the news was shocking.

"Thank you," Baxter told the officer. The man briskly left the room.

As soon as the door closed, Cruz asked, "So, General, what's the scoop?"

"Good news, sir. The special ops team we sent out to find President Conner has come back. They just cleared the main gates and will be in a debriefing room soon."

"Well, anything?" Cruz asked, excited.

"Sir, I suggest we end this meeting and go meet them now," Baxter said, closing his binder.

"What else do you know, General?" Cruz asked, feeling that Baxter was holding something back.

"Sir, it would be better if we discussed this in a more private setting."

"Private? You and everyone else here are my most trusted advisers, we don't need privacy. What else do you know?" Cruz exclaimed.

"The team found President Conner . . ."

"Really? That's good news," Cruz said, jumping out of his chair and making his way toward the door.

"Mr. Vice President. Mr. Vice President, please stop!" Baxter said loudly.

"I have to go see him. How is he?"

"Sir, you didn't let me finish," Baxter said in a pleading tone.

A cold chill came over Cruz as he stopped and turned to face Baxter and said, "Go ahead."

"Sir, they found a body."

San Diego, California

"That was one of the best lunches I've ever had. How do you prepare beef Stroganoff in these conditions?" Sebastian asked after wiping his face and mouth with a paper towel.

"Freeze-dried," Annaliese said, picking up the tray from his bed.

"Freeze-dried?"

"Yes. Now, if you're up to it, my father wants to talk with you."

"Uh, sure,"

"Good, I'll be right back," Annaliese said as she walked out of the room with the tray.

She left the door open, giving Sebastian the ability to hear murmurs down the hall. He couldn't quite make out what the people were saying, but it didn't make much difference as within moments of her departure a man stepped into the room. He was tall, white-haired, clean-shaven, handsome. If Sebastian was to guess, he'd say he was in his midsixties. The man walked to the chair that sat next to the window. He grabbed it and positioned it closer to the side of the bed. Sebastian just stared at him nervously. After the man sat down, he smoothed out his trousers and crossed his legs. Placing his hands on his knee, he cleared his throat and looked at Sebastian.

"Hello, sir," Sebastian greeted the man.

"Hello, Corporal Van Zandt," the man said.

"I want to thank you for rescuing me from the chopper and taking—"

"No need to thank us, it's what we do," the man interrupted.

"Okay," Sebastian said and then shut up. He didn't know what to say. The man made him feel apprehensive.

"Corporal, we have some questions for you, so I'll just begin. We have had someone out near the crash site since the helicopter went down, but no rescue team has come for you, why?"

"Uh, well; that's a tricky one," Sebastian said, sitting up farther. "Go ahead."

Sebastian paused for a moment. His instinct was to be open and honest, but doing so could jeopardize his recovery. Sebastian's recent experiences with "being honest" had put him where he was now. He looked at the man sitting next to him. He was dressed in jeans and a buttoned-up collared shirt. His clothes were clean, but his jeans showed the stains of work. Sebastian studied his hands and saw that they too showed the marks of labor. His knuckles looked rough, and some fresh scratches were visible. At one time this man had worked behind a desk, but now he used his hands. Sebastian didn't quite know which direction to go in, but his instincts won over and he opened up. "I don't think you'll see a rescue team. They probably just assume that if the bird went down we were all killed. I mean, who the hell survives a chopper crash?"

"Well, you did, God willing. Unfortunately, your comrades all perished," the man said, confirming the outcome of everyone else on the chopper.

"You see, the unit I was with is not your run-of-the-mill group of Marines." Sebastian paused; he didn't know how to put it.

"Go ahead, Corporal, I'm all ears."

"The unit I was with mutinied and took control of the ship I was on. I was being dropped off because I didn't agree with what they were doing. They don't plan on helping anyone here. They were just dropping people like me off and picking up others who wish to join them. I couldn't in good conscience follow along." Sebastian quickly spat the words out.

"Interesting. Well, I am impressed to hear that you're a principled man. We might be able to use someone like you here, and with your skills you might be useful."

"Excuse me, but after I'm healed up I need to go find my brother and his family."

"Where is your brother?"

"Not far from where we crashed, maybe five miles. He lives near the Carmel Valley area."

"Well, Corporal—"

"Please call me Sebastian. I'm no longer a Marine. I was discharged, so to speak, yesterday," Sebastian interrupted.

"Well, Sebastian. You broke your leg badly. You're not going anywhere anytime soon," the man said, pointing at his leg.

"Who are you?"

"Sorry, very rude of me. I'm Bishop Sorenson," the man said, reaching out a hand to Sebastian.

Taking his hand and shaking it firmly, Sebastian asked, "Bishop of what?"

"I'm bishop of the Encinitas First Ward of the Church of Latter-day Saints."

"Why am I here?"

"We saw your helicopter crash, and knowing it was military, we went to your aid. That's it, nothing more," Sorenson said flatly.

"Like I said before, not much we or the Marines can offer. My old unit probably already left."

"Where were they going?"

"I heard they were headed to Oregon."

Sorenson just sat for an uncomfortable period of time before he said anything else. Sebastian didn't know how to size him up. He seemed like a pleasant enough man, but Sebastian just wasn't sure.

"I'll let you get back to resting, you need it," Sorenson said, standing up and putting the chair back.

"Wait, um. Can someone go see if my brother is okay? Can you send someone to get them, maybe? He's a good man, he has the same skills I have, and if I know my brother, he'll have supplies and his family will be an asset," Sebastian hurriedly said.

"We have enough supplies and more than enough people at the moment, but I will consider it. Right now you need to rest and we need to continue our preparations."

"Preparations for what?"

"We're leaving, Sebastian. San Diego is not a safe place and it's now time to go home."

"Where's that?" Sebastian asked curiously.

"Zion."

40 miles east of Barstow, California

Per Nelson's request, the group had gathered to discuss Gordon's plan to scavenge near Fort Irwin. Nelson felt the plan was shortsighted and unnecessary. Huddled in a circle, minus Holloway, who was on lookout, the group discussed the new plan. For protection they had tucked the convoy behind a small mountain a couple miles off of Interstate 15. Each person in the group showed the weariness of the previous seven weeks. The weight of the struggle had affected them all in similar ways. Collectively they wanted to get to Idaho, but they also trusted Gordon.

When Gordon had heard about the meeting, his initial reaction was frustration. He hated having to explain himself to everyone. Not really having a choice in the matter, he would do his best to convince them. But in the end, even if they decided against it, he was going.

"By now you know why we've been sitting in the desert for hours," Nelson stated as he started the discussion. "I thought everyone should have a voice in Gordon's plans, as they affect us all." Nelson turned to Gordon, who was not sitting; he stood with his arms crossed. "Gordon, I'm sorry, but I disagree with this plan. It's important for us to keep heading north. I think we have enough supplies, and the more time we're on the open road the greater the chance we have of being attacked. Yesterday was an example."

Unfolding his arms and pointing at Nelson, Gordon answered, "I appreciate a good debate, so thank you, Nelson, for bringing everyone together. Before I get started on why I think it's important for me and Holloway to go scavenge the nearby base, I wanted to remind everyone of something." Gordon paused and looked around. "We have gotten this far because we have the resources and the skills. Yes, while it seems we have a lot of supplies now, they will eventually dry up. The troubles we encountered on the road yesterday are something we may well encounter again. Plus, think about this. Once we arrive in Idaho and settle down, we will most likely have to defend ourselves from raiding parties. We will need not just food but lots of ammunition and heavier fire-power. Yesterday that .50-cal saved us. We need more weapons like that and more ammunition for them. This base might have those things." Gordon paused again and pointed in the direction of Fort Irwin.

Melissa, who was normally quiet, spoke up. "Gordon, I trust you, but I have to agree with Nelson here. Let's just get going. I feel very vulnerable on the road. I want to get to Idaho so we can get our life going."

Following on Melissa's comment was Eric. "Sorry, Gordon, but I agree. You know I always have your back, but let's not stop, let's keep going."

More in the group spoke up, and all agreed with Nelson.

"Okay, I hear you!" Gordon exclaimed, clearly flabbergasted by the opposition to his plan. "Does anyone agree with me?" he asked, looking around. What surprised him most was that Samantha didn't raise her hand; in fact no one did.

"Honey, sorry. Yesterday proved to me that we need to keep driving," Samantha replied to Gordon's hard stare.

Everyone in the group felt the awkwardness, and all fell silent.

Gordon just looked at each person; even Holloway's wife was opposed. He couldn't believe it. He didn't know how to deal with this situation. Everyone's comments were against the plan, but no one told him he couldn't do it. He struggled with how to respond. His thoughts were conflicted because he felt the need to go but knew the importance of having a connected and cohesive group. The seconds passed like hours as everyone remained quiet, wait-ing for Gordon to respond.

"Dad's right," Hunter spoke up.

All in the group turned to see Hunter standing on the edge of the group near his trailer. He looked different now; it wasn't his clothes, but his demeanor was different.

He took a step forward into the circle and repeated his comment. "Dad's right, we will need bigger guns to defend ourselves."

Gordon was taken aback by his son's forcefulness. He was proud and shaken. He had never seem Hunter act like this; it was if he had morphed into a small man.

"Thank you, Son," Gordon said, looking at Hunter proudly.

Hunter just nodded and stepped over to Gordon's side.

"Everyone, I heard you and I agree, we need to keep pressing forward, but we also have to get those things we'll need to protect us. Here is what we will do. Holloway and I will set out in a few hours to recon the base. We will return in the morning. Upon our return we will head north again. It's starting to get dark, and you know we don't move in the darkness. I hope this satisfies everyone; look at it as a win-win."

There was some slight cross chatter, and then everyone agreed to the plan. One by one they all got up and went back to their vehicles until only Samantha, Hunter, and Gordon were left.

Samantha walked over to Hunter; she looked at him, then looked at Gordon. "What is this?" she asked, pointing at the revolver holstered on Hunter's hip.

"I gave it to him this morning, he needs it. If he'd had it yesterday, things would have been different," Gordon responded.

"He's a boy, Gordon! Have you even showed him how to shoot it?"

"I know how to shoot it, Mom. I'm a man now," Hunter interjected.

"No you're not, you're still a boy, you're only eight and your father is crazy for giving this to you!" Samantha replied.

"Now I'm crazy! The world is crazy, Sam, and you better get used to this because he needs to protect himself and Haley. You know better than me, this isn't the world of birthday parties and Disney Junior. He knows how to use it and knows not to treat it like a toy," Gordon answered defensively.

"If you weren't constantly going off leaving us, maybe he wouldn't need it! I can't believe you're taking off to go to that base. What if something happens to you? We need you here!"

Gordon didn't answer because he didn't know how to without upsetting her. He just stood there staring at her.

"Never mind; you're too stubborn and always have been!" Samantha exclaimed. She stormed off.

"Dad, can I go with you and Mr. Holloway?"

"Absolutely not. I need you here in my place while I'm gone," Gordon said, looking down on his son.

"Please, I can help," Hunter pleaded.

"No way, I need you here; plus your mother would skin me alive," Gordon said lightheartedly. He tussled his son's hair and finished by saying, "Let's go eat, we all have a big night ahead of us."

Cheyenne Mountain, Colorado

Julia's heart was pounding hard in her chest. She felt almost faint after hearing the news that one of the search teams had returned and had information about Brad.

When she awoke that morning she'd been greeted with her first bout of morning sickness. She had laughed to herself earlier that all the discomforts of pregnancy are wiped from your memory after you have a baby. The nausea she was experiencing was not unlike her first time, almost twenty years before. After spending most of her morning lying down, she remembered how much she disliked the pregnancy part. She recalled the conversations with her mommy friends then and how she'd said, "Never again." Her pregnancy with Bobby had been tough for her; the first trimester had been one day after another of horrible nausea and a total feeling of malaise. The second trimester gave her some reprieve, but it soon was replaced with constant back pain and overall discomfort.

One other thing she lost during pregnancy was the concern for what others thought of her. She quickly put on a robe, pulled her hair back, slipped on her slippers, and exited her room. The vacant hallways would soon welcome more men and women from bases around the country, and she looked forward to it. The base itself could handle thousands more. It was currently understaffed at less than a thousand, which was only 5 percent of capacity. Brad had often told her how wasteful the government was with its money, but now she was happy they spent lavishly. She was now the beneficiary of that government spending.

She didn't know what to expect when she reached the briefing room door. When she touched the door handle, she said a little prayer and took a deep breath, then opened the door. Sitting around a small table in this stale gray room were Cruz, Dylan, Baxter, and two men she'd never seen before. They were young men; stubble and dirt covered their faces.

It was apparent to her that these men had just arrived. They hadn't even been given the chance to take a shower. The one man she was hoping to see when she opened the door was not sitting there. The expression on each person's face told her the answer to a question she had been asking since she first heard of Brad's disappearance.

"Hi, Julia, please sit down," Cruz said in a relaxed tone. He stood and pulled out a chair next to his.

She just stared at them all and said, "No, no. This is how you do it? This is how you tell me? You bring me down here? I thought that you wouldn't be so cruel. I thought that when you wanted me to come down here it was good news because no one with a heart would bring someone down to a dark, small room to be told her husband is dead."

"Please sit," Cruz said again. He stepped toward her, but she recoiled.

"How dare you, Andrew? If you wanted to tell me my husband was dead, you should have come to my room!" Julia said loudly, tears starting to well up in her eyes.

"Mrs. Conner, we don't know if the president is dead," Baxter blurted out.

Cruz snapped his head in the general's direction in surprise.

"What do you mean, General?" Julia said. Her hands were shaking as she dabbed the tears around her eyes.

"These two men here found what they think was his body, but they didn't bring anything back with them to verify it was his."

"Yes, ma'am, we found several charred bodies," one of the special operations men said, but Julia interrupted him.

"So why do you think he was one of them?" she asked, then slowly walked to the chair and sat down. The combination of the pregnancy and the stressful news made her feel weak.

"Ma'am, we discovered a pile of clothes in the same room, and this was in the jacket pocket," the man said, tossing a wallet on the table.

Julia recognized it as Brad's. She grabbed it and opened it just to make sure.

"We examined the corpses, but it was impossible to ID any of them. That was all we could get before we were forced to vacate the area under threat of force," one of the men said, pointing to the wallet in Julia's hands.

Taking a series of deep breaths to calm herself, Julia felt relieved by the news in some way. The wallet only proved he had been there, it didn't prove that one of the bodies was his.

"So what happens next, gentlemen? We send more teams back in?"

"This is something else we needed to talk with you about," Cruz said as he sat back down.

Not letting Cruz finish, Baxter interjected, "Yes, we send more teams."

Cruz again craned his head in Baxter's direction; this was the second time he'd just blurted out something.

"Actually . . ."

"Actually, what, Andrew?" Julia asked.

"What I'm going to say is that we are beefing up the searches while simultaneously we will start executing the president's plan of setting up the government in Portland."

"And we'll have the manpower to do both?" Julia asked, looking a bit concerned that the search for Brad could be jeopardized by going to Portland.

"Julia, Brad would want it this way. We need to start executing his plan for Portland. We have the manpower and will continue looking for him while I go to Portland and get the government established there for his return."

Julia looked deeply into Cruz's eyes, then brought her attention to Baxter. She was seeking to be reassured. She understood what Cruz was doing and knew that what he said about Brad wanting him to move forward with the Portland plan was correct.

"Who will be in charge of Brad's search party?"

"Mrs. Conner, I will be in charge here and in overseeing the operation for the president," Baxter said.

"Good. I'm glad to hear that the search will continue and that Brad's plans are still going forward. You are right, Andrew, he would want that. Now, if there is nothing more, I will excuse myself. I don't feel all that well," she said. She then slowly lifted herself from her chair. Cruz stood quickly and assisted her.

After the door closed behind her, she felt the tears coming. She dabbed her eyes again and began her walk back to her room. She walked slowly and deliberately through the hallways, stopping frequently to take breaks. She started to experience cramping in her lower abdomen, so painful that it took her breath away. Grimacing in pain, she felt a sensation of vertigo. She attempted to steady herself by placing both hands on the wall, but the vertigo and the light-headedness that followed were too much to bear. She looked down the hall hoping to see someone, but, as usual, the hall was vacant. The vertigo intensified in tandem with the pain. She tried to take a step, but her legs gave out and she collapsed to the floor with a thud, unconscious.

Tijuana, Mexico

The exhaust from the trucks was too much for Pablo. He handed the clipboard to a man next to him and left the warehouse. The cool night air felt good. He looked up at the stars and was impressed how bright they were now that the city lights were not there to mask them. He thought of the days his father would take him to Loreto Bay. They'd lie on the beach at night and his father would show him all the constellations. Those years were innocent for him; he knew nothing about what his father or family did.

His father hadn't always been a cartel boss, but he had been involved in crime from a young age. His father grew up like many in Mexico, in a poor but proud family. His grandfather worked one labor job after another. Lacking a real education or any connections, which are important in Mexico, he never could get a job that could elevate him or his family. Alfredo was smart and wise at even a young age and saw his father's failings. He swore to himself that he would never be poor; he would rise out of the squalor of poverty. This opportunity presented itself when a thug not much older than Alfredo at the time needed someone to "run" something. Alfredo never looked back, and within two years he had his own runners. Heroin was the drug of choice, and the buyers were mainly American. Alfredo's operation grew beyond drugs and into smuggling anything that could make money. He soon became the go-to person for anything in Tijuana.

He leveraged this distinction to connect with the right people. He found that the politicians, celebrities, and big-business types were not unlike anyone else. They had their fetishes, desires, and needs. Alfredo built his business by being the man who could get it for them. Within six years, he ran the largest cartel in Baja California. This level of success didn't come without incident, but he proved to be resilient. By the time he was lying on the beach with his young son, Pablo, in Loreto Bay, he had grown to be one of the top cartel heads in all of Mexico. Within twenty years he was one of the richest and most powerful men in the country.

He did what he could to keep his children out of the business, but Pablo was persistent, so Alfredo made him a deal. Finish college, and then, if you want to go into the "business," it's yours. Pablo graduated from Harvard with honors, and while his father was celebrating his son's achievement, Pablo pulled him aside and told him that he wanted in. Alfredo's cartel ran like a multi-national corporation, with Pablo his chief operating officer. Pablo oversaw a lot of the operations from the ground and reported directly to Alfredo. When the lights went out, everything changed. No longer were cocaine and marijuana the cash crops. Food, water, and energy were now prized possessions and commodities.

Mexico City had been untouched by the North American EMP; however, the northern half of Mexico was not so lucky. The Mexican government was doing all it could to support the north, but getting needed supplies to the people was impossible. Convoys of food, water, and equipment heading north along the western coast soon found their way into Alfredo's warehouses in Baja. Alfredo saw the new marketplace, but Pablo's plans were bigger, much bigger.

Pablo spun around, finding every constellation he knew. He then wondered if his heroes throughout history had stared into the starry sky like he did. His thoughts then shifted quickly to visions of empire. Schooling had taught him about the greatest leaders in history. Alexander, Caesar, Peter the Great, Napoleon, Charlemagne; these men had become his heroes. They had created true legacies, and he wanted that kind of power the way his father had wanted to achieve wealth. Pablo longed for a place alongside those men. This desire had been dreams and fantasies, but now the world had been shaken like a large snow globe and all the flakes were still floating in the air. If he executed his plan correctly, he could be among those revered names in history. The only thing that stood in his way was his father.

He pulled a small cigar out of his jacket pocket and lit it. The glow of the flame lit his face, showing a serious expression. As he watched the flame dance off of the tip of the cigar, he thought of his next steps in this game. He needed to get back north again and regroup his men. This time, though, he would do things differently; he needed some support. As he took a long drag, the cigar's tip illuminated his smiling face. He knew who he'd call. His father's influence had reached across countries and continents. His next call would be to a family friend in Caracas. This friend could get him what he needed: an army.

JANUARY 10, 2014

· · ·

Some choices we live not only once but a thousand times over, remembering them for the
rest of our lives.

—Richard Bach

South of Fort Irwin, California

Gordon liked the desert for different reasons; one was the contrast in temperatures between the day and the night. As he
and Holloway walked back to his truck, unsuccessful in their mission, he took the time to appreciate the cool, crisp air.

Every area of the base appeared locked up tight, and armed
security was everywhere. With the incident of a day and half ago
still fresh in his mind, he wasn't about to walk up to the gate and
ask for help. He just didn't trust anyone, nor could he risk it. The
walk to the truck took about thirty minutes, and then the drive
back would take another forty-five. He'd be able to get a few
hours of sleep; then they'd get their day started on the road. He
was disappointed that the base was locked down, but in some
ways he'd kind of expected it.

Just after starting the truck he heard someone scream. "Sshh,"
he said to Holloway.

"What?" Holloway responded.

"Listen, quiet."

Both men sat in the glow of the dashboard listening. Nothing, just the truck engine.

"Let's get back," Holloway said as he stretched.

"There, again, did you hear that?" Gordon said as he turned off the truck.

Again, both men just sat listening to the quiet desert.

"I swear, I heard someone scream twice in the distance," Gordon said.

"Okay, but what are we going to do about it? It's not our concern, is it?" Holloway asked.

"You're right, let's get outta here," Gordon said as he turned the ignition key again and fired up the truck. Then as if on cue, the scream came again but closer, followed by a gunshot.

"Now I heard that!" Holloway exclaimed.

Just as Gordon turned off the engine again, the voice screamed a third time; this time it was audible and closer. "Dad, help!"

Gordon recognized the voice; it was Hunter. He flung open the door and grabbed his rifle. Holloway followed right behind him, armed and ready. They both ran in the direction from which they'd heard the scream.

"Hunter! Hunter! Where are you?" Gordon yelled, a bit of panic in his voice.

"Dad, over here!" Hunter's voice sounded fatigued and scared.

"I'm coming!"

Gordon ran hard across the desert floor. The uneven ground made him overextend his left leg and almost fall, but he recovered his balance and kept running toward his son.

"Dad!"

"I'm almost there! Holloway, scan the area with the NVGs!"

Holloway stopped, put on the night-vision goggles, and began looking in Hunter's direction.

"I see what must be Hunter, you're close!" Holloway yelled at Gordon.

The night was pitch black. Gordon could not see anything, but he was determined to get to his son.

"Hunter, yell out again!"

"Here, Dad!"

Gordon knew he was close; he pivoted, and in a dozen steps he ran into Hunter.

"What the hell? What are you doing out here?"

"Dad, I, uh, I . . ." Hunter was attempting to answer him but was out of breath.

"Let's go! I need you to keep running!"

"Gordon," Holloway said, "I have a lot of movement out there. I'm counting, one, two, four, at least eight bodies moving out there, and they're heading toward us."

"Get back to the truck, now!"

All three ran. Hunter kept falling down, but each time Gordon pulled him up quickly. No one said a word as each was breathing hard from the exertion.

"Where the fuck is the truck?" Gordon asked loudly.

"It should be around here somewhere!"

"Put the NVGs on, hurry!"

As Holloway put the goggles back on to help find the truck, Gordon held Hunter close. He listened as best he could for any sounds around him.

"Over there, but we have to hurry. Whoever was chasing Hunter is getting close to the truck."

Not hesitating, they all took off in a hard sprint toward the truck.

Gordon was starting to feel panicked. He couldn't see, but he knew people were coming toward him, and his son was there.

"Where the hell is it?"

"Almost there," Holloway stated, now running with the goggles on.

Out of the darkness the truck appeared, but so did whoever was in pursuit of Hunter. All Gordon could feel was something large hitting him in the face. The force of the hit was enough to lay him on his back. He could taste the blood from a large cut across his nose. He shook off the hit and rolled and got back on his feet. The visibility was only feet, but he could hear whoever it was all around him.

"Hunter? Hunter?" Gordon called out. He had drawn his pistol and held it out but didn't shoot because he couldn't identify anyone.

Then gunshots rang out. He didn't know who was shooting, and he still had no idea where his son was.

"Hunter? Where are you?"

From what he could see, there were at least a dozen people around him and the truck. They probably had the same limitations as he did, and from the sounds of only one rifle, Gordon assumed it was Holloway.

"Hunter? Where are you?"

Gordon stepped toward the truck and saw a figure too big to be Holloway. He shot it. He turned and shot another one and another. The next thing he knew he was on the ground again.

He couldn't remember how long he'd been down, but the back of his head hurt badly. The sound of gunfire had ceased. He started to grasp around him for his gun, but all he touched was sand.

"Search him for the keys," a man's voice said, hovering above him.

Gordon tried to scramble away but was stopped when he was hit in the head again. He could still make out some noises, but he couldn't do anything.

"We found the keys on this one," another unknown voice said after going through Gordon's pants pockets.

"Toss him and the boy in the back of the truck," the first voice said.

"What about the other one?"

"He's dead. Samson bashed his head in," a third voice said.

"Two will be fine. Brother Rahab will want to see them."

The men tied up Gordon and Hunter and placed them in the bed of the truck. The last thing Gordon saw before he passed out was his son's bloodied face. With all of his strength, he inched close to Hunter. He placed his forehead against Hunter's head. Just being able to touch his son made him feel a bit better. He kept struggling to stay conscious, but the effort was too much and he passed out again.

USS *Makin Island* off the coast of Southern California

Barone had thought his plan was working up until they began sending in teams of Marines to gather their families. The number who weren't returning was staggering to him. When he'd executed his mutiny, he believed that he could convince many to come with thoughts of treasure and land. On the surface it appeared to have worked, but what was happening now showed that a good number of Marines and sailors were just saying one thing to their commanders and senior NCOs and doing another when they had the chance. All along he knew it would be difficult to convince 100 percent to join him, but now his ranks were decreasing. They had been able to make up for some of the loss by finding Marines at Camp Pendleton and convincing them to join. His men hadn't really known what life was like but would find out; those who had been stateside did and now were eager to come with him.

The thing that troubled him the most was the attempt on his life two days before. When he'd decided to go against all that he had promised to uphold and protect, he knew there were bound to be those who would try to stop him. Taking an entire ARG and then attacking a U.S. military installation was a lot for some of the men to stomach, but this new world they were in was different. His military training and experience went deep, and when he was first briefed on the EMP strikes and the nuclear attack on Washington, D.C., he knew without a doubt his country was gone. Those who kept the faith were like those who believed in awakening a corpse that had been dead for days. It was easy to think that their government could tackle the situation, but only a few understood the enormity of the problem. He understood and knew that to survive he would have to shift his priorities quickly, so he did. The plan was quickly laid out and executed. He felt sorry for those who had decided not to come back; their ignorance would be their undoing. Only when they were face-to-face with the realities on the ground would they know why he'd done what he'd done.

Today would be another new experience for him. The Marine who had attempted to kill him had been taken alive. His court-martial had been swift, and so would the execution of the sentence. The tribunal had found him guilty, and his sentence was death by firing squad. Barone would do something different: Instead of gathering a group of Marines to carry out the act, he himself would do it. If the sentence was to be carried out, he felt the one in command should be the one to do it.

He looked down at his watch; the hour was getting close. His thoughts had been all-consuming; so much had been happening. His stateroom was his sanctuary, and he took advantage of it more now than in the past. Even though he had found his wife and daughter safe, he still could not get over the loss of his son. Guilt racked him. There were moments he regretted his decision, knowing that if he had gone back east, Billy would still be alive. His pragmatic side, though, would not let him sit in this guilt because the conditions in which he'd found his wife and daughter were perilous. It was as if God had made it one or the other. Had he gone back east like a good Marine, he had no doubt his wife and daughter would have starved to death.

He wiped the last bit of oil from his nickel-plated Model 1911 and placed it in his holster. He stood and walked to the mirror to make sure everything was in place on his uniform. He grabbed his belt and holster, put it on snugly, and left the stateroom. Each person he came upon in the passageways of the ship quickly stood next to the bulkhead and acknowledged him. Everyone knew where he was going and what was about to happen on the flight deck.

When he exited the last hatch and stepped onto the black deck, the sun's rays warmed his face. It took a moment for his eyes to adjust to the brightness, but when they did, he saw everyone gathered already. He approached Master Sergeant Simpson and returned his salute. Simpson handed him a piece of paper. He glanced down to see it was the Marine's execution order, and at the bottom of the page it was signed by him. Barone looked around at the group that had been gathered for the execution; every senior NCO and officer had been commanded to attend. Barone did this for two reasons: to show them how violating their laws ended in real consequences and to strike fear into his men. He approached the convicted Marine.

"Lance Corporal Cartwell, you have been found guilty by a military tribunal of attempting to kill a superior officer. The sentence for this is death by firing squad," Barone bellowed.

The young Marine stood firmly at attention with his hands bound behind his back and his legs tied together. The expression on his face showed not a man afraid of death but one defiant as he stared at Barone squarely, not even allowing a blink to interrupt his stare.

"This sentence will be carried out now, but the firing squad is not needed." Barone looked around at all his senior staff and continued, "I will be the one to carry out this sentence. I am the one sentencing this man to die, so it is only right that I be the one to do it. Before I carry out this order, do you have anything to say, Lance Corporal Cartwell?"

"Yes, sir, I do," the man said defiantly.

"Go ahead," Barone responded. He lowered the paper so he could look the man in the eyes.

"I'm not sorry for what I did, no way! This man is a traitor and murderer! You hear me out there, you are following a traitor! Our country needed us and we let them down, we abandoned our people! We are Marines and we have not fulfilled our oath! I only wish I could have been successful. You can kill me today, but I'm not the only one! You will pay for what you did to our country!" the man screamed out.

"Is that it?" Barone asked. He didn't show an ounce of emotion and didn't change his expression the entire time the man shouted at him.

"Just do it, get it over with! Today, I die a patriot!"

Barone rolled up the paper and placed it in his side cargo pocket. He signaled to a couple of men to his right with a nod. They came running over and began to blindfold Cartwell.

"I want to see. I want to see you do it," he said.

Both men stopped and looked at Barone. He didn't respond right away, then signaled for them to leave with another nod. Once the men had taken position back in formation, Barone began. He unholstered his pistol and took aim at Cartwell. He wasn't more than ten feet away, but for him it felt like it was a hundred feet. Barone took a breath, held it, and began to slowly squeeze the trigger. The natural arc of movement felt exacerbated, and for an instant Barone was nervous that he might miss the man. The pressure he kept applying seemed not to be enough. He continued to squeeze, but then the man yelled out, "God bless the United States!" This startled Barone and forced him to apply the final amount of pressure to the trigger. The pistol went off with the bullet ripping through the man's skull, throwing his head back. The man's body then went limp and he fell to the ground lifeless. Barone lowered the pistol and just stared at Cartwell's body. He stood for twenty seconds, then reholstered the pistol.

"Corpsman, over here now!" Barone commanded.

A man in his twenties ran over and examined the body of Cartwell. He looked up at Barone and said, "He's dead, sir."

"Good," Barone answered with a subdued voice.

Barone took a few steps back and stood at attention. He ordered the formation to attention. Simpson walked over and stood in front of him.

"Master Sergeant, dump this man's body overboard, then prepare the ARG, we're done here."

"What about the chopper that's missing, sir?"

"We have to assume they went UA too; time to cut our losses and move on."

"Where to, sir?"

"Set sail for Oregon; our next stop will be Coos Bay."

San Diego, California

Sebastian had never used crutches before, but he was getting the hang of them quickly. He paced back and forth in his room; it was close to lunchtime, and Annaliese would be bringing him his food. After meeting with her father the day before, he had many more questions, especially about Zion.

Right on time, he heard the typical three-tap knock and then the door opened slightly. Her gentle face peered in to see him standing there with a slight smile.

"I have your lunch. Is now a good time?" she asked.

"Sure, come on in. I'm starving. Smells great. What is it, chili?" Sebastian replied. He looked happy to see her as he hopped over to the end of the bed and sat down.

She quickly walked in, placed the tray next to him, and turned to leave, not responding to him.

"Stop, don't leave so quickly," he pleaded.

"I have things to do."

"Just ten minutes, please. I'm stuck in here all day. It's lonely."

She hesitated a bit, then gave in.

"Here, sit down," Sebastian said, pointing to the same chair that Bishop Sorenson had sat in the day before.

She hadn't sat down for a second before Sebastian started peppering her with questions.

"Where's Zion? When are you leaving? Who are you people?"

"I'm surprised my father didn't answer these questions."

"Nope."

"Well, let's see. We are members of the Church of Latter-day Saints."

"Okay," Sebastian replied with a smile on his face.

"I don't know if I can tell you when we're leaving, but where we are going I can."

"Zion?"

"Yes, Zion."

"Where is Zion?"

"It's the Holy Land in Missouri," she replied.

"There's holy land in Missouri?"

"I don't expect you to understand, but yes, there is. We are going home."

Sebastian smirked a bit because the sound of a "Promised Land" in the middle of the Midwest sounded funny. Annaliese caught this smirk and immediately stopped talking. She looked down and shook her head, then stood abruptly.

"Where are you going?" Sebastian asked, now concerned that his inappropriate behavior was the cause of her irritation.

"Mr. Van Zandt, I don't need to sit here and tell you about my beliefs only to have you mock me. You're in my house, and I expect some type of respect. You need to eat so you can get your strength back. I believe you have somewhere to go yourself."

"Listen, I'm sorry. I really didn't mean to do . . . that," he said while motioning to his face.

"Excuse me. I'll be back later for your tray." She nodded to him and walked out of the room.

"Please stay, I'm sorry, truly, I'm sorry," he pleaded, but it was too late. "Damn it, Sebastian, you're such an idiot!" he said out loud. His appetite now gone, he stood and hopped over to the window. His room looked down on a side walkway where crates and large trash cans were stored. He leaned closer to see if he could see anything, but it was useless. The walkway went for yards in either direction. Feeling frustrated with himself and with not knowing what was going on, he hopped back to the bed, grabbed his crutches, and walked to the door. He felt a little hesitation about opening the door, but he asked himself what harm it would do if he went for a short walk.

He entered the brightly sunlit hallway and walked toward what appeared to be a large loft. On the walls hung portraits. He assumed they were her family, and by the looks of it, it was a large one. With each step he took, he felt more like a child sneaking out of his room; the thought flashed and he dismissed it as stupid. The loft was large, fully furnished, and had the appearance of a heavily utilized room. A sectional took up most of the space, a large TV was mounted on the wall, and what must have been dozens of toys were in the far corner.

At the end of the loft was a staircase. He hurried over and stopped. He could hear voices down below. One sounded like Annaliese; the other he wasn't familiar with, but it was another woman. It sounded like they were talking about him, but just as he started to make out what they were saying, a voice from behind startled him.

"Does it hurt?"

"What? Ahh . . . jeez, you scared me," Sebastian said. He looked around to see a young boy. He recognized him from the day before.

"Your leg. Does it hurt?"

"Uhh . . . yeah, kinda. In fact, it's hurting more than usual," Sebastian said, then walked past the boy to the sectional and sat down.

"Where are you from?"

"Now aren't you full of questions?"

The boy walked over to the sectional and sat down next to him. "My sister said you survived a helicopter crash. Was it scary?"

"I'll tell you what, let's play a game. I'll answer a question and then you'll answer a question, okay?"

The boy thought for a moment, then nodded in agreement.

"So your first question was 'Does it hurt'? Yes, it does. So, my question is, What city are we in?"

"Encinitas. Where are you from?"

"I'm originally from Maryland, but I now live or used to live at Camp Pendleton. I guess you could say I'm homeless. I was heading to see my brother when the helicopter crashed." Sebastian looked at the boy. He thought about how well mannered and mature he seemed for his age. He guessed that he was about eight years old. His sandy blond hair was cut short, and his clothes showed a boy who seemed sheltered, a solid-colored blue polo-type shirt, jeans, and white socks. Sebastian smiled and continued. "When are you leaving for Zion?"

The boy looked a bit shocked by this question. "You know about Zion?"

"No way, my turn. When are you leaving?"

"My father wants to leave next week."

"How many in your family?"

The boy waved his finger at Sebastian. "No, way, my turn."

Sebastian chuckled and replied, "Go ahead."

"My sister said you're a Marine. Ever kill anyone?"

Now Sebastian looked shocked. "How old are you?"

"Answer the question."

"Listen, I think we've played this game long enough, okay?"

"I think you have too," Annaliese said. She was standing at the top of the stairs.

Sebastian was surprised he hadn't heard her walking up. He wondered how long she had been listening to his back-and-forth with her little brother.

"Sorry, I wanted to stretch my legs or leg, and I ran into him. What's your name anyway?"

"Away with you. Now go, you have things to do. Go see Uncle James in the garage," Annaliese commanded her little brother.

Jumping up without a word, he walked for the stairs, but before he started down, he turned and answered Sebastian. "My name's Zachary, but you can call me Zach." He smiled, then hurried down the stairs past his sister.

"Nice boy. So, were you spying on us?" Sebastian asked Annaliese.

"No, I heard voices up here so I came to see what was going on," she said, walking farther into the room.

"Listen, I'm really sorry about earlier."

"It's okay, I shouldn't be so sensitive." Annaliese approached the sectional and sat down a few feet away from him. "I know this is all strange to you and that all you know is one minute you were in a helicopter and now you're here. I'm sorry about your friends and comrades. What questions do you have? I'll do my best to answer them."

Being mindful of his previous gaffe, he chose to be as polite and conscious of his facial expressions as possible. He openly asked questions, and she answered as straightforwardly as possible. She told him about Zion, about how their prophet Joseph Smith claimed it to be the place for their people to go at the end of days. She further explained that the Mormons had always been a prepared people, always stockpiling food, water, and essential supplies. When the lights went out, their church was ready. They communicated with old ham radios they had stored in Faraday boxes; some had older vehicles that worked, and they had all the other tools necessary to protect and defend themselves.

She went into detail about what had happened locally after the attack. The reports she'd heard were horrible; she herself had not witnessed the initial atrocities, but some in her group had ventured out to plan a route for their trek away from San Diego. Of course many San Diegans were not prepared for this type of event, and within only a few days many had taken to the streets to look for food. Civil unrest had exploded quickly, followed by a total breakdown in civility. People attacked each other for the slightest bit of food. Rumors that a militia was killing and kidnapping people were being heard a few weeks after the attack. This news caused panic within her group, leading her father to start preparations for an evacuation.

When she finally was allowed outside of her ranch, the things she'd seen and now described to Sebastian were horrific. She paused now and then when she described what she'd seen. The bloated and mutilated bodies were not just commonplace; they were everywhere. She was shocked by the death and carnage. She had only been let outside with her uncle when someone had radioed that ships were off the coast. Rumors then began that the government was there to help, but reality proved otherwise. She told him that she had heard the distant gunfire that hit his helicopter and had seen it go down not far from where they sat.

Sebastian took all the information in. At times he had to remind himself to blink. He was transfixed by every word she said. Even though he'd known things would go to shit, it was still shocking to hear the specific details from an eyewitness. As she went on, his concern for Gordon grew. His brother wasn't the prepper type, but he hoped Gordon was able to keep the family safe. The first four weeks had been a violent and bloody fight for the limited resources in the area. After Annaliese had explained everything she knew, he expressed his concern for his brother and his family.

"I need to go check on my brother."

"You still need to heal; maybe next week."

"No, I need to go. You're leaving next week, and by the way it sounds out there, I have to go. He might need me now."

"I understand. Let me talk to my father," she said and placed her hand on his back and rubbed him gently.

"Can you go now?" Sebastian asked.

"Sure," she said. She stood and walked away.

A queasy feeling overcame him as he thought about Gordon, but more specifically about Hunter and Haley. The thoughts of the horrors befalling them made Sebastian sick. He had to find his brother and he had to do it now.

40 miles east of Barstow, California

The sun's rays cascaded across Samantha's face. She twitched for a minute, then rolled over and attempted to go back into the deep sleep she had been enjoying. She then thought about Gordon. She hadn't seen him off when he left last night. As a couple they worked hard at their relationship, but this time they'd both broken a vow of not going to bed mad. After the group's meeting, she fed the kids, got them ready for bed, and went to bed herself, all without uttering a word to him. Their silence was mutual, as Gordon didn't attempt to smooth things over either. Now, though, she regretted her behavior.

She rolled back on her back and placed her hand on the empty part of the bed he usually occupied. She wondered where he was. Slight concern grew, but she dismissed it quickly because knowing Gordon he was probably outside, "getting something done." Her thoughts were then directed to the little footsteps she could hear coming toward her. Haley was tiptoeing, taking each step gently so as to not wake her mother, whom she thought was still asleep.

"Come here, baby," Samantha whispered.

Seeing her mother was awake, Haley hurried over and jumped into the bed next to her. They both cuddled, and Samantha kissed her daughter on the head.

"Where's Daddy?" Haley asked.

"I don't know . . ." Samantha yawned.

Both of them continued with small talk. Haley had started to role-play more since the lights went out. She would tell her mother that she was Princess Celestia from My Little Pony and that Samantha was her sister. She assigned everyone in the family a role.

Samantha didn't mind this innocence. She would play along with her daughter, creating new worlds and exploring them together.

"Where's Hunter?" Haley asked in the middle of the make-believe.

"He's not in the back?" Samantha sat up a bit to try to see him.

"No," Haley replied.

Samantha again soothed her instinctual concern and imagined her son was out with Gordon.

After another ten minutes of play, Samantha knew she needed to get up and get ready; the group would be heading out soon.

When she stepped out of the trailer, the smells of desert sage and campfire smoke mixed and filled her nostrils. The sky was a deep blue, and the sun felt good. People in her group were packing their vehicles, and she could see Nelson talking to his father.

She made her way over to him and said, "Morning, Nelson. Seen Gordon?"

"Nope."

Placing her hand on her brow to shield her eyes, she scanned the encircled vehicles. She didn't see his truck. A deep feeling of dread overcame her.

"Who was on watch last night?" she asked.

"It was Eric," Nelson answered, then continued, "You all right?"

"Um, I don't know. I'm a bit worried." She quickly walked toward Eric and Melissa's trailer. After a solid minute of banging, Melissa opened the door.

"Eric is sleeping. What is it?"

"I need to know if Eric saw Gordon return."

"He's not here?" Melissa asked, sticking her head out and looking around.

"Please wake him up," Samantha begged.

Melissa could see the worry on Samantha's face. "Sure, one second."

Eric rose quickly and came to the door. "Melissa just told me that Gordon's still not back. They didn't come back on my watch."

"Don't you think that's odd? Why didn't you wake me or tell anyone?" Samantha snapped.

"No, I didn't think anything of it, really. Gordon takes care of himself, and I thought they would be back anytime."

Samantha then turned away quickly. Total fear gripped her as she realized that she hadn't seen Hunter either.

Turning back around, she asked, "Did you see Hunter, have you seen him?"

Eric glanced at Melissa, then answered, "No, I haven't seen him since yesterday."

Samantha didn't say another word to them. She jogged off quickly and went to each person in their group. She asked them all the same question. The responses were all the same. No one had seen him. She then began to scream for her son. "Hunter! Hunter!"

All in the group just stared at her. Nelson approached and said, "Samantha, we'll find him. He probably just walked off to . . ."

"To what, Nelson? Look around. We're in the fucking desert. Where is he?"

"We're going to organize a quick search party, okay?" Nelson said in an attempt to reassure her.

She ignored him and took off running toward her trailer. She flung open the door and grabbed Haley. She took her to Melissa and Eric's and dropped her off with instructions to watch over her.

She then went back to her trailer and grabbed a backpack with some water. Just before she stepped out, she saw the Sig Sauer pistol that Gordon had given her weeks ago. She placed it in her waistband.

Nelson had put together a couple of people to help. They met her just outside her trailer.

Stepping down, she turned to Nelson and said, "Let's go find my boy."

Unknown military installation

Gordon's body was racked with pain from his head to his legs. He was confused about how long he'd been out and even where he was. The only light he saw was coming from the cracks along one of the edges of the room. The odors of mold and dust were intense. Not being able to see, he stood up to walk the perimeter of the room. The first thing he noticed was that the walls were a corrugated metal; the second was that the room was long and narrow. When he reached the end where the light was peeking through, he knew. It wasn't about where he was but about what he was in—a Conex box. He continued walking the narrow interior to locate anything or anyone that might be in there with him. Nothing.

His thoughts raced to the night before, the running, the fighting, Hunter. *Where was Hunter?* He vaguely remembered being hit, then tied up. The memory of the drive didn't exist for him. The last thing he recalled was being placed in the bed of the truck with his son. He felt his wrists; the pain of the tight bands being tied around them was still present. He slowly walked back to the door and began to bang. The metal door gave a deep thud with each impact of his closed fist.

"Open the door!" he yelled. He repeated it over and over.

Finally after what must have been an hour he heard someone on the other side. The sound of a padlock being unlocked was followed by the heavy sound of the latch moving. Soon he'd be face-to-face with whoever took him and Hunter.

"Before we open up, step back! Don't think about doing anything, you understand?" the voice yelled from the other side.

Gordon's initial instinct was to fight, but not knowing where Hunter was, he had to snuff out his flame of resistance. He stepped away from the door. "I stepped back! I just want to speak to someone!"

The anticipation of seeing this person or people gripped him. He took a few more steps back. He didn't know what would be coming in and what they meant to do to him.

A loud clang and bang preceded the door creaking open. The bright light from the outside flooded in, blinding him. Squinting, he tried to see, but his eyes were having a difficult time adjusting. All he could see were two shadowy figures. Feeling even more nervous, he moved back farther. The two figures stepped inside. Gordon's heart raced. Again the instinct to fight was there, but he resisted it. He blinked rapidly until his eyes adjusted and both men came into focus. They were average height, had long hair, and their clothes were soiled. Gordon quickly noticed they were armed with pistols holstered in standard green military side holsters.

"Where am I?" Gordon asked.

"You'll have all of your questions answered soon enough," one of the men responded. They both approached Gordon, one holding some rope, the other what looked like a sack.

"What are you going to do?" Gordon asked, stepping back as far as he could. His back was now against the far wall.

"We're not going to hurt you. We just need to take you with us," one of the men said. Both had now stopped their advance and stood a few feet from Gordon.

"If you want your questions answered, you'll need to come with us, and this is the only way," the other man said, holding up the sack.

Gordon quickly analyzed the situation, sizing the men up. They were both lean and of average build. He had fought more than one man before and won, but these two had an advantage. He finally held up his hands. If he could get in front of whoever was in charge, maybe he could find Hunter and then find a way out of this situation.

Both men stepped forward, tied his hands behind his back, put tape over his mouth, and covered his head with the sack. They turned him around and escorted him out of the Conex box.

Gordon felt the sun's warmth the instant he exited. He could hear some people talking in the distance, but their words were unintelligible. The thick canvas sack made it impossible to get his bearings. He tried counting his steps, but he didn't know if that would be of any benefit. Soon they came to a door, and he went through with his escorts. A couple of turns, one last door, and he was taken into a room. They pushed him down into a chair and forcibly removed the sack and tape. The smell in the air was sweet, like incense was burning somewhere. The room was devoid of anything distinguishable. It was small, just space enough for a table and four chairs. Nothing hung on the garish white walls, and there was no window.

He blinked repeatedly and saw a nicely dressed man across a table from him. The man appeared to be in his early fifties, with long black hair pulled back into a ponytail and a thin beard that covered his face. Gordon again looked at the men who had taken him there; they too had long hair.

"What's up with the long hair?" he asked with a smirk.

The man who sat across from him started to tap his finger on the table.

"Where am I? Where's my son? Why have you taken us?"

"Calm down. I'll answer everything in due time. I have a few questions of my own," the man said. His voice was soft with a slight eastern European accent.

"Where is my son?"

"Your boy is fine, no harm has come to him. He is being looked after."

"Let me and my son go, please."

Ignoring Gordon, the man began to talk. "My name is Rahab, and I want to share a story with you. I came to this country over twenty years ago from the Ukraine. A beautiful country, Ukraine, but nothing like the United States. I was amazed by everything I saw here. You have to remember that I was a child of the Soviet era. We didn't have all the things you Americans take for granted. Just the stores alone were magical. The first time I walked into a Walmart I was in disbelief. I felt like I had died and gone to heaven. So much to buy, so many options, so many luxuries. Aah, I took it all in.

"I immersed myself in the American dream. I worked hard and played hard. I drank from the hedonistic cup that is America and loved it. I let go of all my inhibitions. Nothing was too much for me, you see; I looked at it this way. If America won the Cold War, then they must be doing something right. I can't tell you how much I believed that then as a young man. My gluttony knew no end until I woke up one day and looked around me. I had surrounded myself with people, so-called friends, girls, but they weren't real people, they were shells of people. The excess that is America rotted them out and was rotting me out too. I then found the truth to it all, and that was God."

He paused, thought for a moment, then continued. "I need to clarify something. My journey to righteousness didn't come over time, it was thrust on me one day. I still remember that day as if it was yesterday. I got into my car, high on cocaine and alcohol, and drove it right into a group of children on their way to school. I maimed three children. Do you want to know the irony? I walked away with zero injuries. God came to me when I was in prison. He came down from heaven and wrapped his arms around me. He told me that I had a mission to fulfill for him, that I would be his prophet in this world. He needed me to be his instrument who would cleanse the world of all the debauchery and greed.

"When I was released from prison I immediately began working on God's plan. I found the faithful and started my ministry. Then God sent a new sign, and that was when everything stopped working. I knew then that the beginning of the cleanse needed to happen in earnest. My ministry needed to grow from the few dozen worshiping in a strip mall to a vast movement."

Gordon listened in disbelief. The man he saw across the table was insane. He could see it in his eyes. Gordon wanted to interject but knew it was best to stay quiet. He knew he needed to watch what he said, because anything might set this guy off. Gordon finally took notice of the room he was in. He kept looking for some type of clue as to where he was. Then he saw a stack of folders on the floor behind the man. On the corner of the top binder he saw "U.S. Army." This didn't make sense; was he at Fort Irwin? Were the men he'd seen walking the perimeter these men or men from this group? As Gordon thought about all the scenarios that would have him here, Rahab kept rambling.

"So now all of this brings us here. With you sitting there and me sitting here." The man pointed at Gordon.

"Who are you?"

"No, the question is who are you?"

"My name is Gordon Van Zandt, and you have my son, Hunter. We were in the desert scavenging, that is all. Your men attacked us."

"The devil has many agents. His desire is to stop God's work."

"Just please let us go," Gordon begged again.

"How many are in your group?" Rahab asked.

Gordon hesitated before answering. If these were the same men guarding this expansive base, then Rahab had a small army. Letting him know about the others could put them all in jeopardy.

"It's just us, plus my friend; whom I think you killed."

The man didn't say anything; he just stared at Gordon with his dark brown eyes.

"I swear, it's just us; we were scavenging. We saw the base and thought that maybe we could get something, but we left."

Still the man said nothing.

"Just let me and my son go. We will never come back here and never tell anyone." Gordon said this knowing it sounded clichéd, but he didn't know what else to say. He didn't have much to offer or leverage.

"I don't believe you. I think there are more in your group. We will find them. As for you, that is it for now." Rahab stood up and walked toward the door but stopped when Gordon spoke.

"Can I see my son?"

Looking at the other two men before answering, Rahab turned

and said, "You'll see your son very soon. I promise. Now take him back to his cell," he commanded the men, then left the room.

"What about the others from the other day?" one of the men asked him.

"Ah, yes, prepare them for the ceremony tonight," Rahab commanded.

Both men acknowledged their leader's command, then grabbed Gordon and took him away.

JANUARY 11, 2014

· · ·

Never give up. And never, under any circumstances, face the facts.

—Ruth Gordon

40 miles east of Barstow, California

"You need to eat," Nelson said, handing Samantha a tuna packet.

Samantha looked at the dark blue packet in Nelson's hand, then went back to marking grids on an old map of the area. Using a red marker, she shaded the areas they had searched. Unfortunately for her, most of the map was not touched by the red marker.

"Please, Sam, take a bite. You need the energy," Nelson pleaded.

"Every minute I'm not looking for him is a minute lost."

"How about I feed you while you mark more search grids for us?"

"You think this is a joke? My son is out there somewhere; so is my husband. Something happened. I don't know what, but I can't leave my baby boy out there! He's alone and scared! He needs me!" Samantha lambasted Nelson.

"I don't think this a joke, Samantha. Not at all. I just know if you don't keep your strength up, then you can't keep going. Then you're no good to anyone, especially Hunter."

Samantha had stopped looking at Nelson and was intently making marks on the map. But his last comment caused her to stop what she was doing and put the map down. Grabbing the packet of tuna out of his hand, she exhaled deeply.

"I'm sorry, Nelson, I didn't mean to yell at you."

"I know, Samantha, it's okay. You eat that, and then we'll head back out to the north to look for him."

"You know, I'm also worried about Gordon, but he'd under-stand that I'm prioritizing the search for Hunter."

"Of course he would," Nelson said reassuringly.

"Where do you think Gordon is?" Samantha asked, tossing the empty tuna packet on the ground.

"I'm glad you asked. I wanted to talk to you without everyone else giving their opinion on the matter. I think we should send one team to go look for Gordon and Holloway. We know where they went. Plus, I have to say this: What if Hunter was with them?"

Samantha didn't respond. She sat looking at the map on the ground. The light wind was blowing the edges up and shifting sand grains across the top. She had thought that could be the case but felt that Gordon wouldn't have allowed it, no matter how much he wanted Hunter to be "a man." He would never take their son with him.

"I have thought that, but Gordon wouldn't have allowed it. I know him."

"What if Gordon didn't know?"

Shaking her head in amazement, Samantha said, "It's possible. Oh my God."

"Let's send Eric and my dad."

"Okay."

Nelson left Samantha to finalize the search grid on the map while he instructed Eric and his father on their task. As he walked, he thought that Gordon had truly fucked up by going out to scavenge. He knew his friend, and knew that if he was still alive, he was cursing his decision with every ounce of his being.

Cheyenne Mountain, Colorado

The whispers were the first thing Julia heard. She couldn't make out who it was, but they were in the other room. She opened her eyes to an unfamiliar place. Looking left and right, she didn't see anyone. Judging by the room, she was in the base hospital. When she moved her arm she felt a tug. She looked down to see an IV hooked up to her elbow. The events of the day before were clear in her mind up until she'd blacked out.

She ran her hand across her belly and talked to herself. "How are you doing in there, huh?"

What had happened to her two days ago was new for her. She hadn't blacked out in her last pregnancy, and she couldn't recall ever having such severe abdominal pain.

A nurse entered the room wearing the camouflage uniform of an Air Force tech sergeant. She was young and round with her hair pulled back in a bun.

"Mrs. Conner, you're awake?"

"Yes, I just woke. How long have I been here?"

"You were brought in late, almost two days ago. You fainted in the hallway. Dylan McLatchy found you," the nurse said as she walked around the bed checking on the monitors and attending to her duties.

"I've never done that before. Is everything okay?"

"The doctor will be in shortly to go over everything with you," the nurse said as she took her pulse.

The door opened and a middle-aged man wearing a white lab coat entered. He stepped over to Julia's bedside.

"How are you doing, Mrs. Conner?"

"I'm fine. I was just telling the nurse."

"Everything's normal, Doctor," the nurse said directly to the doctor.

"Great." He smiled back.

After the nurse left the room, the doctor pulled over a chair and sat next to Julia.

"Mrs. Conner, I'm Captain Weatherby, one of the doctors here. You were brought in after being found in one of the passageways unconscious."

"Can I sit up?" Julia asked, looking for the button to operate the bed.

"Sure, here," Weatherby said, pressing the button that raised the head of the bed.

"Thanks. Now I can talk with you and not feel so awkward."

"Mrs. Conner, you came in severely dehydrated. Also, your blood pressure was incredibly high. When we undressed you, there was vaginal blood, so we . . ."

"What do you mean, vaginal blood? Is the baby all right?" Julia asked, concerned. She sat up straight and tense.

"Mrs. Conner, when there is vaginal bleeding, it is a sign that something might be wrong with the pregnancy. We examined you with an ultrasound, and unfortunately found that the pregnancy is ectopic."

Julia's eyes gave away the emotions she was feeling deep inside.

Tears ran down her face and dripped onto the clean white sheets. She tried to speak, but the words would not come out. Losing even the strength to remain sitting up, she fell back into the pillows and gazed past the doctor. She wasn't looking at anything specifically. Her thoughts went to the dreams she had of a new baby. Brad's disappearance was helped by the fact that she had his baby. She consoled herself with the knowledge that even if he was confirmed dead, she would have someone. She would still have a part of him.

The doctor started to talk again, but it sounded like he was in the other room with the door closed. His voice just faded into the background and was unintelligible to her. All she could think of was losing this baby. Ever since she had found out about the pregnancy she had had visions of actually holding the baby and looking into its eyes. Her fantasies even extended to being there every day as it grew up, the first birthday, first steps, first time it said Mama or Dada, all of those precious moments that parents get to experience. Now, without notice, this new life was being taken away. These thoughts were suddenly stopped when Weatherby touched her arm.

"Mrs. Conner. We need to get you prepped for the procedure."

"Get out," she said in a low voice.

"Mrs. Conner, we need to get this done."

"Get out, get out, get out!" she screamed.

Weatherby flinched, but he wasn't shocked. He had been a doctor long enough to know that her response was not unusual. He pushed his chair back, stood up, and promptly left the room.

All Julia could see in her mind's eye was the little baby. She wanted this baby, and for whatever reason, she felt that God was taking it away.

Unknown military installation

Gordon paced his cell hundreds of times. He didn't have much to go on. He had to get out of there and find Hunter. The dreadful noises and screams that had echoed across the area last night foretold a fate he had no intention of experiencing. He couldn't for the life of him understand how Rahab and his men had been able to take this base. All he could imagine was that Rahab had gathered together a large force who were just as crazy as he was. He knew Rahab was an extremist in the purest sense. He was driven by a deeply held belief that his cause was just and divine.

Gordon had run into these types in Iraq, and now they had taken root here. History had dozens and dozens of examples of these kinds of zealots. During catastrophic events, some look to a god to help explain why or to give them hope. Rahab's flock had probably grown tremendously after the lights went out. It took Gordon only minutes to see the charisma and eloquence seeping out of the man. The sheer confidence was intoxicating. Rahab was a natural leader who was hell-bent on further destruction. The vacuum of authority and lawfulness along with Rahab's obvious abilities would have made his climb to power quick. Gordon wasn't scared easily, but Rahab scared him.

The sound of the door unlocking paused him midstride. He looked at the door in anticipation.

Same as the day before. The clang, bang, and creak as the door opened. The same two men approached him; each grabbed an arm and marched him out. This time they didn't tape his mouth or cover his head. They rushed him out of the box and into the sunlight.

What Gordon saw now confused him. This wasn't Fort Irwin.

Ahead of him was a small bermed area that held a fuel truck. To his left he saw a paved runway with *H* emblazoned on some of the areas. He recognized them as helicopter pads. The tarmac stretched for hundreds of feet, two shorter runways running perpendicular to the main one. As he was being paraded through the small base, he saw dozens of people. Some carried guns; all the men had long hair. The women were covered in long robe-like garments. All of the structures he saw were temporary. Two large metal hangars stood at the ends of the shorter runways. He looked over his shoulder to where he had come from and saw another dozen Conex boxes. He thought, *Is that where Hunter is?*

He was attempting to commit the base's layout to memory. He counted each person he saw, how many guns, positions, buildings, what the buildings might be used for, vehicles, and any other useful item that could help him put together a plan to escape. To the far side of the hangars were ten large white structures laid out in two rows with five buildings in each row. Gordon assumed those were barracks. Smaller shacks and random gear were everywhere.

Surrounding the entire base was a dirt berm; beyond it was flat, open desert that ran into towering mountains to the south and west. Everything he saw spoke to it being a military base, but this wasn't Fort Irwin, this was a training area outside the base. Then Gordon's memory from his Marine Corps days kicked in. Although he had never been to the base before, he had heard how large it was. It was similar to 29 Palms in size, mostly vast desert and training areas. He remembered someone telling him Fort Irwin's National Training Center was almost the size of Rhode Island. Gordon didn't recognize the mountains; he had no idea where they were or where Samantha and the group were.

Walking past the closest hangar, he peered inside. It looked like it was housing a classic-car collection. A dozen or more vehicles, one being his truck, were parked in there with some more of Rahab's people working on them. Gordon had counted more than fifty of Rahab's followers. How could this be? he wondered. How could one man put together such a sizable force so quickly? Gordon's thoughts soon went to his own escape. A feeling of dread came over him as he realized he didn't know how he and Hunter would be able to get out of this place.

His trek across the base ended with the two men taking him into another hangar-size building just to the west of the barracks. Gordon's angst quickly turned to confusion as he saw a large group of children playing. He scanned each face hoping to see Hunter, but to his dismay his son wasn't there. They hurried him past the children and into a small side room. Just as he stepped into the room, he heard a familiar voice coming from the group of children. It sounded like Hunter; he tried to step back, but the men forced him into the room.

"Sit down, we'll be right back," one of the men said to Gordon after they placed him on a sofa that was against the far wall.

Gordon didn't answer the man; he adjusted himself and looked around. The room at one time had been an office. Besides the couch there were two chairs and a large desk. He could hear the children laughing in the other room. He didn't know how to act now. He instinctively wanted to call out to his son, but he knew every move he made had to be calculated. He needed to ensure his and Hunter's survival by making sure that he didn't enflame the situation until he could execute an escape plan. The only reason he thought they'd bring him to this building and this room was to see Hunter. He obviously didn't know Rahab, but maybe the man had been telling the truth about his being able to see his son. The walk across the small base had been helpful and informative. The office, though, didn't provide any clues; it was much like the one from the day before.

"God, I got to get the fuck outta here," Gordon said out loud. He knew the longer he stayed the greater the chances were that Samantha and Haley would end up here too. Just when his wife would come looking for them was the only unknown. He knew she would, but when would she find this place? He had given instructions to Nelson to pull up stakes and head north if anything ever happened to him, but he knew Samantha. With Hunter missing, that wasn't going to happen.

Thoughts of regret now filled Gordon's mind. He should have listened to everyone else, he should have listened to Nelson and Samantha. Leaning forward, he planted his head in his hands. A feeling of defeat replaced the regret. He'd tried so hard to keep things together in Rancho Valentino, but for what? Everyone eventually fought each other, and it had torn the community apart, resulting in the deaths of two good friends. He attempted to defend his own doubts by asking himself, *How am I supposed to know and plan for each eventual outcome?* Leading people was not easy, and he found it even tougher to lead when his family's lives were at stake.

Samantha's frustration with him had grown the moment they left the gates of Rancho Valentino. He knew she was upset about Simone, but there wasn't anything he could've done about her suicide. Then had come the attack on the road days ago. In order to lead this group he would have to take risks. His inner self now knew this decision to go out scavenging was a mistake, a mistake that had caused the death of Holloway and now might even bring about his and Hunter's untimely demise.

"You're such a fool," he muttered to himself.

The laughter of the children jolted him back to the present. He stood up and walked over to the desk to see if there was something on it that could help him identify his location.

The desk had been stripped bare. In each drawer he opened he found just miscellaneous items, like paper clips, pens, a penny, thumbtacks. Nothing gave him a location. He then remembered back to the Marine Corps and how they would mark each piece of equipment, including desks, with stickers stating it was government property. Maybe, just maybe, there would be such marking here. He looked under the desk for a sticker—nothing.

The door opened. Gordon jerked and smacked his head as he pulled it out quickly from underneath the desk.

"You won't find anything there worth any value, Mr. Van Zandt," Rahab said, standing in the open doorway.

With a weak attempt at humor, Gordon quipped, "I saw a quarter on the floor."

Rahab just smiled. "Come with me."

Gordon was now very confused. Rahab didn't appear to be concerned with him or remotely afraid that he'd do something. As he stepped out of the office, Gordon looked for Hunter but did not see him among the children.

The children all appeared to be happy and healthy. They were laughing and enjoying themselves, and nowhere in their demeanor did he see any distress.

The walls of the hall were adorned with hand-drawn pictures by the children. Rahab or a Christ-like figure appeared in many of them. Along the wall also hung what Gordon guessed were biblical quotations.

Gordon and his brother had not been raised in an actively religious home. His mother had been a Methodist and his father a Lutheran, but neither practiced their birth religion. During their childhood the family went to church but only on the big holidays like Christmas and Easter. Not having been raised with faith, neither Gordon nor Sebastian took it up. After his two tours in Iraq, Gordon had completely washed his hands of religion. He had encountered many people from different faiths and felt none had a corner on what was right.

The way he was being treated today was so different from the way he'd been treated the day before. Rahab opened a door at the end of the hall and motioned for him to go inside.

When he reached the open doorway, his eyes lit up. "Hunter!" Gordon raced into the room and grabbed his son. They embraced tightly. Being able to hold him and see that he was unharmed brought such relief to Gordon. "Are you okay? Let me look at you."

"I'm fine, Dad," Hunter answered.

"Oh my God, I was so scared for you," Gordon said after looking him over.

Hunter embraced him again and said, "I want to leave."

Gordon didn't know how to answer him. He could see Rahab out of the corner of his eye.

"You see, I told you. I am a man of my word. Now, can you answer my question from yesterday?" Rahab walked in and sat down in the chair next to him.

"I told you, we're alone."

"I already know you have a group and that you have many supplies." Rahab looked at Hunter as he spoke.

Gordon paused; he now knew that Hunter had told Rahab about their group. The next time he opened his mouth could be critical.

"You have to understand that our group is small; we have nothing you need. You have a military base. We mean you no harm. Just let us go."

"Your son, lovely boy by the way, told us your group was heading to Idaho. Why Idaho?"

"What do you want? I don't understand any of this. Do you want our supplies? What exactly do you want?" Gordon asked, now frustrated with Rahab's line of questioning.

"I will be honest with you, as I have nothing to fear. I didn't blindfold you when I brought you here because I wanted you to see for yourself that we are a large group. We have more than a hundred and fifteen people in our ministry. It takes a lot to feed them. We have been going out to get supplies, but as you are well aware, things are scarce."

"So you want to take our supplies?"

"No, I want you to come join our group, all of you."

Hearing this threw Gordon off; he'd never imagined Rahab would ask him to join his group.

"Why would I do that?"

"Our faith requires us to go out and minister to those who will listen. Our flock needs to grow, and we need more able-bodied men and women of faith to take up our mission."

"Not to sound cliché, but what happens if I say no?"

"If you say no? Then we will dispatch you."

"Dispatch me?"

"We will send you to God. We will cleanse you and send you to our heavenly father," Rahab said flatly. He approached Gordon and placed his hand gently on his shoulder.

The words that fell from Rahab's mouth struck fear in Gordon. He'd already feared the man, and now he knew the threat was genuine.

"What do I have to do?" Gordon asked.

"Just let go, be one with God, and pledge your life to us and to God." Rahab pointed up as he spoke.

Gordon looked at Hunter, who to his amazement was quite calm. Every step and decision he made had to be perfect, because one misstep could result in death. Knowing he didn't have a choice, he did what he thought would give him more time. He just stared at Hunter. His sweet son, whom many said was his twin. Even though Hunter resembled him so much, he could see Samantha in the boy's face and eyes. His blue eyes still had an innocence about them. One day those eyes would change and a jaded young man would stare out of them. Today, though, was not that day, and what Gordon said next would determine so much.

Gordon took his attention away from his son and looked at Rahab. "I'm in. I'll join your group."

San Diego, California

Sebastian ran his hand over his tightly bandaged leg. He couldn't stop touching it. Even after a dose of pain meds, the leg still ached. He was grateful that his plea to Bishop Sorenson had not gone unheard. Though Sorenson was busy with preparing his group to leave, he was not a man without understanding. He took care to listen to Sebastian and pledged to help him find his brother. With the offer of a vehicle and two men, Sebastian finally felt that soon he'd be with his brother.

A knock at the door told him that his ride was waiting. Annaliese helped him to the truck, an old Chevy pickup. There he met two men, Willis and Jameson. Both were cousins of Annaliese's and had features similar to hers. Both men were lean, average height, and had striking blond hair.

Jameson put his hand out and introduced himself, then promptly handed Sebastian the gear he had from the chopper. "You'll need this."

"Yes, I will," Sebastian said, putting on his tactical vest.

All the men checked and double-checked their gear. Sebastian was not a big fan of his Beretta mm, but it was all he had besides his M4. He checked the pistol and holstered it in his side holster.

"Find them and get back here before dark," Sorenson said as he approached the truck.

"Yes, sir, we will," Jameson and Willis replied in unison.

Sebastian turned and faced Sorenson with his hand out-stretched. "Thank you again, Bishop. I have to admit, I wasn't asking for all of this, but it helps."

"You're welcome. It's the least we can do for someone who risked his life for us in Afghanistan."

Afghanistan and the life before seemed oddly distant now. Sebastian sometimes felt like he was in a dream. He sometimes thought that he'd wake up on his cot in Afghanistan. But this was not a dream. He was living a nightmare.

"The sun will set in a few hours, we gotta go," Willis said as he sat behind the wheel of the old black truck.

Jameson jumped into the back and sat down on the wood-paneled bed. "Go ahead, take the passenger seat. I like the fresh air."

Sebastian just smiled and got into the truck slowly, being mindful of his leg.

Annaliese smiled and gave a timid wave to him as the truck pulled away and down the long dirt driveway.

Not knowing what to expect, Sebastian pointed his rifle out the open window, not unlike what he'd do in Afghanistan.

When they pulled out onto a small county road, he saw a few abandoned vehicles but no people. He gave very specific directions to Willis, who acknowledged that he knew where he was going. They shared small talk as they crept along the back roads of Encinitas into Rancho Santa Fe. Sebastian was surprised not to see more people, and the few he did see appeared to be wandering with one purpose: scavenging in each abandoned car they could find. It was difficult for him to see through the fragmented parts of the windshield on his side. The truck now bore the scars of the time.

"What happened?" Sebastian asked, pointing to the window.

"A group of kids attacked us with rocks a couple weeks ago. It's not safe out there anymore."

"What have you seen?"

Willis chuckled, then said, "I've seen people kill each other for a can of beans. I've seen children left alone to wander because someone killed their parents. Mr. Van Zandt, hell has come to this world."

When they crested the hill and overlooked Via de la Valle, smoke plumes appeared on the horizon, dotting the skyline in more than a dozen locations.

"What's going on with all the smoke?" Sebastian asked.

"The rumors are a drug cartel has come across the border. They have created an army and are killing and burning everything in their path."

"We heard about them on the ship; a recon team received intel on those guys," Sebastian said. He noticed a few of the plumes were close, too close in fact. As he oriented himself, he now felt certain that some of the smoke was coming from Gordon's area. He recalled Willis mentioning children left abandoned. The thought of little kids on their own in this harsh environment struck him hard. Thoughts of Hunter and Haley then came to mind. If everything worked out, he'd be hugging them soon. "I have to ask, you mentioned kids a bit ago. What happens to them? How do you just leave them alone?"

"We don't."

"You don't?" Sebastian was startled by his response. All he'd seen since the attacks were self-centered and selfish acts. "Sorry if my tone was of doubt; I apologize. I just . . . I just haven't seen much charity since I left Afghanistan."

"The bishop has us take the children in. It's what God expects of us."

Sebastian just stared at Willis. He was amazed by how someone so young could be so grounded and mature. He felt bad about his tone. He thought, *Of course they rescue the children; they rescued me, didn't they?*

"I hope your brother and his family are okay," Willis said.

"Me too. With each mile and turn of the wheel, I get more nervous. I just don't know what to expect."

The old truck slowed to a stop at the bottom of the hill and idled. Willis carefully looked both ways, but as he was about to accelerate he heard another vehicle coming down Via de la Valle on his right.

Sebastian guessed it was an old muscle car because of the rugged and throaty sound.

Willis sat frozen; he gingerly touched the accelerator and moved forward a few feet, then stopped abruptly.

Sebastian could see the car now; it was coming toward them

at high speed. "Ugh, I hate to ask, but what are you going to do here?"

Willis still sat clenching the steering wheel. His grip was an extension of the inner tension he was feeling.

"Hey, buddy, you're kinda sitting out in the road," Sebastian stated, his eyes fixed on the car coming toward them.

It made a last turn before a long straightaway that led to where they were sitting. Once it cleared the turn, the car sped up considerably.

Sebastian tore his gaze from the car and shouted, "Do something, go forward or backwards, but get out of the road!"

Sebastian's voice broke Willis's daze, and he stomped on the accelerator and lurched across.

As they cleared the road, the car was close enough for Sebastian to see two men. One pointed at them and made a motion to the driver to stop, but the car didn't slow down. It kept its pace and vanished around a turn.

The truck sputtered then sped up, and they continued.

"What happened?" Sebastian asked, concerned. He was familiar with seeing men freeze. This reaction to stress was not unusual, but it made Sebastian nervous now to know that one of the men he was going out with might be a liability.

"I don't know, I just didn't know what to do," Willis answered sheepishly.

"How many times have you been out?"

"Umm, a few . . . Listen, I'm sorry. It won't happen again," Willis stated, attempting to sound confident.

"Okay, but I have to tell ya, that made me nervous. Let's not do it again."

"We won't, I promise."

The smoke grew darker as they came closer to the source. Even the wealthier parts of San Diego hadn't fared well. Every gate for a luxury community had been breached. One in particular was a neighborhood just a couple miles from Gordon's. Fairbanks Ranch's main gate and guardhouse had been destroyed by what looked like a fight. Black soot stained the exterior walls, the large panel windows on the front of the guardhouse were smashed, and the stucco exterior was riddled with bullets.

"That cartel must have been here," Willis commented. He had slowed the truck to a crawl as all examined the ruins.

Sebastian didn't say a word; he just stared at the once beautifully adorned gates and guardhouse.

The large iron gates were bent and twisted from the center out. The right gate lay almost horizontal; only the lowest hinge prevented it from touching the ground. Fairbanks Ranch security vehicles, which had been used to fortify the entrance, were smashed and burned and looked as if they had been tossed aside.

"Stop!" Sebastian yelled out.

Willis, obeying Sebastian's command, slammed on the brakes.

Sebastian had seen something he found curious. As the truck idled, he opened the door and stepped out. He hopped on his good leg around to the front of the truck to get an unobstructed view. Lying against the side of the guardhouse were three bodies. Their blood splattered against the wall told Sebastian they had been executed.

"What's up?" Jameson asked, standing in the bed of the truck.

"I just wanted to confirm what I thought I saw," Sebastian answered. He hopped back to the truck and grabbed a pair of binoculars. Positioning himself against the front of the truck, he peered through the binos to get a clearer picture of the carnage.

His count was right, three bodies lay dead. On the wall above their splattered blood was the word *Villista*.

"Villista? Is that the cartel?" Sebastian asked.

"Yes, sir, it is," Jameson answered.

Concern overcame Sebastian. He hopped back to the truck door, tossed in the binos, and jumped in. "Let's go."

The truck cleared the last turn; his brother's community was just ahead. They had found their way there unharmed and had also found the source of the nearest smoke plumes. The main entrance looked eerily similar to that of Fairbanks Ranch. The iron gates were burnt and twisted and flung open to show a pile of charred and crushed cars. The once beautifully ornate sign that had told those visiting or passing WELCOME TO RANCHO VALENTINO was spray-painted with the name Villista.

"Keep your eyeballs peeled and stay frosty," Sebastian said, his rifle securely tucked in his shoulder.

"Stay what?" Willis asked, not knowing what *stay frosty* meant.

"Stay alert, okay?" Sebastian answered, his eyes scanning the area intently.

They drove slowly through the gate; all around he saw smoldering homes, deserted cars, trash and personal effects strewn on the main street, but no people.

"Turn right, then drive up a few blocks," Sebastian ordered. Fear gripped him as he realized that finding Gordon, Samantha, and the kids might not happen. The thought of finding their bodies flashed through his mind, but he quickly dismissed it.

Every single home had damage done to it. Some had been burned, but all had signs of forced entry. A large pile of debris was still smoldering in the central park; neither man in the cab could make out what it was as they passed. After they had driven several blocks and still not seen a single person, Sebastian's fear deepened. Hope of finding Gordon was diminishing with each home they passed.

"Last turn, right here." He pointed.

"This doesn't look good," Willis quietly said, his grip still firm on the steering wheel.

The truck made the turn onto Gordon's street, and finally, after more than seven weeks since leaving Afghanistan, Sebastian could see his brother's house. It was one of the fortunate homes that hadn't been burned, but it had suffered substantial damage.

The blood was coursing through Sebastian's veins, and he felt flushed as the truck slowly came to a stop in front of the house.

Jameson jumped out of the back and was looking in all directions. "Looks clear, not a soul around here."

Sebastian had the urge to tell him to shut up, but he decided to ignore him. "Stay with the truck," he ordered.

"Sure thing," Willis responded; he looked at Sebastian and could see the dread and fear in his face.

Sebastian took a deep breath and got out of the truck with his crutches in hand. The first thing that caught him off guard was the large bloodstain on the sidewalk leading to the front door. He stopped and looked at it; it was hard for him to determine how long it had been there, but from the size, there had been a lot of blood. His focus then shifted to the entire front of the house. The lawn was brown and dead; the flowers that Samantha prided herself on had suffered the same fate. Their petals were shriveled up. The front door was open slightly; the once-solid oak door was cracked at the handle and bullet holes punctured its rustic walnut finish. Dozens more bullet holes surrounded the door and the front windows. The windows themselves were smashed and the screens ripped.

Sebastian stepped up to the front door, and before he pushed it open, he paused. His gut twisted, and he felt a flash of nausea come over him. He took a deep breath and pushed the door. It shrieked at the hinges and, with each inch, gave him a view of more destruction inside. As if waiting to be invited in, he paused again. Finally knowing that he had to get this over with, he stepped inside.

The house had been ransacked. Most of the furniture was turned upside down. Deep feelings of remorse and pain filled his chest; each breath he took was more difficult. He remembered how the house used to look, the squeals of the two kids, the happiness, the Christmases spent here, the many dinners and fun birthdays. All gone now. In a billionth of a second, it was all stripped away.

Knowing there wouldn't be a response, he called out anyway, "Gordon!"

Jameson came in behind him, stopped, and said, "I'll head upstairs."

Sebastian just nodded and continued to walk through the lower part of the house. The floor was covered with smashed decorative items; candles, toys, dishes, and glass was everywhere. One thing specifically caught his eye, and he hobbled over to it; seeing it upset him more than he'd been in a long time. He grunted as he bent down and picked up the paper. His eyes filled when he saw that the handwriting was Haley's. Tears ran down his face and dripped onto the coloring page when he read that it was "to uncle seebastan, from haley."

He remembered she gave him this the last time he was there.

She ran to him, like she always did, so happy, so full of life. He reflected on how he was proud of her, but he also remembered rushing off to say hello to Gordon. How foolish he felt now. If he could be there again, he would hold her and kiss her and tell her she was the best. He thought of how we take things for granted; just the pure gift of love from a child is amazing. Children want to give you the most precious thing that life has, and that is time. The tears kept coming, he couldn't control them. He didn't want to take another step; he was afraid of what he'd find.

"Sebastian!" Jameson called out from upstairs.

He turned and shook his head. "No, no, please, God, don't do this," he softly said to himself.

"Sebastian!"

"Yeah," he answered, clearing his throat. He wiped the tears, folded the coloring page, and put it into his cargo pocket.

"Nothing up here, sorry."

"Okay."

Taking a moment to get his head straight, Sebastian headed farther into the home. Nothing but overturned furniture and debris. Finally he found himself in Gordon's office. The room was a mess. Papers were all over; the drawers of the desk had been removed and emptied onto the floor. He took one of the ends of a crutch and attempted to sort through the inch-deep stack of papers and other items. Frustrated, he asked himself, *Where are you?*

Jameson's loud footsteps caught his attention; Sebastian stepped out of the office and ran into him.

"Hey, I saw two people outside, down the street, looked like kids."

Jameson rushed toward the front door. Sebastian was close behind him doing the best he could do on crutches.

"Did you see anyone?" Jameson asked Willis upon exiting the house.

"No."

Sebastian came out and asked, "Where did you see them?"

"That way," Jameson responded, pointing to their right. "They were running in the direction we came in."

"Jump in," Sebastian ordered.

They turned the truck around and headed toward the kids.

• • •

After spending almost twenty minutes looking for any signs of the kids or anyone else left in the community, the men were about to give up when Jameson yelled out, "Over there, to our right. I saw them. They're running toward the large park."

Willis sped up and took a hard right turn in front of the large central park.

"Straight ahead," Jameson screamed.

From behind a row of parked cars two kids started running toward the park. Their clothes were tattered and hung from their lean bodies.

"Stop the truck!" Sebastian commanded.

"Why?" Willis asked.

"Stop the truck!" he yelled again.

Willis slammed on the brakes, causing Jameson to hit his head against the rear window.

"The kids are running because they're obviously scared. Look around you, no one is here. Everyone left, and somehow they were left behind. They must have seen what happened here. They probably think we're bad guys," Sebastian explained.

"You're right," Willis admitted.

Sebastian opened the door and stepped out. He walked to the edge of the expansive park and hollered, "We won't hurt you! I'm a Marine. Everything is fine now, we're here to help."

No response.

"My name is Corporal Van Zandt with the Marine Corps, and we're here to help. Everything will be okay. I promise we won't hurt you," he pleaded. He scanned the area. It was hard to know where the children had gone. The park was the size of three football fields. Large eucalyptus trees shaded the edges; tucked in each corner were tables and barbecues, and a single playground lay silent in the corner closest to Sebastian.

Jameson came up alongside Sebastian, rubbing his head. "We're going to have to leave soon," he said.

Looking up at the darkening sky, Sebastian responded, "I know, but we should try to help those kids. Go that way and I'll go this way. I saw them last over there, so cut through the park and I'll walk alongside the edge, near the road," Sebastian said, pointing.

Jameson acknowledged and started walking briskly across the dead grass in the direction of a large pile of debris.

Sebastian hobbled along on the edge and kept hollering out to the kids. His arms were beginning to feel the fatigue and pain of walking with crutches. The wind had changed, and the smell of the smoldering pile wafted over him. When it first hit him, he thought it was odd; his nostrils filled with the stench of burnt meat.

"Sebastian! Sebastian!" Jameson screamed.

Sebastian pivoted and looked at Jameson, who was standing near the pile. "What is it?"

"I think I found everybody!"

A look of utter shock washed over Sebastian as he realized that the fifteen-foot-high, thirty-foot-long pile was what was left of the residents of Rancho Valentino.

Tijuana, Mexico

"How do I know you'll honor our arrangement?" Pablo asked the unknown voice on the satellite phone. He was pacing the large parlor of his father's house. Beads of sweat rolled down his temples. He had conducted many deals in his life but not one this large. "I know we've known each other for a long time, but . . . Yes, I know. I will have the gold when you arrive. What would the time frame be for arrival?"

The heavy brass door handle on the main door always made a mechanical sound when turned. That sound now echoed into the room.

Pablo turned nervously to see who was coming.

In stepped an older but finely dressed woman. She was short, no more than five foot two, with black hair that was pulled back and pinned up. Long golden earrings dangled from her ears, and a large diamond ring adorned the index finger of her petite left hand.

"Excuse me," she softly said to Pablo after noticing he was on the phone.

As she was retreating, he waved her to come back in. "Everything sounds in order. I'll expect to see you in two weeks' time then. Thank you." He touched a button on the phone and placed it into his pocket. "Good evening, Mother. Please come sit with me," Pablo said, pointing to a large sofa in the center of the room. He walked over and sat down.

"Are you sure? You look busy," she asked, hesitant.

"All done. Please, come sit with me. I don't get to see you much," he begged, tapping the seat on the sofa next to him.

"If you insist. I just know how busy you and your father can be," she said as she walked over.

"How has Father been? He and I don't talk much. What I mean is we don't talk about personal things much. I'm worried about him, he looks stressed."

"You know your father, all business. He's been that way since the day I met him."

"Yes, I know. Ever since I can remember he was always working and always on the phone."

"Not unlike you, though, I would say," she quipped. She reached over and patted his leg.

"Like father, like son, they say." He smiled. "I just worry about him, all this stress and at his age. It can't be good."

"Ha, listen, Pablo. Your father will die with a phone in this hand, a glass of scotch in this hand, and a cigar in his mouth. If you're insinuating that he should retire, it won't happen. The only one he'll listen to about retiring will be the good Lord," she joked. "You know what's funny? Even when he's standing at the pearly gates with Saint Peter, he'll ask for a phone."

"What's happened, all of this that has happened around the world, this is above Father's head." Pablo sat up and turned to face his mother. His tone changed. "I'm worried that he doesn't understand the opportunity we have, the responsibility we have as a ruling family to change the course of events."

His mother cocked her head and listened to him intently.

"I see this new world and our place in it. What Father sees is the old world. Instead of stepping out of the shadows and taking our place as a leader, he still operates behind the scenes, making backroom deals to have the electricity restored. There is more out there; now is the time to take control, real control."

"Sweetheart, you have always been a dreamer. You are the passionate one who looked up in awe at the stars and asked why. Your father is not that man; it is because he was born with nothing. I will defend him by saying this: What you have around you is because of him. You had the privilege of looking up at the stars; you had no concerns as a boy growing up. He didn't have that; he had to fight for everything.

"You might be right that this is a new world and things have changed, but I still trust that your father will know how to take care of this family. I'm sorry if what I'm telling you isn't what you wanted to hear, but it's true. Go, talk to him. Tell him what you see. He's a smart man. If you can convince him that our place as a family is somewhere else, then he will do it. I have known him for thirty years; there is one thing your father is not, and that is a fool. He calculates everything and doesn't make rash decisions. Take your time and present to him your plan," she said pointedly. She reached over to touch his hand, but Pablo pulled it away.

This had been the second time in three days that he had presented his case, and both times it had been rejected. His mother didn't even want to know what his plan was. Just knowing that Alfredo wasn't interested was enough for her to side with him. Pablo stood up and walked toward the large window.

"I see that I've upset you, and for that, I'm sorry. It was not my intention to hurt you, but I have to agree with whatever your father says. He has given me so much. I lived a life of poverty not unlike his. I knew what it meant to be truly hungry. When he looked into my eyes and promised me that I'd never know poverty again, he kept that promise. I want you two to work together, but

I won't have you make me take sides against my husband," she finished. She stood and walked up behind Pablo.

He didn't turn around or respond to what she'd said. He just looked out the window.

She placed her hand gently on his shoulder and rubbed his back.

A moment of uncomfortable silence fell between them.

Finally realizing he was being immature and impatient with his mother, Pablo reached back and grabbed her hand with a gentle firmness. He turned toward her and said, "I know Father is a good and wise man. I will do my part as a dutiful son and support what he needs. I will be more patient, and if I have ideas, I will strive to ensure those plans don't collide with the overall goal for our family. Thank you," he said, then placed his hand on her face and kissed her forehead. "I now need to go, I have things to do."

She embraced him and kissed his cheek. "Go about your day."

After their embrace Pablo immediately marched toward the door and left the room. He pulled the phone out of his pocket and hit the redial button.

Moments later the unknown voice answered. "Hello?"

Pablo didn't respond. He paused as his attention was drawn to a portrait of Porfirio Díaz, the Mexican president who served on and off from 1876 to 1911.

During President Díaz's tenure, Mexico had realized what some called its Golden Age. It prospered and was an economic superpower that rivaled European nations. His presidency didn't go without criticism, as he was also known as a dictator who imprisoned his political foes and kept a tight noose on the electoral process. But Pablo respected him and saw in himself the same talents, abilities, and aspirations.

"Hello?" the voice on the phone asked again.

"Yes, sorry. I will increase the amount by twenty percent if you can deliver a week early. Can that be done?"

"We can do that."

"Great, and I'll make sure my father is there when you arrive. I want him to see the surprise I have for him," Pablo said, then hung up the phone.

JANUARY 12, 2014

• • •

The pessimist complains about the wind; the optimist expects it to change; the realist adjusts his sails.

—William Arthur Ward

Cheyenne Mountain, Colorado

Cruz quickly glanced into Julia's room through the small window in the door. She lay silent, her back toward him. He couldn't tell if she was asleep or not.

"Excuse me, sir," Weatherby said, after clearing his throat.

"Ah, yes. Thank you for coming down," Cruz said, quickly turning around. He felt a bit like he had just been caught peeping on someone.

"No, thank you, sir. You obviously received my message."

"Yes, yes, I did. So, she still hasn't given approval for the procedure?"

"No, sir, and now it's critical we do something about this or she risks dying. I can't stress—"

"I understand, Doctor. Let me see if I can convince her," Cruz said, cutting off Weatherby.

"Please, inform her this is now a critical time."

"I will, Doctor, thank you." Cruz stood with his hands on his hips. He turned and knocked on the door. He again glanced through the window; still no movement from the first lady. Not wanting to waste time, he opened the door and walked in. The air in the room was warm and had a strong medicinal smell. Cruz disliked hospitals. For him they represented death. His first childhood memories of hospitals were of visiting his dying grandparents. Between the ages of eight and sixteen, he had helped take three of his grandparents to the hospital but never took them home. Even when he was with his wife at the birth of his children, he always had a bad feeling. Somewhere, whether down the hall or from outside, he'd hear the sounds of sirens or doctors being summoned to care for a person who was near death. He thought that even now, he was about to convince his best friend's wife to undergo an emergency surgery or face death.

"Julia, are you awake?" he asked softly. He could see her body move ever so slightly from her breathing. When he reached the side of the bed and looked down, he saw that she was awake. Her eyes were wide open; she was just blankly staring at the far wall. He extended his arm to touch her, but just before he could she turned her head.

"Hi, Andrew. I know why you're here." Her face was pale, almost lifeless. "You don't need to come convince me. I've already made the decision."

"I'm so glad to hear. We should get you in right away."

"Not yet. Please sit down."

Cruz looked around for a chair, then grabbed it and pulled it over next to the bed. "How are you?" he asked, then shook his head. "Sorry, that's a stupid question. This whole thing is horrible."

Her frail hand reached out and touched his arm. She gently squeezed it.

Their eyes locked. He had not seen her in this condition before. She had been through so much since the attacks seven weeks ago. First she lost her son, then lived through the turmoil of the attacks, Brad's disappearance, and now this, the loss of her unborn baby.

"Andrew, please be honest with me. Do you think Brad is dead?"

The question shocked him. Because he was a politician, many ways to answer her ran through his mind. He just stared at her, not knowing how to respond. Deep down he held out hope, but he felt that Brad was probably gone for good. If he told her this now, how would she receive it? Was she just looking for a bit of good or inspiring news to keep her spirits up?

She noticed his hesitation and reassured him by again squeezing his arm. "Andrew, just tell me. I'm asking because I want to go into this procedure knowing if you think my husband is dead. I am owed that at least. Please."

"Julia, things don't look good; but I still hold out hope. The news we received from the special ops team did discourage me, I won't lie. I promise you again, I will still keep looking."

"Once a politician, always a politician. You guys just can't give a straight answer. For God's sakes, Andrew. I asked you a simple question. Never mind, please leave me alone." Julia rolled back onto her side, facing away from him.

Cruz knew he was attempting to walk a fine line in his answer. He knew what he thought, but expressing that could mean the difference between her having hope and just giving up on everything, including herself. The struggle to open up to her was difficult. He then asked himself, If he couldn't have the strength to talk openly with a friend, how could he lead a country? "Julia, I'm sorry. I know you need a straight answer. Yes, I think he's alive. I'm not hoping. I know he's out there, and I won't rest till I find him and bring him home."

A moment passed before she rolled back to face him and said, "You really think so?"

He reached out and touched her hand and said, "Yes, I do."

A tear formed in her left eye and slid down the side of her face. "Thank you, Andrew. Please go tell the doctor I'm ready when he is for the operation."

Cruz stood without hesitation and left the room. After the door closed, he leaned his full weight against it. Fatigued from his brief conversation, he reflected. He admired those who could be open and honest without a second thought. Deep down it was something he knew was right, but it wasn't something he could do with her. His political career was not unlike others; all politicians had an unspoken rule: "The truth, while preferable, always takes second place to getting what you want."

San Diego, California

The failure to find Gordon and his family was at the forefront of Sebastian's mind. Visions of them being burned along with the others haunted his thoughts. He refused to believe they'd perished; he knew Gordon was too smart and would have left before that had happened. The discovery of the remains was frightening nonetheless. Each body was stacked on top of the others like wood. The fire that had consumed them must have been intense because the flesh was burned off and only bones remained.

Willis and Jameson hadn't talked to him since yesterday. The sight of such an atrocity haunted them.

Sebastian's stint in the Marines had exposed him to such cruel and inhumane acts. It wasn't as if he was impervious to these sights, though; he just knew how to compartmentalize them.

He enjoyed the warm afternoon sun as he walked toward the guesthouse at the corner of the property. He hadn't yet been able to explore the more than six-acre property, but he planned on becoming more acquainted with it now that he was getting around on crutches.

The perimeter was surrounded by an eight-foot fence with large eucalyptus trees every dozen feet. This provided cover from any eyes that might be attempting to see what was happening inside. Bishop Sorenson had four armed men constantly patrolling the fence line and two at the fortified iron gate. Each day strangers approached the gate looking for food or aid. At first Sorenson had provided comfort to those starving souls who came seeking it. Soon, though, the reality of the situation made it impossible to do any more. It pained him, but they had to turn everyone away now. Survival of his own group became the priority when he realized that there would be no government response.

Sorenson would make an exception if it was an abandoned child. After the discovery of the bodies, Sebastian and his companions had been successful in finding the two children.

Sebastian was surprised the children had survived the attack and subsequent massacre. He didn't know for sure what had happened because neither talked. Both showed signs of malnutrition, and their hygiene was nonexistent.

Jameson had found them hiding in the pump house of the community swimming pool. At first they'd struggled, but Sebastian had been able to convince them they would not be hurt.

Sebastian had two things he wanted to accomplish when he

saw them today. First was to see how they were doing, and second was to find out what information they had about Gordon.

As he hopped up the stairs of the guesthouse, the front door opened and Annaliese stepped out with the kids' soiled clothes in her arms.

"Sebastian? You should be resting," she exclaimed.

"I'm fine. I want to see the kids. How are they?"

"I know you think you're fine, but if you don't rest more, especially after yesterday, you could do more harm than good."

"Whoa, that smell is horrible," Sebastian said with a grimace.

"I know," she said, referring to the clothes. "Since you won't listen to your nursemaid, don't come crying to me if you hurt yourself again." She stepped down, then turned. "The kids are fine, still not talking but doing much better than when they came in last night. Go ahead on in. I need to go toss these away," she said and hurried past him.

Sebastian grabbed the doorknob and paused. He reviewed how he would ask his questions. He knew the kids were in shock, and if he wanted to get the info he desired from them he would have to be gentle. Opening the door, he glanced in and said, "Hello?" No response.

It was a quaint little single-level home. The front door opened into a living room and kitchen. The furniture was dated; he felt like he was stepping back into the 1980s. He made his way farther through the house until he found the boys sitting on a bed whispering to each other.

When they saw him, they both fell silent.

Sebastian stuck his head into the room and said, "Hi, guys. How are you? It's Sebastian, remember me?"

Both boys looked at him quickly but then turned their eyes away and didn't answer.

Sebastian could see how uncomfortable they were; their body language said everything. Their frail arms had become rigid and pressed against their bodies. Their now clean but uncut hair hung down and covered their tan faces. Since the grime and dirt had been wiped away, they looked even younger. He guessed that they were only eleven or twelve.

"Can I come in? I have just a couple of questions and then I'll leave you alone," Sebastian said softly. He stepped into the room and leaned against a chest of drawers just inside the doorway. "I know you're both scared and not sure what our motives are. I can only imagine what you must be thinking. I can assure you that these people are good and you are now in safe hands."

The boys just kept staring at the floor.

"Hey, there was a family that lived in your community. I want to know if you know them and if you know what might have happened to them. The Van Zandts—do you know them?"

One of the boys looked up at Sebastian, met his eyes briefly, then turned away.

"Do you know them?" Sebastian asked that boy urgently. "Gordon Van Zandt is my brother. Have you heard of him? Do you know what happened to them?"

The boy who'd looked at him looked up again. His mouth opened to say something but stopped when the other boy spoke up. "He left. He left us all."

"He's alive? He left before . . . before the bad people came?"

"Yeah, he and a few others left after the big fight," the second boy said. He swept his long bangs out of his face and cocked his head.

"What fight? What happened? Are they all okay, Samantha, Haley, Hunter?"

"I don't know a Samantha or the other two. Gordon was in charge of the neighborhood security until he was shot . . ."

"Shot?" Sebastian asked; his voice grew louder with each question.

"Yeah, all I know is one day he was there and the next I heard he had been shot."

"But he didn't die, right?"

"No, he lived. He and his friends ended up fighting another group in our neighborhood. They killed a lot of people and then left. That's the last I heard of him. I don't know where he went."

"Oh my God, oh my God. He's alive, they're alive," Sebastian blurted out.

"My dad said he was an asshole," the first boy said loudly.

"Yeah, well, that's my brother. He's a bit of the shoot-from-the-hip-and-mouth kinda guy," Sebastian cracked.

"After he and his friends left, the Villistas came and killed everyone," the first boy continued.

"I'm really sorry about what happened. Why didn't more people leave with my brother?"

"My dad asked if he could go, but your asshole brother said no," the first boy shot back.

"Sorry. I can't even begin to explain my brother, but I'm sorry."

"Whatever," the first boy said. His tone had grown angry. He stood up and stormed out of the room.

"Hey listen, I'm sorry," Sebastian called out to him.

"His parents were killed in front of his eyes. He doesn't blame your brother, he's just angry," the second boy said. "I don't blame your brother. He tried to help us, but everyone started to turn on each other. Nothing worked. No running water, no food, only a few cars. It didn't take long before everyone tried to kill each other."

"What happened to your parents?"

"Dead, I figure, like Brandon's parents, but I didn't see anything. When those men came, my mom and dad hid me in an attic space in the garage. I never saw them again. I heard a lot of guns shooting, screaming, and then nothing.

"The men came into my house and tore it apart, and then they left. I was so scared. I didn't leave the attic till the next day. When I did, I couldn't find my parents. I looked everywhere, but didn't find anyone except for Brandon. I'm guessing they killed everyone else and burned them in the park."

"I'm so, so sorry," Sebastian said. "What's your name?" he then asked as he stepped over and sat on the bed next to the boy.

"My name is Luke," he said. His eyes showed the pain of the events he had witnessed.

"You don't have to be afraid anymore, everything will be okay now."

"No it won't. That's the same thing your brother told all of us. That's the same thing that my dad told me. You know what? It wasn't okay. Your brother left us and my dad was killed by those monsters. So don't tell me it will be okay. I might only be eleven years old, but I know that none of us are safe anymore. It will never be safe again!" Brandon said loudly from the doorway. He had returned without either noticing and had overheard their conversation.

"I can say this," Sebastian told the boys. "Everything has changed, but I will do whatever I can to protect you both. I promise you that."

"I don't believe you, you're just like every other adult. You lie!" Brandon snapped back.

Sebastian's only experience with children had been his niece and nephew, but that too was limited. He wasn't sure how to handle a child who had witnessed such horrors. His last attempt to soothe Brandon felt contrived. He wasn't lying when he said he'd do whatever he could to protect them, but he knew he'd have to prove himself to these two boys. Words were not enough; he'd have to show them that not everyone in the world was bad.

Unknown military installation

Gordon's first full day as a member of the Children of God had started early. His restless sleep ended with the loud bangs of a drum in the barracks. His agreement to join them gave him one benefit: He no longer was kept locked up. They had transferred him to the men's barracks; the large room was similar to the squad bay–type barracks he was accustomed to in the Marine Corps. Each side of the long rectangular room was lined with bunk beds. He shared the barracks with other followers. While they readied themselves for what would be a long day filled with physical labor, he attempted to chat with his "roommates." Everyone shied away from him, though; no one would even look him in the eye. Failing to get any particulars about his new home from them, he was determined to keep his eyes wide open once he left the barracks. Any detail could be the linchpin in his escape. But escaping with Hunter was complicated because Hunter was housed somewhere else.

The unrecognizable mountain range to the west had a steep slope that almost touched the main entrance of the base. The mountains to the southeast were high and sloped gradually down, with the western part of them almost connecting to the western mountain. From the air it would have looked like an upside-down horseshoe with the base being positioned near the bottom. If he could get Hunter, Gordon knew he'd head south over the sloping hills. There he thought he'd run into the interstate.

• • •

His first working party consisted of filling and stacking sandbags. As thoughts of escape processed through his mind, his pace slowed down.

"Keep moving!" one of Rahab's men yelled to him. The man was one of the guards he had met just after his capture.

Gordon didn't acknowledge him, he just focused on the task and picked up his tempo. The job he and his fellow workers had been given was to reinforce the base entry. This told Gordon that even Rahab felt vulnerable. Also, the fact that he and the others were being forced to work under the watchful eyes of several armed men told him that they weren't truly part of Rahab's following but slave labor.

"Do you work like this every day?" Gordon whispered to the man next to him.

The man didn't look at Gordon; he kept right on grabbing the sandbags in the pile behind him and placing them like bricks.

"What the hell? Is everyone here deaf and dumb?" Gordon rhetorically asked louder.

"Please be quiet and just work," the man whispered while still working. He kept his gaze away from Gordon.

"Why? Why can't we talk, if we're part of their group?"

The man ignored Gordon again.

Now frustrated, Gordon spoke a bit louder. "Hey, buddy, unless you answer some of my questions, I'll just keep talking to you and get us both in trouble."

"Fine, later tonight after dinner. Volunteer for the working party," the man said, still not looking at Gordon.

"Good, I will," Gordon answered, then asked, "What's your name?"

"Derek. Now shut up and get back to work."

USS *Makin Island*, off the coast of Coos Bay, Oregon

Barone stared at the map of Coos Bay that hung on the wall in the briefing room. Red circles populated the map, showing target areas for the ships to moor and strategic locations for his group to set up. His recon teams had reported back that the port was abandoned save a few people who were camped out there. The port was large; it stretched fifteen miles around the city of North Bend and Coos Bay. The deepest mooring areas were all right next to residential areas and the city of Coos Bay. Bringing the ships in covertly would be impossible. Barone knew that he couldn't start a new country without people, and so he would go in as a liberator. He kept a few teams back to lock down the port facilities they would need and to meet with what city elders they could locate. He wanted to limit his contact with the civilian population until he'd properly established a beachhead, so he wanted to recruit the local leaders to keep the civilians calm.

One by one, his command team entered the situation room and sat down. By now his team had become accustomed to his style of briefing: blunt and direct.

Turning around, he stared at each man as they sat waiting. All looked rested, as if they'd just come back from a long leave. The addition of the families and loved ones on the ship had helped with morale. The stress and concern about their whereabouts and condition had been put to rest upon the Marines' landing in Southern California over a week ago. With the elimination of the group that had attempted to assassinate him, Barone felt more empowered to walk the passageways alone. He knew that some men might still hold misgivings about their new mission, but he aggressively moved to temper them. He pledged to retrieve the families of those men who lived elsewhere upon their landing in Coos Bay. His plan called for teams dedicated to their retrieval no matter where they were. Another item he had promised and knew he must deliver on was to reward them with gold. He hadn't really planned on how he'd get that gold, but when they settled into their new home that would be a priority.

He too felt more at ease in some ways. Of course, not a day went by without thoughts of his son, but having his wife and daughter with him brought great solace. The look on his wife's face when he broke the word of Billy's death was worse than he'd imagined. The age lines that already etched her face seemed to grow deeper as the reality of never seeing her son again sank in. Maggie had hidden herself away in his stateroom for two days but then emerged with new purpose. She had many questions for him but never assigned blame for Billy's death. After dutifully following and supporting him all these years while he served in the Marines, she had hardened herself and knew that this life brought great risk. She knew that Billy had died doing something he loved, and even though his death came during an upheaval in their country, she knew he died fighting for what he believed in.

Still scanning the happy faces of his men, Barone decided he would take a more personal direction in this briefing. Today, he wanted to have a conversation about where they were, not physically but where the men's hearts were in this new mission he had brought them on. He walked over to the side of the room, grabbed a metal folding chair, and placed it in the front of the room with the back facing them. He straddled the chair and sat down.

Some of his men looked curiously at him as he did this. His signature briefings never had him sitting, and when they saw him sit, it was never this casually. Since his son's death he had grown unpredictable, so seeing him do this made some of them a bit uncomfortable.

"Good morning, gentlemen." Barone's tone was remarkably sanguine.

In unison, all the men in the room replied, "Good morning, sir."

"We've come a long way. Not just in miles but in the transition from men fighting for our country to pioneers of a new land. I know now that on that day weeks ago when I assembled some of you and told you of my plan to come back to California instead of the East Coast, not all of you were one hundred percent behind me. I understood then as I do now how difficult it would be for you to voluntarily join me. Some of you, I'm sure, were against it but felt you had no choice. Most of you were concerned but didn't know what else to do. Believe me, I get it. I don't want to beat a dead horse here, but for those of you who were reluctant because you felt we were abandoning our country, I would ask you this: What does country mean to you? I want you to process that question because I asked it of myself over and over.

"At first when I heard about the attacks, I went into gung-ho mode and vowed revenge upon those who did it. However, when I finally, truly understood the devastation that had occurred and the foolish mission the new president was sending us on, I reflected. I met with some of you and started our plans for the recovery effort.

"It was in that briefing that a young intel officer raised his hand like a schoolboy and asked this question: 'Sir, if nothing is working at home, who is taking care of our families?' That question alone struck me because I didn't have a good answer. I retired to my tent after that first briefing and reflected. I thought about my own family and who was taking care of them. For years the Marines have been tasked with being the tip of the spear in protecting the United States from its enemies. I am a proud Marine who has served many years and risked my life for my country many times. But before, I knew my family was safe. I knew they were being taken care of. Now it's different. Do you understand what I'm saying, gentlemen?" Barone asked, his tempo increasing slightly.

"As I sat in my hooch after that first briefing I decided that my country is not my government. I knew then that we fight for the safety and freedom of our families and the people. Only twice in the country's history have fighting men been away while their loved ones were under attack at home: the American Civil War and the Revolutionary War. What was different in those times was there were standing armies and you knew your enemy. Now the enemies at our doorsteps are starvation, pestilence, and the mob. I have been questioned and even attacked for my actions. I accept that, but what I'm not is a traitor."

Barone stood now, taking his normal towering posture. "We swore an oath to defend our country. I go back to what it means, our country. To me, it means the people, but most importantly, our families. What have I accomplished if I go and attempt to fix what can't be fixed? I accomplish nothing. The traitors to their own people are the fools who listen to orders that do more harm than good. So I ask those who have challenged me, would they have gone and allowed their families to starve? Really? If a man knowingly leaves his family to die, he is not a man of honor but a mindless fool," Barone said. "I know you didn't want to go through this again, but I have never given anyone except those few the true time line and reasons why we are where we are.

"After I thought that day, I attempted to contact someone of higher authority. Because of the attacks and the catastrophic failure of all the infrastructure nationwide, I couldn't reach anyone but a general at an Air Force base in Oklahoma. I knew then the sheer damage done. Gentlemen, my decision has created many different consequences, some bad; but overall we now have our families next to us."

Barone paused and looked at his men, all still staring wide-eyed at his openness. "Many people, specifically civilians, think of us as robots, that we are somehow emotionless and only listen to commands and mindlessly obey. When I joined the Marines many years ago, I did so because I wanted to defend my country. I ask again, what is country?" He looked at each man's face, seeing if somewhere in their expressions they were processing this question. "Gentlemen, I feel vindicated after having seen with my own eyes the damage and chaos in San Diego. If I hadn't made that tough decision, we'd be spinning around our anchors off the coast of Virginia. Now we are sitting off the coast of Oregon about to take another turn in our new lives. Out there offers us a chance to rebuild a country and to help those Americans who want to join us. The old way is gone, taken from us. We didn't ask for it, but it happened."

Again he paused. This time he looked back at the map on the wall. On it he saw a new world for him and his men. Turning back to face them, he drew his speech to a close. "Men, I will finish my little explanation by telling you something that I've never mentioned before. When I spoke to that Air Force general over seven weeks ago, he explained to me what had happened and commanded that we follow standard operating procedures by departing Afghanistan and heading back east. I asked him about our families out west and what was being done to help them. He explained that he wasn't sure about our families back in California because a lot of communications were down and almost nothing was working.

"I wasn't satisfied with his answer, so I again stressed the point about finding out about our families. He then pointed out what he called the 'fact' that we were Marines and our obligation was to our government. I paused when he said that, 'our government.' No, I thought, our obligation was to our country. I could hear the frustration in his voice, and this is where he made everything clear to me. He said, 'Colonel Barone, the priority right now is not taking care of the people, it's government continuity.' This statement told me everything I needed to know to make my final decision."

He grabbed the chair he had been sitting in and put it back. The room was very still. He took his place in front of the room again and said, "Now that I've gotten that out of the way, let's dive into the briefing." His tone had gone back to his typical professional and direct tenor.

The briefing went on for approximately thirty minutes as he

explained that his recon Marines had located safe mooring for all the ships. He covered in detail his plans for incorporating the civilian leadership at some levels, but they would not have any real operational control.

He then discussed with them his long-term plan of making their way to Salem, the capital. There he wanted to establish his own seat of government. The task ahead would be tough, but Barone knew exactly the advantage he had. Even though he had lost a significant percentage of both battalions along the way, he had been able to replenish a lot of the losses from all the bases back in the San Diego area. His force now stood at more than four thousand combat-tested Marines with more than twelve hundred naval personnel. He had tanks, dozens of light armored vehicles, dozens of helicopters, half a dozen jump jets, over one hundred Humvees, dozens of artillery guns, thousands of rifles, millions of rounds, and tons and tons of potable water and food. Barone had a force to be reckoned with and he knew it. The two MPS ships they had taken from Diego Garcia were not included in the count. Once they landed in Coos Bay they'd be able to see what bounty was hidden in those ships' hulls.

Barone assured his men that no harm would come to civilians unless they threatened his force. He knew that in order to establish a new country he would have to win the hearts and minds of the people. As he paced the room answering his men's questions, one was posed that many hesitated to ask but all wanted to know the answer to.

"Sir, what are we prepared to do about the remnants of the U.S.?"

Barone stopped pacing, looked directly at the Marine who'd asked the question, and responded forcefully, "We mean them no harm, so if they wish to do us harm we will defend ourselves. I have to admit, though, it's now over seven weeks since the attack and I can't imagine what force is left of the U.S. that can be effectively deployed. Some of you who went ashore saw for yourselves the chaos and anarchy. Where was the government, much less the military? They're hunkered down taking care of themselves. So what we're doing is no different than what they're doing. I don't expect much resistance now from what is left of the federal government. I hope that answers your question, Captain." Barone finished and looked at the young officer, who nodded back. He looked at each face; these would be the faces he'd create a new country with. With no more questions to be answered, he closed the briefing with one final statement. "Men, before I dismiss you, I want to say thank you. Thank you for believing in me, thank you for letting these ships reach our families. Together, we will make Operation Rubicon a success and build a new country."

Cheyenne Mountain, Colorado

"General Baxter, now is the time to continue forward with our mission to Portland. I will be leading it. Please put together a team and make all arrangements," Cruz said to his secretary of defense.

Both men were relaxing in Cruz's office, a large room built for the commander in chief to be used for just this type of circumstance.

"Sir, can I ask you what your thoughts are on the president's status?"

Cruz chuckled then answered, "Sorry for the impolite laugh, but I had to laugh because of the coincidence of the question. You see, earlier today, the first lady asked me that identical question."

Baxter just looked at Cruz; he didn't respond to his comment but again asked a similar question: "Mr. Vice President, do you think he's dead or alive?"

"General Baxter, at the moment, I don't know how to be quite honest. Between you and me, I would say my friend's chances are dimming with each passing day. This doesn't say we stop looking. But we can't hold off on his plan of going to Portland to get a new capital up and running. I agree with the president. We must show that the federal government is here and doing something. It's time to leave the bunker and take some real action."

"Agreed, sir. I'll get working on that ASAP."

"How long before we can be ready to depart?"

"Give us a week, sir. Our advance team is still in Portland in a secured location. They've made contact with the governor in Salem. So a week should be all I need to make sure your trip out there is safe."

Baxter closed his leather binder and stood up, but Cruz stopped him. "Hold on, General."

"Yes, sir."

"Sit down, please." Cruz pointed back to the seat his secretary of defense had just been sitting in. "Do you drink at all?"

"Yes, sir, I do. I have to admit I haven't really enjoyed a drink since the attacks last month," Baxter said. He sat upright in his chair, a bit apprehensive.

"I have some quality sipping tequila, will that do?"

"Sure, that sounds fine, thank you."

Cruz walked to a cabinet against the far wall. The furniture in the office was from the 1990s, the last time the bunker had been renovated. He opened the top cabinet door, pulled out a bottle, and grabbed two stemmed glasses.

"I have to laugh now because Brad gave me a hard time about

all the luggage my family had when we joined him in Florida. I told him that I had some nonnegotiables. Plus, I didn't know if I'd ever go home again. I wanted to make sure I had some things that I enjoyed and that reminded me of a different time. That's this here," Cruz said, holding up the bottle. "If you haven't had it before, I can tell you, it's magnificent."

"I'm not familiar. What is it?" Baxter asked. He squinted to see if he could read the label as Cruz poured the tequila into the glasses.

"This is AsomBroso La Rosa reposado tequila," he said as he handed the general a glass. Cruz then held his glass up, swirled it, and continued. "It's aged over eleven months in French oak barrels used once for vintage Bordeaux. It's one of the best, if you ask me." He then brought the glass to his nose, closed his eyes, and sniffed. "Aah, perfection."

Baxter watched Cruz's performance. He'd never seen the vice president like this. It was interesting to him to witness what people found pleasure in. While he didn't hold tequila in the same regard as Cruz, he did like a good drink. He too smelled the tequila, but he thought it smelled like any tequila. Without waiting another second, he took a sip. The liquid felt good against his lips and mouth. The slight burning in his throat was a welcome feeling. He instantly felt more at ease.

"It's good, right?"

Looking at the glass, he answered, "Yes, sir, it is."

"Good, good." Cruz sat down after taking a sip himself. He relaxed into the chair and opened up on why he wanted to have this more casual meeting. "General, you're aware of what happened before with Conner and Griswald. You see, I don't want us to have that type of situation. Maybe we can prevent that collision of ideals if we really get to know one another. I took the liberty of looking at your personnel file. Very impressive, but I'd have to say that we as people are more than profiles or files." Cruz closed the folder and tossed it on his desk.

Baxter didn't know what to say. He looked at the glass he held, now resting on his leg. He took a quick sip to give him a few more seconds to think.

"Sir, I'm not much of a conversationalist, so I'll tell you straight. I agree that we need to prevent another situation like before. If assurances are what you need from me, you have them. I'm on board with everything. I'm a dedicated officer and will give you my counsel when asked, but when given an order, I will comply," Baxter finally said. When he finished he took another drink.

"Good, glad to hear that. Like you, I'm a team player. My family came to this country as immigrants from Cuba. I grew up seeing my parents go from struggling to prospering. This country saved me in many ways, and this is why I intend on saving it. I won't just roll over and let her die. I will fight and do what is necessary to ensure she rises again. Knowing that you're with me makes it easier. Our first step toward getting her back on her feet is to let the people know we're still here."

"Sir, sorry to interrupt, but what if we don't find the president before you leave? What do you plan on telling the governor?"

"Aha, the eight-hundred-pound gorilla in the room. What do we say about the president? For the moment, I think we should just keep it quiet. Say that he's back in the bunker to remain safe."

"So, just stick with the story we told him about why we never made it out there at first?"

"Yes, no need to panic them any more. Just tell them after the attack on the president we feel it's better to keep him here."

"That's easy to do for now, but you do know that eventually we'll have to make a decision the other way."

"Don't remind me. I think about it all the time. Right now, it's not critical that we inform anyone of anything. Let's just keep moving forward with his plan and keep the hunt for him active."

"Yes, sir," Baxter said, then took a final swallow of his drink.

"Here, have another," Cruz offered.

Holding his hand out to cover the top of the glass, Baxter said, "I'm good, but thank you. I still have a few more hours left on the clock."

Cruz smiled and poured a bit more in his glass.

"If that is all, sir, I need to go."

"Sure, you're excused."

Baxter stood up, holding his binder, and headed for the door. As he turned the handle Cruz asked a final question.

"General, do you think the president is still alive?"

Baxter turned and answered, "Yes, sir, I do."

Unknown military installation

Gordon couldn't find the appetite to eat the MRE he had been served. He had only gotten as far as ripping open the thick plastic bag and removing its contents. Lying before him were cardboard packaged "food-type" products. It had been years since he had eaten one, and his memory told him it wasn't a pleasant experience. He picked up the largest packet and read the box it was in: "Spaghetti with meat sauce." His stomach ached with hunger, but the slight depression he was experiencing prevented him from opening the container. As he glanced around the room, the waning sun's light made it hard for him to make out each person's face.

By a rough estimate he counted almost forty people. People like him, imprisoned by Rahab. He asked himself how each one of them had ended up here. How did they fall prey to this man? Were they just looking for food and came into contact with him? Were they attacked like he was?

Whatever the reason, they all had the same purpose: escape. Rahab had done a good job at segregating everyone. Gordon knew there were women because he saw them working on the base too. However, that was as far as contact came with them. The women slept and ate in different locations. He already knew the outcome of the children, sent to live with Rahab and his inner circle; there he assumed they were being brainwashed and indoctrinated.

When the guard asked for volunteers for the working party, Gordon promptly raised his hand. He wasn't sure what to expect or what type of work he'd be doing, but if it meant he could find out critical information, he was up for it.

One of the guards instructed Gordon and the other volunteers to line up against the wall. Gordon made sure he stood next to Derek. The guard came by, tapped each one, and gave them a location. When he tapped Derek's shoulder the guard asked, "Latrines?"

"Yes, sir, I know what to do," Derek said.

"I'll help him," Gordon spat out.

The guard nodded and proceeded down the line.

· · ·

The guard didn't say a word as they trekked across the darkening base to the makeshift latrines outside the male barracks.

One of Gordon's unfavorable memories from the Marine Corps was doing latrine duty while on a training operation outside of 29 Palms. After leaving the Corps, he never imagined he'd be handling large quantities of human waste beyond changing diapers. The smell of feces filled his nostrils, causing him to cringe with disgust.

"So what do we have to do?" Gordon mumbled from behind the hand that covered his mouth and nose.

"Here," Derek said, offering him a surgical mask to wear.

"Thanks," Gordon answered, quickly placing the mask on his face. His first breath through the mask introduced him to the smell of lavender.

"Before you ask, during another working party I found some body sprays in a locker. The lack of decent hygiene has made this stuff come in handy. It especially helps for this duty."

Gordon looked around; the sun's rays were quickly fading behind the mountains to the west. He swiveled his head in all directions to look for the guard. Only he and Derek were there now.

"Where did the guard go?"

"I always pick this job because the guard never stays around. The smell might be bad, but it's good for us. Plus, they take this time to go over there," Derek said, gesturing with his head toward the female barracks.

Gordon looked in that direction; the female barracks was similar to theirs.

"They're over there having sex with the women?"

"If you want to call rape sex, then yes," Derek said as he opened a hatch to expose a fifty-five-gallon drum cut in half. He put on a pair of work gloves and carefully removed the drum.

The sloshing of the contents made Gordon feel nauseous for a moment. Once the drum was removed, Derek stopped and looked at him.

"Get over here and help me."

A handle had been cut out near the top edge of the drum, making it easy to carry. Both men picked up the drum and started to walk very slowly toward the runway. Just ahead of them were two structures that resembled large Xs. Gordon had seen them the day before and was curious about what they were. They stood more than six feet tall with a three-foot separation between them. They were constructed with an almost black stained wood resembling railroad ties. At the top and bottom of each arm of the X were leather straps. Seeing those straps, Gordon knew they were for restraining people. He wondered if these had anything to do with Rahab's ceremonies.

The sight of structures and their presumed use added to Gordon's somber mood. They both walked slowly and steadily down one of the short runways toward the southern berm of the base. Gordon hadn't been this far out, so taking advantage of the diminishing light, he looked around. Once they reached the berm they stopped next to a large pit and dumped the contents of the drum.

"Now you can see why I asked you to volunteer," Derek commented.

"Yeah, I can. No one is around, and this gives us a chance to get a better perspective of the base."

"I know you have a lot of questions, but let me give you a bit of sound advice first. Watch yourself here; these people are bad and will kill you without thinking twice. You saw those two large Xs over there, didn't you? That's where they execute people. So when I tell you to shut up, shut up."

"I heard some screams the other night. Was that an execution?"

"Yeah, it was."

"So what exactly is going on here?" Gordon asked with a pleading tone.

"The first thing you need to realize is that Rahab is a psychopath and his followers are a bunch of Kool-Aid drinkers who will kill for him. Be careful what you say or do, okay?"

"I will. How long have you been here?"

"Almost four weeks now. I came with a group from San Diego. We saw the signs for the main base. While we were driving there they attacked our cars. They killed two people in my group and took the rest of us prisoner."

"You came from San Diego? Whereabouts?" Gordon asked.

"Near downtown, but none of that matters now. What is important is that if you're looking to get out of here, I want to go too but we have to play the game."

"Here's a problem I have. My son is here too. He's being—"

"Yes, I know, Rahab has him. That complicates things a lot," Derek said, interrupting Gordon.

"How many men does Rahab have? He told me over a hundred."

"Oh, I would estimate almost fifty loyal followers. The rest he counts are people like us. He has about fifteen in his inner core; they are the same bunch of whack jobs that followed him before."

"What do you mean by followed him before?"

"Rahab has been around preaching his insanity since before everything went to shit. He had a *church,* or a better word would be a *cult,* in San Diego. I first ran into him when he came before the city council to seek rezoning for a building in Claremont Mesa. We shot him down right after several abuse cases came to our attention."

"Wait a minute, now I know where I know you from," Gordon said.

Derek didn't respond, he just looked at Gordon, waiting for the answer to spew forth.

"You're that gay guy who ran for mayor a couple years ago, aren't you?"

"Why is it I'm the gay guy? I don't say, 'Oh wait, you're the straight guy who did XYZ.'" Derek shot back, clearly irritated.

"I'm sorry, but it's not every day you see a gay Republican run for mayor of San Diego. It's kinda like seeing bigfoot," Gordon said, attempting a bit of humor.

"Do you want to know more about Rahab and this place or do you want to keep going with this?"

"I'm sorry, I really am."

The sun finally dipped below the mountains to the west, creating an eerie orange glow in the sky.

Derek pulled out two headlamps and handed one to Gordon. "Here, put this on; we're required to wear them at night."

"What happens if we don't?"

"Just put it on."

"How do we get out of here?"

Derek turned on his headlamp. The light splashed across Gordon's face.

"I don't know. If it were you and me, I would say we make a run for it on a night like this. The guards usually keep themselves busy with the women, so we can pretty much do what we want. With your kid being here, I don't know how we get him and then get out without being noticed."

"Do you know anything about where they keep the kids?"

"As much as you. They sleep in the same building as Rahab and his council."

"Who is this guy? Where did he come from?" Gordon asked.

"I'll tell you more of what I know as we finish," Derek said.

As both men walked, Derek explained what he knew about Rahab.

Rahab's view of Christianity didn't fit with any of the churches he attended in San Diego. One by one they asked him not to return. His deeply held views on the end of days turned many away from him. However, they did attract a few, and those few were as fanatical as he was. He eventually started his own ministry, and his church grew.

When Derek ran into Rahab that day before the city council, Rahab had already created a solid core of followers. The city council was set to vote to allow his rezoning when the stories of Rahab's legal troubles were brought to light. Several people were suing him, and the local police were investigating him and his church for possible kidnapping and fraud. The council immediately changed course and denied his application. Rahab was able to avoid the legal trouble based on a few technicalities.

Knowing that he was now a target in San Diego, Rahab took his followers into the desert, just a few miles from where they were now. He set up a compound and kept his head down. His flock grew, but not by much. He took to the Internet like many did to preach his word of the end and the coming purge, as Rahab called it.

As Derek kept detailing what he knew, it triggered a memory for Gordon.

"I now remember reading about this guy. A few men sued him because they claimed their wives had been coerced into giving him their life savings," Gordon said excitedly.

"That's him," Derek replied.

On their final return to the latrines, Gordon abruptly stopped at the X structures. His light illuminated the bloodstained wood.

"What happens here?"

"I've only seen it once. One of my staffers who had come with me was wearing a pink triangle necklace . . ."

"A what?"

"It's a symbol for gay pride. Anyway, they found it. They asked him what it meant and he stupidly told them. Without hesitation they brought him here." Derek pointed to the large X. He just stared at the ominous wood structure, its shadow long against the tarmac.

"Never mind, I get the picture," Gordon replied quietly.

"No, you don't. They tied him up and then Rahab came out. He said a few things out of his book and then plunged a large knife into Chad's chest. It was awful."

"Come on, let's go," Gordon said and stepped away from the X and Derek.

After a few steps he noticed Derek wasn't coming. Gordon turned; he was holding the empty drum in one hand.

Derek was now touching the center of the X. His fingers were shaking as he ran them across the rough wood surface. Looking up at Gordon, he said, "You know what they call this place? They call it the 'cleansing cross.' " He paused, his hand still touching the cross. "We can't allow this to be our fate. We will find a way to get your son and get out of here."

JANUARY 13, 2014

• • •

Courage doesn't always roar. Sometimes courage is the quiet voice at the end of the day saying, "I will try again tomorrow."

—Mary Anne Radmacher

40 miles east of Barstow, California

Nelson tapped on his watch to make sure it was working. He even brought it to his ear. It was ticking. He looked over at the door of Samantha's trailer. Any moment she'd come out and be ready for another day of searching. The past two days had been unfruitful. They had driven morning to night. Slowly they were marking off the grids on her map. Today they were planning to go near Fort Irwin. Because of the discontent and the disagreement the group had with Gordon and Holloway, Gordon hadn't felt the need to leave a clue about where they were actually going. All everyone knew was that he was going to the base.

Nelson looked at his watch again. Samantha was running ten minutes late. Assumptions ran through his mind—*she must have overslept.* He knew how important this was to her, so he walked to the door and tapped twice on the glass window.

Movement inside let him know she was there. The door creaked open, and out stepped Samantha. Her eyes were puffy from crying.

"Just give me a minute to get Haley ready," she said softly, wiping tears off of her cheeks.

"Sure, take your time," Nelson answered. He thought about asking her if she was okay but stopped short. He knew why she was crying; he already knew she wasn't okay.

Samantha stepped back in and closed the door. Inside he could hear movement and murmuring. Moments later the door opened again and Samantha stepped out holding a tired and clingy Haley. She was wrapped in her blanket and was resisting Samantha's requests to wake up.

"Just give me a minute to drop her off," Samantha said, walking toward another trailer.

Nelson watched her. He couldn't imagine what she was feeling. He didn't have children, much less a spouse. Gordon had opened his home to him and his parents, and for that he was eternally grateful. It had been only three days, but a couple of people were already asking him how long they were going to sit around. He knew the grumbling would grow the longer they sat. Without a single sign of what had happened and knowing Gordon's prowess, Nelson himself was coming to the regretful conclusion that his friend might be dead. He hoped today was the day they'd find them or find a clue as to where they might be. That way he could keep the search going.

• • •

"I suggest we go near the south gate of the base and work our way around to the east, then north along the perimeter," Samantha said, focused on the map in her lap. She traced her suggested route with her right index finger while she held a lensatic compass in her left hand.

"Okay, so which way do I go?" Nelson asked, peering out through the bug-covered windshield.

"Just keep heading straight."

They drove without a word save for Samantha's directions. Nelson had attempted to start a conversation, but Samantha's monosyllabic responses told him she didn't want to talk.

"At the top of the rise, stop," she said.

Nelson followed her instructions and stopped just short of the skyline. They both got out and crouched until they reached a spot to lie down and survey the valley that stretched out before them to the north. With binoculars, they looked for any sign that might help. Two to three miles away, they could see the southern fence line of the base. Nelson panned his field of view to his right. There he saw a circling flock of birds.

"Samantha, hey, I think I might have something. Look that way," he said, pointing east.

She trained her binoculars on the birds, then strained to see what they were circling: something large—large enough to be a person.

She jumped up without concern for skylining herself and ran to the truck. Nelson was right behind her. She got behind the wheel and started the engine. Nelson could see the determination on her face.

Her forehead wrinkled, and the crow's-feet around her eyes became more prominent as she focused on the task. She put the truck in gear before Nelson had a chance to close the passenger door. The truck spun out and threw dirt and rocks as she accelerated east along the ridgeline.

The silence between them continued, now brought on by the fact that both of them thought the worst.

She turned the wheel to the right and went down a dirt road. The road crested the hill and doglegged down the opposite side to the valley floor. The truck whined with each abrupt turn. Samantha barely slowed to compensate for the turns. Nelson's body was tense, and he gripped the armrest tightly with each anticipated turn. The desert dust was filling the cab with a brown haze.

Samantha prayed: *Please, God, don't let it be Hunter or Gordon, please.*

They both knew they'd find a body; whose it was, was the question.

Samantha slammed down on the accelerator once they cleared the dogleg and entered the straight, flat valley floor. Both were bouncing up and down in the truck as they raced over each mound and hole.

She slammed on the brakes just short of the body. The turkey vultures that were picking at it flew off with haste, their loose feathers floating through the air.

Samantha opened the door, stepped out, then paused.

The body that lay before them was that of an adult. This gave her some consolation that it wasn't Hunter. The horrible condition of the body—from the severe bloating to the dry, bloodied tissues left hanging by the scavengers—made it impossible to identify from their perspective.

Nelson climbed out of the cab and carefully approached the body, acting as if might explode. With each reluctant step he too prayed that it wasn't Gordon.

"Is it him?" Samantha yelled from behind the truck door, as if the door shielded her from the reality of what was lying dead out there.

Nelson drew closer. The body was that of a man, left to rot on his stomach. The clothes he was wearing were ripped and torn from claws and teeth.

Nelson knew Gordon had similar clothes, so they didn't rule him out. He stepped over the body. Judging by the degree of decomposition, the man had been dead for a few days. Nelson went to grab the body and turn it over when he saw a sign he had wanted to see. Above the right rear pocket on the pants was a name tag—it read "Holloway."

"Sam, Sam it's not Gordon! It's Holloway!"

Not able to answer, she fell to her knees and began to sob. Looking up to the sky, she quietly said, "Thank you, God."

Nelson did a quick examination of the body to see if he could find the cause of death. But the vultures and Mother Nature had made it impossible.

"I don't know how he died, but I think this might be a good sign for Gordon and Hunter."

Pulling herself together, Samantha stood up and sat back in the truck.

Nelson walked over and said, "Let's put his body in the truck and continue to look."

"One sec," she said. The tears had stopped flowing, but her nose was congested by the crying.

"Take your time."

"Sorry, as soon as you told me it wasn't Gordon I felt such relief but I also felt helpless. Where is he? Something bad has happened to them. Look! Holloway is dead and Gordon and Hunter are missing. Hell, I don't even know if Hunter was with them. We've been looking for days, and the first sign is a dead body. Where are they, Nelson?"

"I don't know, but today we know we are on their trail. I don't know what happened here, but not finding Gordon alongside Holloway tells me that he just might be alive somewhere. I think the next place we need to go is right there." Nelson pointed in the direction of the base.

Cheyenne Mountain, Colorado

Julia kept touching the stitches on her belly. The nurse had already told her not to do it, but she couldn't help it. The little one-inch incision was all it took to remove her baby. How sad, she thought. When Brad returned, she hoped he'd understand. It wasn't her choice; for whatever reason they weren't meant to have the baby. She did intend on trying again after he came back. But when would that be? She felt so lost without him. She needed something to take her mind off of what had happened. The doctor had told her she'd have to stay under their care for another day or two. Typically after laparoscopic surgery she would have been able to go home within two to four hours, but not having anyone to care for her, she'd have to stay there.

She decided she would take this time to reflect on everything. So often in her life she had tried so hard to control every little aspect of things. Her focus so often in the early part of Brad's career as a congressman was ensuring that everything looked "just right." This tight control put her at odds with her son, Bobby. She felt it important to be a member of any number of charitable groups. The salary Brad made along with the benefits gave her the ability not to work, but she felt she couldn't just sit at home. It was the job of the wife of an up-and-coming congressman to be active, so she set to it. Even with the cries of her toddler son to stay at home and play with him, she had places to go. She now wished she could go back and change it all. *The things we think are important truly aren't,* she thought and laughed to herself. All her baby Bobby wanted was her time, but she couldn't give that to him.

Regrets, so many regrets. Why does it take the loss of someone you love to awaken you to what is important in life? Again, she laughed to herself, thinking that it was a cruel joke by God. She didn't have the courage to tell Brad her regrets about Bobby. Now Bobby was dead and Brad was missing, possibly dead.

She put that out of her mind. Every time the thought that he'd never return came creeping in, she quickly vanquished it.

Maybe God killed my baby because I'm not a good mother, she thought. Again, she rid her mind of those negative ruminations. *How can there be a God?* she then asked herself. *How can God allow what happened seven weeks ago to happen?* So many thoughts passed across her mind. She now didn't feel alone; she knew many others were having the same doubts and questioning it all. To what purpose? Why? Who did it?

Not being able to stop the thoughts, she hit the call button. She needed a distraction.

A moment later the door opened and a young nurse came in. "Yes, Mrs. Conner? Is everything all right?"

"Yes, I'm fine. Actually, I'm bored. Do you have anything to read?"

"Aah, let me go see."

"Wait a minute. Come sit down for a moment," Julia beckoned.

The nurse looked apprehensive but obliged her. She pulled the chair from against the wall and sat down.

"So tell me your name," Julia asked.

"I'm Nurse Belicheck," she said. Her hands were clasped in her lap.

"No, what's your first name?"

"Oh, my name is Stacy."

"Where are you from, Stacy?"

"I'm from Sioux Falls, South Dakota, ma'am."

"Don't call me ma'am, my name is Julia. Please call me Julia."

"Okay," Stacy answered, clearly feeling uncomfortable.

"Is that where your family is?"

"Yes, it is."

"Have you heard from them since the attack?"

Stacy looked down at her hands. She began to fidget with the waist string that hung from her pants.

"I'm sorry, I shouldn't have asked you that," Julia said. She now felt foolish asking this young nurse these questions.

"If you'll excuse me, I need to get back to work." Stacy stood up quickly, placed the chair back, and left the room.

When the large, heavy door closed, Julia let out a huge sigh.

The door opened again, but this time it was the surgeon.

"Mrs. Conner. How are you today?"

"I'm fine, Doctor. Just bored."

"Can I get you something?"

"I already asked the nurse to find me something to read."

"Good, good. Let's see here." The doctor looked at her chart and then said, "As you know, everything came out okay. All we want to do now is monitor you for a day or so. Any questions?"

"No."

"I'll remind the nurse about finding you something to read," the doctor said, then promptly left the room.

When the door closed a second time, Julia said out loud, "Mr. Personality there."

• • •

Nurse Belicheck returned fifteen minutes later with a stack of magazines.

"I scavenged and found these. I hope you're fine with them?"

"Oh, thank you so much. Hey, listen, I'm sorry about the questions earlier."

"Don't be. I'm just upset about my family is all," she said, looking sad. "If there's anything else I can get you, let me know."

"Thank you."

Julia began looking at the magazines.

"She really did scavenge for these," Julia said out loud. There was a vast assortment here. She fingered through the pile and tossed out the ones she didn't want. Aside went *Men's Health*. Aside went *Guns & Ammo*. Aside went *Wired*. She stopped when she saw the cover of *Time* magazine. Her hand went to the picture of Brad on the cover. She looked at the date: July 8, 2013. Below his picture the line read, "Will 2016 be his year?"

She chuckled to herself recalling the photo shoot and interview they both went through before the article was written. The camera crews, makeup people, and the pretentious writer who visited their Washington, D.C., home that day were torture. She took it all in stride, though, as it was part of the job. As she thumbed through the magazine to find the article, she passed over ads promoting health-care products, pet medicine, makeup, real estate in Tennessee, and insurance. The magazine was so full of advertising for things that everyday people thought were important then. So often people never think something bad can happen to them.

She remembered how full-circle events went for Brad. He had always been very hawkish about defense. People think politicians don't talk politics when they go home or go out, but they do. Many times Brad would want to discuss the happenings on Capitol Hill with her, but she refused to listen after a few years. She was so tired of the endless fighting and infighting, the petty politics and agendas. She played her part as the dutiful wife and was willing and ready to assume her role as the first lady if it ever came to that, but she never thought it would happen like it did.

After September 11, Brad had felt his worldview had been vindicated. He knew that something would happen stateside, and when it did he didn't waste time pronouncing that he had predicted it. At that time he was only the majority whip, but his ambition was not short-lived. When his boss, Speaker Canning, retired, he ran and won the speakership. He held that position until the attacks came and washed him onto the shores of the presidency. It was something he had thought about, but he could never have even guessed it would have been through the line of presidential succession. The question about his running had come up in the interview that hot and humid July day, but it all seemed so weird now for her. It seemed like a different life, and in many ways it was.

Julia wondered where all those people were who had put this magazine together. Where was the young writer/interviewer? Was she alive? Julia remembered that she lived in the D.C. metro area. Did she perish in the nuclear strike on the city? All those people in her house that day. She didn't talk to most of them, and now many of them were probably dead. It felt so odd. The circumstances had taken them out of harm's way and saved their lives. If Bobby hadn't been in a car accident, then she and Brad would have died. It was as if Bobby dying had saved their lives.

Julia was having the hardest time distracting herself from these dark thoughts. Wanting not to be reminded for a moment of her situation, she tossed the magazine aside and began to seek something that would feed her mind nothing but entertainment.

But it was too hard; even when she picked up the *People* magazine and saw the photo of a celebrity couple and the headline about their most recent breakup, she couldn't help but think of the event. Anything she picked up was a reminder of what was or what had been lost. Frustrated, she pushed all the magazines off the bed and lay back.

"Where are you, Brad?" she asked out loud. Thoughts of where he might be ran through her mind. *Are you wounded? Who has you? Why have they taken you?* Then the thought that she kept at bay for so long crept back into her mind: *Are you dead?* If Brad truly was dead, then none of this made sense and her going on made no sense. If she were to get confirmation that he was dead, she wondered if she'd have the strength to end her own life.

San Diego, California

"How do you plan on getting to Zion?" Sebastian asked. He had been invited to eat breakfast with Sorenson and didn't want to waste time with casual chitchat.

"Ha! Why not at least take a bite of some of eggs and enjoy your breakfast before we get into the heavy conversation," the bishop quipped.

"Sorry. I have been waiting to ask you since we last talked. I hope you know I can help with the planning and route."

Not looking at Sebastian, Sorenson cut his fried eggs and began dipping his bacon in the runny yolk. Holding the dripping bacon, he answered, "I realize you're an asset, and I would like to share our plan with you. Why don't we sit down later today and go over it? I'm hoping you'll give me some insight into what we should do."

Sebastian perked up with that comment. "Thank you. I look forward to it," he replied. He'd just begun to dig into his food when the screen door opened and the two boys stepped in.

Both continued to hang their heads low as they sat down at the large dinner table.

"Good morning, boys," Sorenson said cheerily.

Both mumbled, "Morning," as each took a seat.

"Did you boys sleep well?" Sorenson asked. He was clearly attempting to engage them in conversation.

"Yeah," Brandon said.

"Yes, sir," Luke replied.

Brandon picked up his fork and began to cut his eggs.

"Uh, don't you say grace before you eat?" Sorenson asked.

His question made Brandon pause a moment, but then he continued cutting his eggs.

Luke put his fork down and answered, "Yes, sir, we, aah, I mean I used to."

"Please go ahead," Sorenson implored the boy.

Luke looked nervous. He looked at Brandon, who had impolitely ignored the bishop. He then sheepishly looked at Sebastian, who raised his eyebrows then winked at him.

"Um," Luke blurted out, not knowing what to say.

"Brandon, how about a little courtesy?" Sorenson reprimanded.

Tossing his fork onto the now-empty plate, Brandon shot back, "I'm done anyway." He stood quickly, wiped his mouth on his sleeve, and left.

Sorenson just watched Brandon. He wasn't shocked by his behavior. He knew the boy had been through a lot and his actions were most likely the result of PTSD.

Luke watched in fear as Brandon left the room. He again started his prayer but stopped.

Sebastian could not only see but feel the awkwardness oozing out of the boy.

Sorenson just waited for the boy to try again.

Not wanting Luke to feel tortured anymore, Sebastian said a quick prayer. When he was done, Sorenson thanked him. Luke, feeling a weight lifted, began to eat his breakfast.

"So, who do you think killed these people in your brother's community?" Sorenson asked Sebastian.

"Luke here has been a big help. He mentioned a group called the Villistas, some type of former Mexican drug cartel. Apparently they have been going from community to community, almost house to house, killing and looting. As we found, they are ruthless. This is one of the main reasons why I wanted to talk about your route and about trying to expedite the trip. If we can, we need to leave ASAP."

"Villistas, huh? Mexican drug cartel? Well, I agree, Sebastian, we need to get going, but not before we're ready."

"What are you waiting for?"

"We need some more cars for the trip."

"I see. Well, what can I do to help?"

"Not much on the outside with your bum leg, but we are close. We need three more cars; then we'll have enough to caravan everyone out of here with all of our supplies."

"Can I suggest something? I know it might be kinda harsh and I'm guilty of it. That might be a bad word to use, but I did it as well. Stop taking in people," Sebastian said. He took a moment to glance at Luke. His comment didn't provoke a response.

"I hear the earthly and pragmatic side of you coming out, but we will take more children in if God puts them in front of us."

"But with what I saw at my brother's community, we may not have much time. We need to get those cars and go."

"Your urgency is noted and we are in agreement that it is now time to leave, but for the time being we must keep looking for more cars, and if other children in need show up, we will take them in."

Knowing that pressing the bishop wouldn't work, Sebastian decided to drop the debate. "Can I help with the perimeter security? I used to be a sniper."

"I don't see why not. I will have one of the men give you my old Winchester Model seventy. I think you'll appreciate that," Sorenson said to the eager Sebastian.

The screen door sprang open and in came one of Sorenson's men. He was sweating and out of breath.

"Bishop, we have more people at the gate."

"How many?" Sorenson asked.

"Too many to count."

Sorenson wiped his mouth off with a napkin and stood up.

Sebastian followed, hobbling on one leg until he reached his crutches.

Sorenson wasted no time leaving the house.

Before he could follow, Sebastian turned to Luke and asked, "You want to come?"

"Sure," the boy said, jumping up.

They both proceeded to the main gate.

• • •

The sound of what must have been dozens of people resonated off the brick wall that lined the drive and the iron gate that stood between them and the outside world.

Sebastian moved as fast as someone could on crutches. He cursed with each step, frustrated by his injury.

Ahead of him Sorenson was standing on top of one of their trucks. It was parked behind the gate and provided a platform for him to see what was happening.

The people outside were begging for him to open the gate and let them in. Even with all the death, there were still hundreds of thousands of San Diegans alive and on the hunt for more food and a safe place. During times like this, rumors were the only source of information. Rumors had spread that the Mormon community had plenty of food and other resources. The group now at the gate were people from the bishop's surrounding area.

Sebastian couldn't make out the back-and-forth between the group and Sorenson until he reached the truck where the bishop stood.

"People, everyone, please stop yelling!" Sorenson called back to the unruly group. With every surge the gate bowed in and hit the side of the truck Sorenson was perched on.

"People, please calm down!" the bishop yelled.

The only response he received was multiple people shouting, "Let us in! We know you have food! We are starving!"

Sebastian knew what people were capable of when their only choices left were finding food or starving. This situation could easily escalate and spill over into their little sanctuary.

He looked at the three armed guards present, all of them appearing apprehensive and unsure.

Sorenson's plea for calm wasn't working. These people wanted in. They were hungry and desperate.

With everyone's focus on the gate, nobody saw a few in the group climb the fence about thirty feet away.

"Help!" the wife of one of Sorenson's followers screamed from the barn that sat adjacent to the fence.

Sebastian turned and saw a man grabbing her and yelling, while two others ran into the barn.

Sebastian was not fazed by the sight of chaos. After his several months in Afghanistan, his mind was sharp. He hopped over to one of the guards and demanded his handgun. The guard, a middle-aged man, complied without hesitation.

Sebastian nestled the pistol in his waistband and moved as fast as his crutches would take him toward the barn.

"Hey, you, stop!" he yelled at the man who was shaking the woman.

The man looked up, let the woman go, and ran into the barn.

The barn was a single-story building with a high ceiling. It provided stalls for the few horses that Sorenson had. It now also served as a storage area for supplies his groups brought back from their runs outside.

A crashing sound caught Sebastian's attention to his right near the fence. Two more men had jumped over. One was heading toward the guesthouse and the other toward the main house. The situation was quickly deteriorating. Sorenson was still attempting to calm the group at the gate, and his guards were now nervously pointing their guns at them.

Sebastian's instincts told him to just start shooting these people, but his conscience wouldn't allow him. Ignoring the two outsiders, he pressed on toward the barn. He needed to protect what supplies they had.

The three men inside the dusty barn weren't trying to be discreet; all were ripping apart packages and eating like wild animals. Their attention was only on the food in front of them;

their hunger had transformed them into caricatures of human beings.

Sebastian dropped his right crutch, grabbed the grip of the pistol in his waistband, and pulled it out. He pointed it at the unaware men and yelled, "Stop. Just stop what you're doing and leave!"

The men stopped instantly and focused on him. They all looked middle-aged. Smears of dirt covered their unshaven and darkly tanned faces.

Time slowed down for Sebastian like it always did when he was faced with a life-or-death scenario. He had the gun trained on the man closest to him but was looking at each one carefully to see if any of them had a gun.

The man farthest from him bolted toward the back of the barn. His quick movement startled Sebastian briefly.

The other two men continued to stare at Sebastian; both were unsure what to do. The one closest to him finally spoke up. "Hey, listen, we're hungry. You have plenty here." He motioned with his arms to the large cache of food before them.

"This is ours and you need to leave now," Sebastian ordered firmly.

The man who had spoken looked at the other. They locked eyes and then turned their attention back to Sebastian.

Only ten feet at the most separated them from him. If they ran, Sebastian would let them go, but if they took a step toward him, he would have no choice but to shoot them.

"Come on, man. Let us take some of this food with us to feed our families," the other man said.

"I can't let you do that. I need you two to leave, now," Sebastian said louder.

The tension in the air was thick. The men's hunger, coupled with their basic human instincts, was telling them not to move. What sat before them meant survival if they could keep it.

The sounds from outside were giving Sebastian a picture that things were now collapsing. He needed to do something about these two so he could address the pandemonium in the compound.

A shot cracked behind the men. Sebastian saw the telltale muzzle flash but couldn't see who had shot. What he did see was the man closest to him clutch his chest. The bullet had entered his back and exited his sternum. He fell to the ground, dead.

The other man, unsure of what to do, dropped to his knees and begged for his life. His pleas were short-lived as another shot silenced him forever. The bullet ripped a gaping hole in his head. The man fell facefirst into the boxes of food.

Sebastian still couldn't see who was shooting, but because the two men were the targets, he assumed whoever it was was on his side.

"Who's there?" Sebastian called.

Out of the shadows stepped Brandon, holding Sebastian's M9 Beretta pistol.

"Brandon?" Sebastian gasped.

"I took care of what you couldn't, obviously," Brandon said as he stepped over the bodies and walked past Sebastian toward the front doors.

Sebastian just stood in awe of what he had witnessed. He'd seen many things, but never had he seen a child act out in such a vicious way. It unnerved him.

· · ·

The scene outside the barn had turned tenuous. Sebastian no longer saw Sorenson. Only two guards were now occupying the main gate, which still held, but the numbers coming over the fence, men and women, were too many for Sorenson's group to stop. Fortunately for them, none of the people coming over were armed. People were running everywhere. Up at the main house Sebastian could hear glass breaking and more screaming.

To Sebastian's left, about fifteen feet away, he saw Brandon walk toward the fence with the pistol and immediately shoot the woman who had just scaled it.

The sound of the gunshot instantly escalated the chaos. The two guards on the gate, already tense and nervous, let off a volley of fire into the group.

The yelling from the deranged group turned to screams of horror as the bullets rained down on them.

Brandon was calmly and diligently walking up to each person who had breached the compound fence and shooting.

Gunfire soon erupted from the main house, followed by harrowing screams.

Panic now gripped those who had forced their way in as they realized that the death they were trying to avoid was happening.

With the main house under siege, Sebastian's concern for Annaliese spiked.

"Fucking leg!" he yelled out as he moved as fast as he could on the crutches.

More gunfire came from the main house.

The distance from the barn to the house seemed like a hundred miles.

People he didn't recognize came pouring out of the house with arms full of food, followed by Annaliese with a shotgun. She brought the shotgun up, placed it firmly in the pocket of her shoulder, and pulled the trigger. A man no older than twenty was struck in the back by the bird shot. He collapsed to the ground; the food he was carrying spilled out across the dead brown lawn. Annaliese pumped the action of the shotgun and shot again, this time hitting a woman in the back.

Sebastian's hesitation to shoot these people now subsided. Finally, after seeing Annaliese, he knew this was about survival. The rules had changed, and he'd better change too. He stopped, raised his pistol, and shot a man coming near him. He then took aim on another, then another, then another.

San Ysidro, California (10 miles south of San Diego)

Pablo grabbed the man by his hair and lifted his head. He stared into the dark brown eyes of the man who once was a Villista comrade.

Tears, sweat, and blood covered the man's face. He attempted to say something, but his broken jaw distorted the words as they fell from his mouth.

"I sent word days ago to stop the brutal attacks on civilians. I gave very, very specific instructions about how our people were to conduct themselves in my absence," Pablo whispered loudly into the man's ear.

The man was one of five lieutenants Pablo had working for him in San Diego. Pablo had the Villistas grouped in five divisions by geography. Those divisions were then broken down into smaller and smaller units. For all intents and purposes, Pablo had created a chain of command with which to maintain control over his group. When his father called him back to Mexico, he had given detailed instructions that the harsh attacks, the murders, rapes, and other brutality the group had been carrying out had to cease.

Pablo found it odd that his father had such criticism of his actions with the Villistas, as his father was not known to be easy on his opponents. However, his father believed in a code, and that meant innocents were not to be harmed. Your enemies, in contrast, played the game and knew the consequences.

Pablo looked at the man he had just spent the last hour torturing and beating. This man had played the game, so any treatment he received was to be expected.

Gripping the man's black, sweaty hair tightly, Pablo slammed his face into the table he was sitting in front of. The man let out a groan. Pablo let go of the man, who out of total exhaustion and pain slumped in his chair, blood oozing from his mouth and nose.

Pablo grabbed a towel from the table and began to wipe off his hands. As he wiped he started to pace the room. A row of four other men stood a few feet away, their arms tied behind their backs. They were flanked by several armed men. Each man had the look of deeply held fear. They knew that they were about to experience what the man in front of them had just gone through.

"I leave for a short period of time and when I'm gone you think you can defy my clear orders. You think that you can do what you want," Pablo said loudly. He tossed the soiled towel back on the table and grabbed a bottle of water. "This torture business works up quite a thirst," he said after taking a long drink. He stepped up slowly to the first man in the row and looked into his eyes.

"José, I've known you for a long time. I trusted you, and this is how you repay me? You disobey me?"

"Patrón, please. I'm sorry. I won't . . ."

"Silence!" Pablo yelled at José. He then continued. "Timing and patience are essential in what we want to accomplish. You were all my trusted division leaders. I thought we would conquer this country together. But alas, I was wrong. What's that stupid American saying, 'When the cat's away the mice will play'? You played, but what you didn't realize was that you were playing with your own lives." Suddenly he stepped away from them, grabbed a machete lying on the table, and swung it at the man slumped in the chair. With precision and force, he cut off his head. The man's head hit the floor with a loud thud and rolled so his lifeless face stared at Pablo.

Two of the other men began to plead for their lives, another started throwing up, and the last man just stood stoically, seemingly reconciled to his fate. Pablo tossed the machete on the table, reached down, and picked up the man's head. He walked over to the four others and said, "This is what happens to those who disobey! José, you're next!"

Two other guards firmly grabbed the lieutenant and placed him in another chair at the table.

Pablo handed the head to one of his guards with instructions to not throw it away.

When he walked up to José, he sniffed and cringed. "Did you shit yourself, José?" Turning to his guards, he laughed and said, "José shit his pants." When he faced José again, the laughter left his face and he looked pointedly at him and said, "You piece of shit. Just for that, I'll torture you slowly."

Pablo spent the next two hours torturing all four men before he beheaded them all the same as he had the first.

• • •

Hygiene and cleanliness were important to Pablo, so after he had dealt with his division leaders he washed up and put on fresh clothes. He pulled a cigar out of his pocket and placed it under his nose. The strong aroma of the blend of tobaccos filled his nostrils. As he prepared the cigar to smoke, one of his guards approached from behind.

"Patrón, what do you want us to do with the heads?"

Pablo didn't answer right away. He continued preparing his cigar by clipping off the butt end.

The guard stood anxiously, awaiting his response.

If fear was a goal of Pablo's, it had worked. The guards all had fear seared into them.

Pablo thought about the events that had just transpired. He liked those men he had killed, but if he'd done nothing then his position as their leader would have been weakened. The world they lived in now required direct action, deliberate and confident behavior, as well as the willingness to get your hands dirty. Respect and fear were closely linked, and for many they meant the same thing. The Villista movement was still strong but could not grow stronger if the men didn't have structure and discipline. If he was going to create a new Mexican Empire, he had to know that his words would never be disobeyed again, for he believed that he was the only one who had the clear vision needed to accomplish this.

He spat out a few pieces of loose tobacco before he finally answered the guard. "Have each head transported back to the man's division headquarters. Have it displayed on a spike for all to see. Do not remove it, ever. I want it there as a reminder of what happens to those who don't listen."

40 miles east of Barstow, California

Samantha couldn't stop talking. Even though the rest of their search that day hadn't given them another clue, she felt strangely comforted that the body wasn't Gordon's or Hunter's. The whole ride back to camp she talked about how she believed they'd find them.

Nelson now was the silent one. She had insisted on driving the rest of the day, so on their way back he just stared out the window. He thought about Gordon and Hunter. He didn't know what to think in some ways, whether they were alive or not. Oddly, he began to think about the hundreds of thousands of people who were now just wanderers. They saw them on their drive through Palm Desert. People by the thousands had taken to the roads and were heading west. He could only imagine they thought the coast would be safer than the desert. Maybe they were right; come summer the desert heat would start to leave its deadly impression on those survivors. Electricity had enabled mankind to populate the desert by the millions. It brought not only light but precious water and air-conditioning. Without power the desert cities would all eventually be abandoned. He wondered what the people in the large desert cities, those in Phoenix or Las Vegas, were doing. Images of herds of people migrating to the coast or mountains came to mind.

It all seemed unreal. The pace with which it all had collapsed was what shocked him. Once people became aware that the government was ineffective or nonexistent, panic set in; then fear rippled through a population totally unprepared to actually survive. He was a capable man, but he knew having a solid team that included Gordon would help ensure his longevity in this world.

"Hey, are you listening to me?" Samantha lightly tapped his arm.

"Ugh, sorry. I was in deep thought," he answered.

"I asked about which one of us is going to tell Beth about . . . ," she said, motioning with her thumb to the bed of the truck.

"Oh, aah, maybe you should. Maybe having a woman console her would be the best idea."

"I was thinking you should, and if she needed a shoulder to cry on, then I can help."

"Sure, that's fine. Poor guy. I liked him. I didn't get a chance to really know him, but he seemed like a solid guy. It's his kid I'm most worried about. Hell, it's all of the kids I'm worried about. All this death. What kinda world have we given them?" Nelson was just rambling now.

Samantha didn't answer. Nelson talking about children touched a nerve with her. Her own children now consumed her thoughts.

Nelson went back to staring out the window; he didn't want to talk anyway. He couldn't wait to get back to camp and just be by himself. A weird sense of doom had come over him. He wasn't one for getting depressed, but how could one not have moments of dread living in the world he was now calling reality?

When the camp came into view, something seemed out of place. Parked outside the circle was an old AMC Gremlin that had a small, uncovered U-Haul trailer attached to it. Nelson was a lover of old cars, but that one was a classic clunker and he couldn't believe somebody had found one that still ran.

"Ugh," he muttered.

"Yeah, I see them," Samantha said. Her foot began to lessen its pressure on the accelerator.

Nelson checked his handgun and had it at the ready.

The truck slowly rolled to a stop thirty feet away from their camp. Both of them stared intently to see if everything was okay.

Samantha could see the kids playing; seeing Haley chasing after a ball put her at ease.

Nelson saw his father walking around with a rifle slung over his shoulder.

No one seemed to notice them.

"What do you think?" Samantha asked.

"Everything seems fine, let's head in."

They slowly approached and pulled the truck into the center of the circle of cars and trailers.

Haley ran to the truck and cried out with joy, "Mommy, Mommy, yay, you're back!"

The sight of Haley happy almost brought tears to Samantha's eyes. She quickly got out of the truck and hugged her.

Haley gripped her tightly, then whispered, "Did you find Daddy and Hunter?"

Samantha hated to say it, but she had to. "No, honey, Mommy didn't find Daddy or Hunter. But we will, I promise."

"I miss Daddy," Haley whimpered.

"I know you do, honey," Samantha said, tears welling up, but she fought them off. She knew the real difficult task was coming.

Nelson was greeted by his father, who said, "How did it go, Son?"

"Good or bad, depends on how you look at it. What's the deal with the Gremlin?" Nelson asked, motioning to the car parked outside their camp. He was searching but couldn't find anyone new.

"Good or bad, depends on how you look at it," his father quipped.

"What . . . ?" Nelson began to ask. Then he spotted Beth Holloway coming toward them with her daughter in her arms. "Excuse me, Dad," he said as he intercepted Beth before she reached the truck.

"Hi. Any clues today?" Beth asked. She looked flustered.

Nelson couldn't imagine the pain she must be going through not knowing. He only hoped having closure would be a consolation. "Beth, can we go back to your trailer?" he asked.

"Why?" she responded, looking over his shoulder toward the truck.

A few others had gathered near the truck like they did every night upon their return, but this time they were all remarking on something in the bed of the vehicle.

"Can we please not do this here?" he pleaded.

"Do what, Nelson? What are we getting ready to do?" Beth said, her voice starting to crack. She tried to step around him, but each time he blocked her.

Nelson grew weary of the back-and-forth and reached out and held her still. He looked into her eyes and was about to tell her when she just fell to her knees.

Gasps could be heard from their small group as all were now focused on them.

Samantha put Haley down and ran over to Beth. She took her daughter, Presley, who was three years old, a sweet and gentle little girl who had long, straight black hair. "Sweetie, go play with Haley," Samantha told her.

Nelson couldn't bear what he was seeing. Reassured that Samantha was taking control, he walked back to his father.

Samantha carefully helped Beth up, and both of them walked

back to her trailer so she could tell her friend in private what they had found.

Nelson couldn't shake the feeling he was having, but before he could rest he still had to remove and bury Holloway's body. He also wanted the story on the Gremlin.

That story revealed itself when two strangers appeared from behind one of the trailers. One was a man, middle-aged, with long hair and a beard, the other a woman, average height with short, dark hair. He squinted hard because the woman looked familiar. He rubbed his eyes and looked again, thinking that somehow his vision was playing tricks on him.

"Seneca?" Nelson asked.

The woman walked up and hugged him. "Oh my God. It is so good to see you. When we came up to your group we didn't know what to think, but we took a chance. We were running on fumes and had maybe a day's worth of food."

Nelson was in complete shock at who was hugging him. He glanced toward his father, who shared his sense of humor.

His father winked and shot him a shit-eating grin.

"Well, aren't you going to say anything?" the woman asked.

"I can't believe you're here, sorry. It's been a long day. Seeing you wasn't something I thought would happen."

"Nelson, this is Mack. He's a friend of mine. We got the hell outta town right away. We have been hiding out in Palm Springs. We kinda took over a house there, but that didn't last long. The owners showed up, and needless to say, they weren't too happy we were there."

"Mack, nice to meet you." Nelson shook the other man's hand. The thick calluses were a clue of a man who had lived a hard life before the attacks.

"Mack, this is Nelson, my former fiancé."

Unknown military installation

Derek had been a wealth of information on Rahab and the base where they were being held. The entire day, Gordon had been committing to memory the guards' rotations. He also was examining, as best he could, every building entrance, sidewalk, window, road, anything that could help to identify a way to get Hunter and safely escape. He looked at patterns of movements Rahab's other people, especially his council, made.

Today's working party was the same as yesterday's, filling and stacking sandbags at the entrance. This afforded Gordon the time to examine the perimeter as well. He studied everything he saw. He knew time was not on his side, and as soon as he could find a weak spot and exploit it, he would. While he was digging up sand for the bags, he spotted Rahab walking with two of his followers from the main building, where Hunter was being housed. Gordon wanted to talk to him again. He had a request that he hoped Rahab would grant him.

"Brother Rahab! Brother Rahab!" Gordon yelled out.

The guard watching over the working party instructed him to shut up.

But Gordon persisted. "Brother Rahab! Please, this is Gordon. May I have a word with you?"

Rahab looked over at Gordon and stopped. He addressed the two people he was with, and soon they moved on. "Brother Jonathon, please bring Brother Gordon here," Rahab ordered.

Jonathon obeyed without question and took Gordon to him.

"Brother Rahab, thank you."

"Yes. How can I help you?"

"When you brought me here, you stripped me of all my personal possessions. I was hoping I could have them back."

Rahab looked at Jonathon, who nodded.

"May I ask what it is you want specifically?"

"My watch, my wedding band, and I had a letter that I keep with me at all times."

"A letter?"

"It's a good-bye letter for my wife. With all the uncertainty, I thought I should have something that expresses to my wife how I feel. You know, in case something happens to me."

"I don't see why that should be a problem. Jonathon, make sure Gordon gets his things tonight after dinner. Now, is that all?"

"No. When can I see my son?"

"We can arrange a supervised visit sometime this week. I'll let one of the guards know when."

Gordon noticed a long-bladed sheath knife on Rahab's hip. He had not seen it before. This, he thought, must be the infamous knife that had killed Derek's friend.

"Thank you, Brother Rahab," Gordon said. He hated the way he had to express himself with this madman. He longed to reach out, strangle him, then plunge that knife into his chest.

The double doors to the main building opened, and all the children came out in a single-file line. They were "marching" in lockstep toward the runway. Gordon's attention had been so focused on the children that he didn't notice Rahab had walked off.

Jonathon reached out and pushed him back toward the working party.

The shove pissed Gordon off. He snarled at Jonathon but returned to work.

• • •

Gordon hadn't been back at the sandbag wall for ten minutes when another guard approached and informed Jonathon that they all had to proceed to the cleansing cross.

Everyone in the working party looked at each other. All had expressions of fear; they weren't sure who was about to be put to death.

Similarly to the children, the working party was marched over to the runway.

Gordon couldn't stop looking at Hunter, who stood with the children on the opposite side of the cross. His son now looked so frail. He wondered how he was doing. It took every ounce of strength Gordon had not to run over and grab him. The guard who looked over the children had features similar to those of Rahab. In fact, his hair and facial structure made him look almost like a younger Rahab. Then the lightbulb went off in Gordon's mind: This must be Rahab's son. Whoever it was, Gordon didn't like how he touched the children. With some he was rough, but others, including Hunter, he rubbed. The next thought that crossed Gordon's mind made him see red: *That son of a bitch better not be touching my boy.*

Gordon's dark thoughts were interrupted when the drum began. About ten feet in front of the cross, one of Rahab's followers banged a slow, rhythmic beat on a bongo-type drum.

Up the long tarmac from the direction of the buildings came a small procession. The leader of the group held a large book; Gordon assumed it was a Bible. The second person was a woman. Her thin hands were bound by a bloodstained rope. Bruises covered her face, arms, and legs. Behind her came Rahab, adorned in a brown cloak. To Gordon he looked like a monk from the Middle Ages.

Gordon wondered what that poor woman had done to deserve this. Did she say no to one of her rapists? Did she fight back? Did she attempt to escape? Whatever the "crime," her punishment was to be extreme and unjust.

She seemed at peace with what was about to transpire. She didn't resist when they tied each arm and each leg to a corner of the large X. As Rahab read out her "crime," which was "refusing to comply with the will of the Children of God," Gordon just burned with hatred for him.

Gordon's position in the crowd allowed him to see her face. She was young, midtwenties, with shoulder-length brown hair. Her face showed the abuse she had received from Rahab's men. Stains from tears covered her bruised and swollen cheeks. But it was her eyes that were telling. They begged for it all to end. She kept her gaze toward the sky and didn't say a word.

Rahab finished his sermon and pulled out his long knife. He held it up in the air as if he was offering it to God. Taking the knife in his right hand, he brought his arm back slowly.

The woman closed her eyes as tears flowed from them.

Rahab lunged forward and drove the knife deep into the center of her chest.

The young woman gasped loudly, and within seconds her head fell forward.

No one in the crowd said a word. There was not even a gasp or whimper for this poor woman. All of them lived in fear that they'd be next.

Gordon looked over at Hunter, who blankly stared at the woman.

Rahab withdrew the knife, cleaned the blade, and sheathed it. When he finished, he spoke loudly. "Praise be to God, the cleanser of this impure world. We worship and give thanks to you. For in you is the true heaven. Please take this poor soul back. We have released her from her earthly pain. Praise be to you, God."

Gordon stared at the knife on Rahab's belt. He determined then that one major part of his escape plan had to be killing this maniac.

Coos Bay, Oregon

"Sir, the chopper is ready to take you to Salem," a young Marine told Barone.

Barone had changed his mind and was going to meet the governor of Oregon today. His forward recon teams had reported that the governor was still alive. Raymond Pelsom had been a U.S. senator for several terms before winning the governorship two years before.

Holstering his pistol, Barone grabbed his jacket and headed out the door to the flight deck. He was still on the ship with his family. Even though the port was safe for him, it lacked the amenities the ship had. His crews were working nonstop alongside civilian crews to get the port's main equipment online. The heavy crane would be a big help in off-loading the two MPS ships. The crowds from town were getting larger by the hour. They peered through the makeshift fence line the Marines had set up. Barone's plan to work closely with the local leadership had been paying off.

Of course they had many questions about why Barone and his men were there and what the government was doing to help bring back the power. Unfortunately for them, Barone didn't have many answers, and some of those he did have were flat-out lies. He explained to them that Washington, D.C., had been destroyed and that most of the federal government had been decimated. He neglected to mention that he had taken the ships and that he wasn't there on official orders. Barone immediately ordered stockpiles of food to be distributed, but he knew he couldn't feed the local population of more than twenty thousand for long.

The cities of North Bend and Coos Bay had not experienced much violence. Yes, they'd had their problems with looters, and some of the people had mobbed the town hall asking for answers, but overall the troubles here were minimal compared to those of the larger cities. They had expanded their police force so they could close off the highways that led into town. This was done because after two weeks, roving gangs had attacked dozens of homes in search of food and resources. The local leadership had also imposed new laws right away, the first of which was a zero-tolerance law against looting. Anyone caught looting or robbing others was arrested and taken out of the town. They were never allowed to return. All violence was dealt with severely. When the local government said "zero tolerance," they meant it.

Barone was proud in many ways of how these Americans had pulled together. Again, nothing was perfect, but they were surviving. He thought how in some towns people must have come together, but in others they must have turned against each other. What was transpiring across the country wasn't uniform. Reactions to the attack were all different. Barone had assumed that he'd pull into Coos Bay and see total chaos, but it wasn't that way. He imagined the smaller the towns, the more manageable they were. Things had reversed; the large federal government had become ineffective while the small local governments could actually help the recovery in their specific areas.

The cool breeze and the smell of the salty sea air was refreshing. The hum and chop of the rotors from the CH-53 always made Barone feel like he was about to go on an adventure. Before he stepped onto the chopper, he looked out at the town and the houses in the distance. If he didn't know, he'd think that nothing had happened. The roofs of all the houses were unscathed. Smoke from dozens of chimneys drifted into the air. He saw children riding bikes and playing in the streets. These people had welcomed him and his Marines, but would that warm welcome remain if and when they found out what had happened? Barone intended to make sure it did by being the best guest he could be. Not wanting to delay his surprise visit to Governor Pelsom, he stepped onto the chopper.

Salem, Oregon

The flags that encircled the oval lawn outside the capital building flapped wildly as the chopper came in for a landing. His team on the ground was there to meet him, as were some representatives from the governor's office.

When the ramp lowered, Barone didn't see the governor. He stepped out, and two aides for the governor approached him and put their hands out.

"Welcome, General," a middle-aged man said. He was wearing dark jeans and a brown pullover.

The other aide was a woman; she was in her early fifties and attractive. She was short and had her dark brown hair pulled back into a ponytail. The ponytail was fast becoming the hairstyle for women in this post-attack world.

"General, we weren't expecting you for a couple of weeks," she said.

"Who are you?" Barone asked both of them.

"I'm Jeanne, and this is my colleague Jason. We work for the governor."

"Where is the governor?"

"Sorry, he couldn't make it; he's meeting with the city council and legislature about how we can facilitate you off-loading the supplies your ships have," Jeanne said.

"Supplies, yes, supplies," Barone said, playing along. He looked over her shoulder at one of his MARSOC Marines, who nodded, signifying approval of Barone playing along.

"I'd like to see the governor as soon as I can," Barone said.

"Yes, sir," she answered.

"Before I go, I want to talk with these Marines here," Barone said. He stepped away from the aides and over to the two Marines who were part of the recon advance team.

"So, what do you know?" he asked them.

"Sir, we made liaison like you commanded. The governor welcomed us and was excited. He mentioned that we were weeks early. We didn't want to contradict him, so we went with the story. You made it clear not to mention who we were."

"Okay, so there must be another Marine unit en route. This is good intel, very good intel. Good job, Marines," Barone said, patting them both on the shoulder. "Now, things are going to go down a bit differently than I thought. I assumed he would have met me out here. Looks like we will have to do this inside. Where is the rest of your team?"

"Two more are near the front of the capital, and the other two are on the eastern lawn."

"Have them all meet us . . . Wait one minute." Barone stopped to ask Jeanne a question. "Excuse me, where are we accessing the building?"

Not thinking at all about the question, she quickly answered, "The west entrance will take us to the governor's office; from there we will have an operational meeting with the legislative leaders and the mayor."

"Great, thank you," Barone responded, then turned his attention back to his men. "You heard her; have them meet us there. Radio the strike teams back in Coos that we are a go."

"Roger that, sir."

"Good man; now let's go see the governor."

San Diego, California

Sebastian tried his best to help with the cleanup, but his leg was hurting badly and during the ruckus he had torn open his stitches.

Annaliese attended to his leg while he sat on the front porch steps.

"Ouch!" he yelped after she poured some antiseptic on the reopened wound.

"Oh, you'll live. I thought you were a tough Marine," she quipped.

"I think we need to get out of here, I don't know how many of these mobs we can handle," he said, looking at everyone working around him. The bodies were far more numerous than he had thought. He had never really seen how many were at the gate, but from the looks of the carnage inside the compound, there must have been almost forty people. "Where did they come from? Who were they?"

"I don't know most of them. I did recognize the woman I shot.

She lives a few houses down on a small plot. I would guess that these were our neighbors," she answered, looking up only briefly to gaze at the bodies.

"How's your father?" Sebastian asked.

The question made her pause.

"Hey, you okay?" he asked. Looking down, he saw she was weeping. "Hey, hey, it's going to be all right. Your father seems like a tough guy." Sebastian touched her shoulder, causing her to weep more.

"Sorry, I just have never seen or been through anything like that before," she said softly as she reached up and grabbed his hand.

"There's no reason to apologize. I've seen my fair share, but not like what happened today. I've never had to shoot, uh, people. My entire time in the Corps it was easy for me to kill the enemy. I know what we did was right today because if we don't stand up for ourselves we'll die, but it's just so strange to shoot regular people. I know it all sounds weird, but I don't know if I can get used to it."

"I don't know what came over me. When they came into the house I was trying to hide the kids. They burst in and . . . My dad tried to stop them, but they just, like, ran over him. When one of them hit him in the head with the vase, I lost it. I just lost it. I had the shotgun and started shooting them. That's all I remember. My dad fell and I started shooting them."

Sebastian gripped her hand tighter and reached over with his other hand to touch her face.

She didn't resist his affection but responded by gently rubbing her cheek against his palm and looking up at him.

The front door bursting open cut off their brief intimate encounter.

"Annaliese, hurry, it's Dad!" Zach, her little brother, yelled.

"I'm coming! What is it?"

"I don't know, but he's having a convulsion or something. Hurry, please!"

Unknown military installation

"I know I asked before, but every night they go over to the women's barracks?" Gordon asked after noticing the guard was not around to oversee the latrine working party.

"Every night, like clockwork," Derek answered as he pulled the first barrel out.

"For us, that's good. I think we have our window then," Gordon noted, grabbing the handle on his side of the barrel.

"What I'm thinking is we have the women help us out on the inside to stop the guards," Derek mentioned.

"How do we do that? We don't have access to them."

"Let me figure that one out."

The two men talked quietly as they made their way to the ditch. The setting sun cast their shadows long against the black tarmac. When they walked past the crosses, Gordon spoke up.

"We need to kill that son of a bitch."

"I agree. If ever a man deserved to die, it's him. But trying to kill him could really jeopardize our escape," said Derek.

"Let me worry about him," Gordon said defiantly.

"Don't be a fool!" Derek scolded. He stopped walking, causing the contents of the barrel to slosh and splatter onto Gordon's pants.

"What the fuck?" Gordon snapped.

"Don't be an idiot. Rahab has men around him all the time.

Just getting into the building will be one thing; getting upstairs where he sleeps only adds to the complications. We risk the entire thing by doing that. We get your son and go, simple."

Gordon just stared at him; he liked to be in control and liked to be right. But he resisted saying anything. However, anger filled him; he was tired of taking orders from people. He just stared at Derek, his LED headlamp illuminating the deep wrinkles on his companion's brow.

An odd silence settled between them. Neither said anything. The cool desert breeze ruffled their hair. It felt good against Gordon's throbbing temples.

After what seemed like minutes, Derek broke the silence. "Are we good? I can see a troubling look in your eyes."

"Yeah, we're good. Let's finish this shitty job and call it a night," Gordon answered stoically.

Derek attempted more conversation as they delivered one barrel after another to the pit. But Gordon just gave him one-word answers.

After they dumped the last barrel, Derek grabbed Gordon by the arm. "Hey, are we good?"

"Yeah, we're fine."

"You don't seem good."

"Listen, Derek. I know you've spent a lot of time in politics and you think you run things, but in my group, I'm the leader. When we get out of here, you will have to follow my orders. I don't run a democracy; I just want that to be clear."

Derek was surprised by Gordon's response. Not wanting to get into another heated exchange, he just said, "Crystal."

"I'm tired and want to go to bed. We can discuss more of our plan tomorrow, but it needs to happen soon."

"Soon is great, but we should make sure we can do it."

"It needs to happen *soon*; my wife and daughter are out there. I know they're looking for us, and if they come here, you know what will happen. I can't risk that. We need to get down to brass tacks tomorrow night and start working on putting this into operation soon."

"I haven't even found a woman yet; that will take time," Derek countered urgently.

"Like I said, let's talk more tomorrow. I need to sleep on this," Gordon said, then reached down for his end of the barrel.

Their timing for ending the conversation was perfect as a large light burst across them.

"You two, hurry up!" their guard yelled from about thirty feet away.

"You think he heard anything?" Derek asked quietly.

"I don't think so, but if he did, we're leaving tonight. Let me take the lead here. Grab your end; let's go."

Derek's stomach tightened as they drew closer to the guard, who hadn't let them out of his flashlight's beam since he first called to them.

When they walked by him the guard asked, "What were you two arguing about?"

"Oh, that. This asshole spilled some shit on me," Gordon answered quickly.

The guard didn't answer, nor could they see his face.

"Can I take a shower?" Gordon asked.

"No. But you can leave your clothes outside and one of the women will wash them tomorrow."

"Okay, I'll do that."

The guard walked behind them the entire way back. He had

returned early from his nightly excursion in the women's barracks.

After they put the last barrel away, both Gordon and Derek were heading back to their barracks. The guard stopped Gordon.

"One second."

"Me too?" Derek asked.

"No, you go on ahead."

Derek walked on into the darkness. Gordon's body was racked with anticipation of a fight. He clenched his fists, ready to strike.

"Here. Brother Rahab said to give this to you." The guard handed him a gallon-size zip-lock bag with Gordon's personal effects.

Seeing the bag dangle in the bluish light of his LED headlamp eased Gordon's tension.

He grabbed the bag and said, "Thanks."

• • •

Gordon emptied the bag's two items on his rack. The one thing he most wanted was there: a letter he had written for Samantha. If something happened to him here, she'd never read it. Carrying a farewell letter was something he'd adopted as a Marine. It was important for him to control the last thoughts and words that his loved ones would read from him. The letters he'd carried with him in Iraq twice were written to Sebastian. Before they had left for Idaho almost ten days ago, he had written the letter he now had back. He hadn't anticipated this type of problem. In fact, what he and Hunter were going through had never crossed his mind as a possibility. Eight weeks before, he and Samantha had been planning their trip to Idaho under different circumstances. If someone had told him then that he and Hunter would be prisoners of a religious zealot, he would have laughed at them.

Rahab had also given Gordon his wedding band. He'd thought that would have been gone for good. Strange, he thought, that it was still there. Gordon rubbed the smooth sides of his platinum ring. Still wearing his headlamp, he could see the thousands of tiny scratches etched across the circumference. Each scratch represented a time and a place. Many of those came from times with his wife and his kids. He missed them so much. He was so worried about them. Rahab had threatened to go after them, but in some ways Gordon felt Rahab didn't want the fight.

Gordon couldn't figure out Rahab's long-term plan. Why had he chosen to set up on a military base? One good reason was it had supplies and resources, but didn't they risk an attack from the main base close by? Was Fort Irwin still manned with a fighting force? Gordon assumed it was; he had seen sentries walking the perimeter. Maybe they were just hunkering down. This small base wasn't an asset worth losing men or precious ammo over.

Gordon's mind raced through so many things: his family, escaping, the rest of the drive to Idaho. He didn't often think about the status of the government. After spending so many years in the Marines, he knew that the government's main priority would be to take care of itself until a plan could be formulated. His two tours in Iraq had shown him how great and how awful the government and military could be. The military and certain government personnel cared deeply about doing what was right, but the "machine" was a behemoth so large that the left hand didn't know what the right hand was doing. So much waste and incompetence. With the chaos of the attack and the absence of any authority for weeks afterward, he assumed the attack had left the government paralyzed. Once people knew no one was coming to help, the wheels had come off.

His thoughts were disturbed by the loud snore of the man in the bunk next to his. Not wanting to listen to it, Gordon took his pillow and hit him. He awoke briefly, shifted to his side, and fell back to sleep sans the snore.

Samantha would have to do that to him sometimes, especially after a few drinks. He wondered again where his family was. He prayed that Samantha and Haley were safe. Regret filled his mind. He cursed himself for going on the recon mission with Holloway. If he hadn't gone, he and Hunter would be with them and they'd be closer to Idaho and some sort of safety.

Gordon thought about all the decisions he'd made after the lights went out. Some he thought were sound, others he now questioned. Running around half-cocked, as others said, was something he had always done. He wasn't one to sit and ponder. If something was happening, he quickly assessed the situation and acted with what came first. In retrospect, he thought he should have just left for Idaho. He should have just found a camper and headed north with Jimmy. He couldn't remember why he had stayed. Now it all seemed like a stupid plan. Jimmy would have done what he told him to, and if he had decided to go north, Jimmy, Simone, and Mason would still be alive.

The regret kept coursing through his mind. Gordon hated regret, but he knew his impulsive and risky plans had gotten him and Hunter captured. The earlier conversation with Derek now came to the forefront of his mind. Even though it pained him to admit it, Derek was right. Trying to kill Rahab was stupid; he should just get Hunter and go.

Feeling the fatigue creep up, Gordon turned off his light and tucked his letter under his pillow. He placed the ring back on his finger and rubbed it.

He began to run through each detail of his escape plan. He envisioned entering the main building to get Hunter. Everything ran smoothly except when he saw Rahab in his mind's eye. He again reminded himself that Derek was right, he must stick to the plan. However, in Gordon's dream plan, Rahab would make himself an easy target. With defiance Gordon convinced himself that only if Rahab made it easy would he take the chance to kill him.

40 miles east of Barstow, California

"It's just so strange to see you here. I mean, what are the odds?" Nelson said to Seneca. He, Seneca, Mack, and Eric were sitting around a small fire.

"I know. I didn't think I'd see anyone I knew again," she replied. She sat across from Nelson. The glow of the flames illuminated her olive-toned skin.

Nelson couldn't get over how much her look had changed. When they were engaged, years before, she'd worn her hair shoulder-length and blond. Now it was cut short and dyed black.

After they had split up, she had explored one of her passions: motorcycles. Within six months of their breakup she had bought a classic Harley-Davidson, cut her hair, and worn the clothes of a biker whenever she could.

"So how did you end up here?" he asked, motioning with his arm to their camp.

"After we were run off from the house, we thought we should find another place to go. Mack has a cousin in Antelope, so we were heading that way when we pulled over to go to the bathroom. Mack said he saw something reflecting out here. We have been scavenging since everything happened, and we thought maybe there was something here. You know, some houses where we could find food, a safe place to sleep."

"You guys don't have any food?" Eric asked.

"We did, but we had to leave in a hurry," Mack answered.

Eric looked at Nelson.

"To continue, we were driving down the dirt road a few hundred feet away when we saw your little camp. We thought we'd come over and see if we could barter for food," she said.

"Which way did you go to get here?" Nelson asked.

"Through Barstow," Mack answered. He was burly man, with short-cropped, graying hair. His skin was tan and leathery from a lifetime of being outside. His red nose, covered in small burst blood vessels, showed signs of countless years of drinking.

"We tried to go through there, but we were attacked a few days ago. We lost a family and a car," Eric said as he poked the fire with a large stick.

"Really? We saw a burned-out car along the highway. Was that you?" Mack asked.

"Sure was," said Eric somberly.

Nelson asked the question that all had been thinking about. "What's your plan going from here?"

Seneca looked at Mack, then answered, "Well, we were hoping we could stay with you."

"Um," Nelson muttered.

"I don't know if that's possible," Eric said.

"Why?" Mack asked.

"To be honest, Mack, we don't know you, and our rule is to

only take in people who have something to contribute," said Eric. He was following Gordon's selective recruitment plan.

Nelson didn't say a word. He let Eric take control of the conversation.

"Can we do an exchange?" Seneca offered.

"I don't see why not," Nelson quickly interjected. He couldn't keep his eyes off her. He hadn't really stopped loving her. Their breakup had not been a mutual decision; she had been the one to initiate the separation. Even though he never forgave her for that, he still loved her.

Mack took notice of Nelson's intent staring and drew closer to her.

"Hey, Nelson. We can't just change things. What would Gordon do?" Eric said.

"I heard he's been missing. I'm so sorry," Seneca added. Upon her and Mack's arrival, Nelson's father and mother had told her everything about the group, including that Gordon and Hunter had gone missing.

"We'll find him, and I think Eric is right. I don't know if we can spare food," Nelson said.

"So who's in charge here, you or the Chink?" spewed Mack.

"What did you call me?" Eric asked.

"Mack, calm down," Seneca begged. She held his arm tight.

"I thought you were in charge, but it seems like this slant-eye is the one giving the orders."

"Really? Seriously, man, this is how you thank us for feeding you tonight and giving you shelter?" Eric said, almost shouting.

"Get off of me," Mack snapped at Seneca before he laid into Nelson. "So who's in charge here? We have things to trade. We need food, and I think you'll like what we have."

"After those bullshit comments, you're not getting anything!" Eric said loudly.

Nelson had to redirect this conversation. He still couldn't stop looking at Seneca. The fire crackled and the flames kept highlighting her face, with its high cheekbones and blue eyes.

"So the Chink is in charge and you sit there eye-fucking my girl!" Mack said, his voice now even louder.

"Please, Mack, don't do this," Seneca pleaded.

"Fuck them. If they don't want to help us then they can go fuck themselves," Mack screamed.

"Calm down, buddy. I'm willing to see what you have," Nelson interjected.

"Nelson, we don't have food to spare. We will need it all for the trip and the winter in Idaho," Eric snapped.

"We have guns, lots of them. We stumbled upon a vacant police station in Palm Springs," Seneca said calmly and directly to Nelson and Eric.

"Fuck them!" Mack exclaimed again.

"Listen. We have kids here. We don't need you yelling and screaming," Eric scolded.

"Fuck you, you fucking Chink," Mack yelled. This time he stood up and pointed at Eric.

Eric, not intimidated by Mack, stood too. Both started yelling at each other over the fire.

Nelson knew he needed to stop this before it went too far. "Shut up! Everybody, just shut up!" he yelled.

Neither man listened. Seneca was also standing now, with her arms crossed. Her attempts at calming Mack down were being ignored.

Then Mack pulled a knife and threatened to cut Eric.

Nelson had reached for his handgun when out of the darkness the barrel of a shotgun was placed against Mack's head. "Put the knife down. Drop it now!" Samantha commanded.

The cold steel of the muzzle against his head said it all. Mack held his arms up and dropped the knife.

"Now both of you. You too, Seneca. Go sit down over there." Samantha pointed to a rock a couple feet away from Mack's dropped knife. Both Mack and Seneca sat down.

"Sam, I'm sorry. I really am," Seneca said.

"We have enough to worry about. We don't need this type of behavior here. Every day we fight for our lives. If we have enough food, we will make a deal for your guns. And if you wish to join us, then we will take a vote on that. But no more of this. You hear me? No more racist name-calling or fighting or you're both out."

Samantha had lowered the shotgun, but she still stood at the ready in case Mack had a change of heart.

Nelson had never seen Samantha this way before. He was impressed. She was now fully adapting to the new world.

Eric stood poised to attack Mack. His hand rested on the hilt of his knife.

"Whatever you say, Sam, we'll do," Seneca answered with a consolatory tone.

Mack had his arms folded and didn't answer.

"Mack, what about you?" Samantha asked him.

He kept looking at the fire and not at her.

"Answer her, Mack," Seneca chided him.

"Yes, okay," he said regretfully to Samantha.

"Good, now let's take a look at the guns you have."

JANUARY 14, 2014

. . .

You can never plan the future by the past.

—Edmund Burke

Salem, Oregon

The Pioneer statue atop the Oregon Capitol looked out upon the city of Salem. It represented the pioneering spirit that had created the great state. For Barone it signified a time that was long gone, until now. He and his men were the new pioneers. Like he had told his men several times, their days of being subjects to the political class were over.

A smile cracked his rugged and typically stoic face. He liked the new world they were living in. There was opportunity if one seized it, and that was exactly what he was doing.

Smoke billowed out of the many windows and doors of the building. The dark soot stained the white sandstone walls of the impressive three-hundred-plus-foot structure. Barone stood outside watching his men gather up what legislature there was left. Those who resisted were shot; those who obeyed were sequestered in the upper chamber. He would interrogate them one by one to find where everything of value was.

His original plan in coming to Salem had been to pay a visit to an old adversary and see if the city would be a good place to establish his government. But upon landing and hearing that more Marines were coming, he knew his days there were numbered. "Adapt and overcome" was one of Barone's mantras, and whenever situations occurred, one needed to adapt or die. He had always adapted, so without much thought he changed his plan regardless of how it would go down. When his Marines landed and instructions were given, local law enforcement and the few Oregon National Guard troops could do little against his superior numbers and firepower.

Changed was his plan to take the city. Flying over Salem, Barone saw it was too large for him to provide adequate support for the population. He would lose too many precious resources in an attempt to satiate the local civilians. His plan shifted to sacking and plundering what he could from the government stores.

With the Capitol secure, he could now have the conversation he had been wanting to have with the governor.

Barone thought the appropriate place to have this "meeting" was the governor's ceremonial office. The colonel would forever cherish the look on Pelsom's face when he saw it was him there.

Barone settled into the large leather chair behind the oak desk. He kicked his feet up and relaxed while he waited for his men to bring the governor in.

The large, solid alder door creaked as it opened to show the man who had at one time pledged to end Barone's career.

When Pelsom had been a U.S. senator, he had maneuvered himself to chair several powerful committees, one of them being the Armed Services Committee. This was where Barone had met Pelsom. He was a thin man who didn't stand taller than five feet five inches, and had thick, curly brown hair. His high-pitched, nasal voice was consistent with his small frame.

Barone remembered the day, almost ten years ago, when he first saw Pelsom. It had been a beautiful spring day in Washington. Cherry blossoms adorned the trees along his walk toward the Dirksen Senate Office Building. The pundits were already saying that Barone would be the fall guy for what had happened in Iraq. Pelsom had personally declared that Barone should take full responsibility for what his Marines had done. Barone knew how to cope with stress, but what he called a political witch hunt forever seared in him a hatred for the political class.

"Senator, oh, I'm sorry, Governor Pelsom. It's a pleasure to see you again. Sorry we couldn't catch up yesterday," Barone said sarcastically.

"When the president finds out what—"

"I've already spoken with the president. I talked to him weeks ago. Let's just say that we're no longer on speaking terms," Barone quipped. He took his feet off the desk and stood up. "Sit him right there," he ordered his Marines.

Pelsom looked smaller than he remembered.

"What do you want, Colonel?"

"That is a good question." Barone continued with his mocking.

"Let my staff go; don't hurt them."

"I don't plan on hurting anyone unless they fight back. I have given very loose rules of engagement to my Marines. Please share that with your people when you go back to your holding area."

"Just tell me what you want and then leave."

"Senator, you're being very accommodating. Thank you. I want to know the locations of every emergency storage facility in the city and around the state."

"You can't take all of our emergency stores; the people need them."

"My people need them too. We have the guns, and so we will take what we need," Barone said as he walked around the large office. On the walls hung beautifully framed awards and certificates. He stopped and looked at each one as he talked.

"Why are you doing this? Don't you love your country anymore? Why would you steal ships, attack U.S. military bases . . . kill Americans?"

"Because we have time, I will explain why, even though I don't think you deserve the answer. When the attacks happened, I was serving my country in Afghanistan. On my third tour in nine years, mind you. When word came down that our country had been attacked, like many I was shocked, then angered. We were then given orders to float to the East Coast and support a recovery effort around D.C. Can you believe that? A recovery effort. It's as if the leadership was treating the attack like a hurricane or some sort of natural disaster cleanup.

"I wasn't about to take orders that would result in more death, so I did what I thought best. I seized the ships and turned them around. What happened on Diego Garcia was out of my control; we had no intention of hurting anyone, but we will defend ourselves if we are attacked. I know this all doesn't mean a thing to you, because you have lived a life of privilege. You bring in millions a year because of your influence as a politician. Heck, you went into politics an accountant making thirty-six K a year, and now you're a multimillionaire, or I should say were. Did you earn that? No, you peddled influence and sold your vote to the highest bidder—"

"That is a lie!" Pelsom fired back.

"Hmm, a lie? I think not. I know you politicians. You like to say you're in 'public service.' Since when did public service include getting rich? You whore yourself out and sell your votes, then buy votes to get elected by giving away welfare and freebies. It's a vicious and corrupt system whose day has come and gone."

"I have faithfully and honestly—" Pelsom said quickly, before he was interrupted.

Barone marched across the room and grabbed him by the throat. "Shut the fuck up! What is it you'd say? 'You're out of order'?"

Barone towered over Pelsom like a father does a child. He squeezed his hand tighter around the smaller man's neck until Pelsom began to squirm and yelp with pain.

"Raymond, you're going to tell me where every single warehouse and storage facility is located or I will slowly torture you and all of your people."

Pelsom, gripped with fear, started to nod.

"Good, I'm glad we agree on something," Barone said, then let him go.

Coughing and hacking, Pelsom bent over to let the blood flow back into his head. He felt dizzy and foggy. Barone's grip had almost caused him to black out.

Stepping away from Pelsom, Barone began to search the desk drawers for a pad of paper and pen.

"There's nothing in this desk," he said, frustrated.

"This is my ceremonial office; nothing is kept in here," Pelsom answered, still rubbing his neck.

"Lance Corporal, get in here!" Barone hollered.

The heavy door opened and a young Marine came into the room.

"Go get me a pad of paper and a pen. Make it fast!" Barone barked.

The Marine turned and left the room.

"Colonel, I don't know how you think you'll get away with this. There's a Marine detachment coming soon."

"Tell me about this other Marine unit," Barone queried.

"Whatever you have planned won't work. Every active military unit is heading this way."

"Tell me, why would they be coming here?" Barone was truly interested in what was happening. Since hearing about another Marine unit on its way, he had ordered Captain White to take the sub out as soon as they were able. If they were truly coming, he wanted to know more about them.

Pelsom, fearful for his life, told Barone about the president's plan to establish the new U.S. capital in Portland. He hoped the revelation would strike fear in the colonel and force him to abandon Salem.

Barone listened intently to everything that Pelsom had to say. Intelligence was always valuable to a mission; this time it was critical. The new capital's location concerned him. He also knew that Pelsom was probably overstating the president's resources. His immediate internal reaction was to get what he could and flee Coos Bay in search of a new place. Then Pelsom gave him the biggest gift.

"Colonel, like I said before. You should just go. Go before they come. Go before the president comes."

"Wait a minute. The president is coming here?"

"Yes, uh, no. He's coming to Portland."

"President Conner is going to Portland?" said Barone, his interest really piqued.

"Yes, he will be arriving within days. He's personally going to oversee the recovery and establishment of the new capital. Don't you see? You can't win, Colonel. Just leave us. If you leave I won't say anything to the president."

"Now that is the dumbest thing I've ever heard."

"I promise. Just leave us," Pelsom was begging.

"You know why it's dumb? Because we just attacked your capital. How do you plan on keeping everyone quiet?"

"Only two people ever talk to the president or his people. That's me and my lieutenant governor."

Barone stared at Pelsom, covered in sweat and groveling. Nothing was more pathetic than a groveling man. He thought of the lance corporal he had executed days before; now, that man had honor. Barone knew Pelsom was lying; the minute his men left he'd contact the president. Leverage was what he needed, and without his people there he didn't have it. But then an idea flashed across Barone's mind. It excited him so much that he stood again and walked to the door.

"Where the hell is that paper and pen?"

"Sorry, sir, coming now," said another Marine who was standing guard outside.

Barone closed the door and thought about what he should do with this new information.

A knock at the door disturbed his thoughts.

The lance corporal stepped in and handed the paper and pen to Barone.

Still full of excitement about his new idea, Barone hurried back to Pelsom.

"Here, write down every location of stockpiled food, water, and supplies."

The governor looked at Barone uneasily. His having been forthright with so much information didn't seem to have dissuaded his old foe. Not wanting to get strangled again, he began to write.

Barone took the time to pace and think. He knew that one day they'd encounter more U.S. forces. However, he and his men had come far, too far to turn tail and run. Maybe this was what they needed: a fight. And if he was going to have one, he'd better be ready for it.

40 miles east of Barstow, California

Haley enjoyed watching the ants climb all over the piece of bread she had tossed on the ground. What had started out as only a few had turned into dozens. Their tiny bodies were picking apart bits three times their size and carrying them away. She decided she'd create obstacles for them, so she put rocks in the path the ants were taking. Adjusting quickly, the ants made their way around each rock. She picked up a stick and carved out a groove in the dirt. Again, the ants figured out a detour and kept going. Growing impatient with her inability to stop the ants, Haley started hitting them with the stick. She then took the tip of the stick and jammed it into the centers of some of the ants, separating their bodies. She marveled at how each part still moved. Laughter erupted from her when she began to smash each ant. She now turned hitting the scrambling ants into a game.

"Haley, stop that," Samantha ordered after seeing what she was doing.

Samantha was having a hard time focusing on the map. She at first blamed it on Haley, but her lack of sleep probably also played a part. Beth Holloway's crying had kept many up last night.

"Mommy, are Daddy and Hunter not coming back?" Haley asked, leaning up against Samantha.

"Of course they are, they're just lost," Samantha quickly answered. She felt bad having to hide the truth.

"Joey said they aren't coming back," Haley said sadly.

"Joey said that to you?"

"Yes, he said Daddy is probably dead," Haley answered, now upset.

"What? When did he say that?" asked Samantha, her attention now focused on Haley. Holding her daughter tightly, she looked around for any member of the Thompson family. Seeing Joey's father, she called out, "Mike, you got a minute?"

"Ah, yeah, of course. What else do I have going on?"

Mike Thompson was very tall and very lean, almost six feet seven inches. His hair was black except for the gray coming in on the sides. He had a pleasant personality and was smart. It was hard to get to know him, because he didn't talk much. Many had complained that getting him to talk was like pulling teeth. Gordon had selected Mike and his family to come for two reasons. Mike was a structural engineer, and his family was big in the prepping community. The entire back courtyard of their house in Rancho Valentino had been a hydroponics system.

Haley held to Samantha's arm tightly as she walked over to talk with Mike.

"Good morning, Samantha. What can I help you with?" he asked.

"I'm troubled by something Joey said to Haley."

"What's that?"

"Apparently, Joey told Haley that Gordon and Hunter were probably dead. Where would he get that kind of notion?"

"Samantha, I'm sorry. He must have heard Sandy and me talking."

"So is that what you believe?" asked Samantha, hurt.

"Hey, listen, it's not what you think," Mike said, attempting to backpedal.

"We're going to stay here and keep looking for them. No matter how long it takes. My husband and son are out there; they aren't dead. I would appreciate it if you kept any other thoughts to yourself!" barked Samantha.

When Samantha's voice rose, Haley clung tighter to her leg.

"We didn't mean for him to repeat what we said to Haley. Sorry."

A voice in the distance bellowed something unintelligible, causing Samantha and Mike to look.

The zipper on Mike's tent opened, and out came his wife, Sandy. They were an odd couple proportionally; while he was very tall, she was very short. She stood at five feet four inches with a stocky frame. Her light brown hair was cut just long enough to pull back into a small ponytail. As she came toward them, Samantha could tell where this was going by the sour look on her face.

"No way, Samantha. You don't stand here and berate my husband for speaking the truth," said Sandy.

The tension among them caused Haley to whimper and cling even tighter to her mother's leg.

"How can you say that Gordon and Hunter are dead? If it were Mike and Joey, we'd be out there every day like we are now, looking, and we wouldn't give up!"

"I don't think so. I've gotten a chance to know Gordon, and I think he'd forget about us if he could."

"That's not true. He'd be out there looking, unlike your husband, who just sits around," Samantha said, pointing at Mike, who stood, hands in pockets, silent.

"Mike stays busy here keeping the cars working so when the day comes and you finally realize that Gordon is not coming back, we can move on!"

Fury began to rise in Samantha. "Sandy, you're unbelievable. Have you forgotten everything that Gordon did for everyone here? If you remember, he approached Mike about coming with us. He didn't have to do that!"

The women's yelling caught everyone's attention. All eyes were now on them.

"We would have been fine."

"How's that possible? You didn't have a car; Gordon let you take the second jeep after Fowler was killed! You know something, Sandy, this is bullshit. If you want to go, then go. I don't know where you'll go, but don't bother going to Idaho. We don't want you there!" Samantha screamed and walked off with Haley still clinging to her tightly.

"Mike, we don't need them," said Sandy loud enough for everyone to hear.

The heated exchange with Sandy and Mike started to sink in for Samantha. Coupled with the stress of Gordon and Hunter's disappearance, it made her feel like she was on the verge of a breakdown. She reached her trailer but couldn't steady her hand to open the door. She quickly sat in the chair next to the door and put Haley on her lap.

Haley too was feeling the bad energy from the argument. Sandy's accusations filled her young mind with images of her dad and brother dead, their eyes staring out of lifeless skulls.

Not wanting to let Samantha be, Sandy fired off another cutting barrage, which she finished by saying, "Everyone here but Nelson and you thinks they're dead. You're delusional, Samantha, completely delusional!"

Unknown military installation

Gordon held Hunter close. By his smell and the condition of his clothes he could tell that his son had been getting washed and his clothes cleaned. Gordon wanted so much to be able to tell Hunter everything, but they were under a watchful eye.

"Dad, remember when I shot that man?"

Looking at Hunter oddly, Gordon said, "Yes, I remember."

"Brother Jeremy agreed with you. He said it was a good thing I did that," Hunter said, his eyes now on the man in the room with them.

"Did he now?" Gordon replied. He too glanced at the man in the room.

"Yes, he said I was doing God's work by cleansing him."

"Excuse me for a second, Hunter," Gordon said, then stood up and approached the man. "Hi, I'm Gordon," he said. "Who are you?"

"I'm Brother Jeremy. I have the honor of watching over the children."

Brother Jeremy was the man Gordon had noticed the other day. Looking into his eyes, he could see the same insanity that plagued Rahab.

"Hey, sorry to ask. Are you related to Brother Rahab?"

"Yes, he is my father, but most important, he is my light to God's truth," Jeremy said. He was just as tall as his father, with the same dark hair and dark eyes. There was no mistaking they were related.

"I thought so. Um, so tell me. What goes on every day with the kids?"

"Why, we look after their entire well-being. We feed, clothe, and give them their spiritual nutrition through daily readings and exercises."

"Exercises?" Gordon asked.

"We challenge the children to tap into the true meaning of sacrifice by doing role playing."

"Role playing? Like what?" Gordon's tone had shifted. He was getting upset as he had a dark vision of child abuse or molestation, but he wanted to hear Jeremy say it.

"We don't divulge our ritualistic exercises to those who haven't been baptized," said Jeremy directly.

The blood was rushing to Gordon's face. He could feel the anger building up, but he knew exploding at Jeremy wouldn't work out for him. Quickly he was processing how he could kill Jeremy, snatch Hunter, and make a run for it. He couldn't leave his son with these people anymore; he had to do something. The touch at his hand brought him back from the brink.

Hunter grabbed his hand and said, "It's okay, Dad, I promise you. I'm a young man now, remember?"

Gordon knelt down and looked at him. "Of course I remember, but thanks for reminding me. Have I told you about the time you were born?"

"Only a hundred times," Hunter said, rolling his eyes.

"Please indulge me," said Gordon as he took his son to the

chair and replayed his birth with him in detail. Gordon was thankful for Hunter's ability to sense the situation was getting out of control. He had proven he was a young man by interjecting himself.

After a few minutes of going down memory lane, Hunter's laughter reappeared. It was so good for Gordon's soul to hear him laugh. It had been too long since he had that experience.

"Dad, you remember when Haley and I colored your face with the markers?" Hunter asked with a slight giggle.

"Ah, yeah, I do. What I remember the most was that Haley used permanent markers. The worst part was I had to meet a client that afternoon," said Gordon, playfully giving Hunter a stern look.

"That was so funny," his son replied.

"I'm glad I've always been the one who gets laughed at or gets hurt by you kids."

"Of course. You're our dad."

"Why does Haley think that hurting me is so funny?"

"Because it is. Remember when she threw the golf ball and hit you in the face? I've never seen her laugh so hard."

"Yeah, that was *so* funny," Gordon said sarcastically.

"Dad, I miss Mommy and Haley," said Hunter as he took Gordon's hand.

"I miss them too," said Gordon, reaching out with his other hand and caressing his son's face.

"Time is up." Jeremy interrupted Gordon and Hunter's moment.

"We've only had about twenty minutes. I want more time with him!" exclaimed Gordon.

"That is all the time you'll get," Jeremy shot back sternly. He knew he held the advantage.

Gordon stood up, his face flushed with anger. Before he could take his first step, Hunter grabbed his arm.

"No, Dad."

As if a bus had hit him, Gordon stopped in his tracks. He looked down at his ever-maturing son, staring into his blue eyes. The strength that emanated out of them inspired him to keep his cool.

"Fine, let me say good-bye for now."

Jeremy looked at Gordon, then focused on Hunter, then back on Gordon again. "Sure, one more minute. Then you need to go back to work."

Gordon knelt and hugged Hunter. "I love you, Son. You definitely didn't get your old man's patience or lack of. You're smart like your mom, thank God for that."

"Here, Dad," Hunter said in a whisper. He poked Gordon in the stomach with something hard.

Gordon glanced down to see his Spyderco folding knife. Shocked, he whispered back, "You've had it hidden?"

Aware that Jeremy was looking and might notice something, he whispered again, "Slip it into my front pocket when I hug you."

Hunter gave a slight nod.

They embraced again. Hunter slyly slipped the four-inch knife into Gordon's front pocket and whispered in his ear, "I love you, Dad."

San Diego, California

Watching Annaliese wash and prepare Sorenson's body for burial was something Sebastian had never experienced before. He remembered reading in history books about how the family took

care of the corpse and then displayed it in their home. One ame-
nity that modern society had long taken for granted was the coro-
ner and funeral home system. Without them, the family of the
deceased had to become the mortician and undertaker.

Annaliese's eyes were red and swollen from the heavy tears
that had flowed following Sorenson's death.

The strike to his head with the vase had been fatal, causing
massive brain injury, hemorrhaging, then death.

Sebastian almost felt like a voyeur watching her perform her
daughterly tasks.

She took the warm washcloth and, as if she were caring for
an infant, slowly and gently washed her father's entire body. She
then took his favorite cologne and applied it modestly. When she
began dressing him in his favorite suit, she looked to Sebastian
for help.

With much care and respect, he turned and lifted the fallen
man's lifeless body while she put on his clothes.

Sebastian knew that what had happened today was going to be
the norm until the bloodletting stopped. He knew eventually it
would come to an end, but before an equilibrium was established,
millions more would die.

He excused himself when they were done and proceeded to the
porch. His leg was hurting, and weariness was weighing heavily
on him. He found the large rocker on the far end of the porch
welcoming.

As he closed his eyes, a voice jolted him from his slumber.

"I heard what Brandon did," said Luke, who towered over him.

"Ah. Yeah. Is he okay?"

"I think so. He's in the guesthouse sleeping."

"So can I help you? Not to be rude, but I'm really tired."

"Sorry, I, uh, just wanted to ask you a question," said Luke sheepishly.

Sebastian waited for the question, but when he noticed Luke wasn't going to ask right away he said, "Spit it out, boy, I'm tired."

"Ah, sorry. When are we leaving for Zion?"

"I don't know if we're going to Zion now. With the bishop and two others killed today, our plans might have changed. Plus, why are you asking me?"

"Because you seem like the most logical one to be in charge now."

"Do I? Well, until someone pins that rank on me, I'll just help out," Sebastian said. He really didn't want to have this conversation. Then an idea came to mind: If he could be in charge he'd take the spot, but he wasn't going to force his way on the others. "Of course, I'd step up if they wanted me to."

"I was talking with Jameson and Willis. They like you and trust you. I just think we need to go somewhere safe. All of this seems like we're heading toward the same outcome as my family," said Luke, pointing to the now-buried bodies of the attackers.

"You and I agree that we need to get out of here, but not until we bury the bishop and the other two. Then we can start talking about leaving."

"Okay, sorry for bothering you. I'll leave you be," Luke said and turned around quickly.

"Wait a minute."

"Yeah?"

"Where do you want to go?"

"Don't matter to me, anywhere but here."

Just then, gunfire cracked in the distance.

Sebastian sat up, his fatigue replaced by adrenaline.

"So who—"

"Ssshh," Sebastian said.

More single-fire gunshots echoed in the distance.

"Sounds far away. Looks like we're not the only ones having issues," joked Sebastian.

"Hey, what are you going to do about Brandon?"

"Nothing. I'm not his parent, and looking back on yesterday, I have to say I think what he did was right."

"But he's only twelve years old," said Luke, shocked by Sebastian's cavalier attitude.

"Luke, I don't know you, but I'll open up a bit. What I've seen from almost day one after the attacks is people doing crazy things. I judged them for their lack of morality. I placed myself on this pedestal as some kind of moral authority. I've witnessed a lot of crazy shit in my day, but what happened yesterday was the most fucked-up shit I have ever seen. You know something? I froze yesterday. I found these men in the barn, I held them at gunpoint as if I was waiting for the police to come. I looked at these people as people. But what I have come to realize is that I've been the crazy one. I've been a fool. Brandon sees the world for what it's become.

"If we think we can apply the same moral code we had almost two months ago, we will end up dead. Those people who came in here were once neighbors and acquaintances of the bishop's. Something changed for them, though: They were hungry; they figured we had something and they were going to take it." Sebastian paused for second to think about how he wanted to express himself, then continued.

"The lightbulb finally went off when I saw Annaliese step outside and start shooting. These weren't her neighbors anymore, they were her adversaries. We have to pick sides in this long battle now. You, for one, have seen the horrors played out. I know you're looking for structure and something to help explain this chaos. Why somebody attacked us weeks ago and caused all of this is unknown, and frankly it fucking doesn't matter. What matters now is we have to protect our own. We have to fight and be willing to kill, like Brandon. You sounded shocked that I didn't jump at scolding him. Hell, I kinda applaud him for taking the action I should have taken. He was able to see the trees through forest."

Sebastian stopped again. He hated people who preached, and he knew that was exactly what he was doing now. Tiring of his own his voice, he finished by saying, "If I were to go back weeks ago, before all of this, I would agree with you. But I'm now awake. There's no one coming to save us. It's up to us, plain and simple."

40 miles east of Barstow, California

"When were you going to tell me this is how everyone felt?" Samantha shouted at Nelson.

"Calm down, Samantha," he pleaded.

"Don't tell me to calm down. Don't you dare! My husband and son are out there, and what you're now telling me is everyone here wants to leave because they think I'm delusional, as Sandy said. What would *you* do? Huh? Would you leave your family, or would you search and search? I can't give up, Nelson, and I won't!" Samantha's screaming had the entire group staring.

"Of course I don't think we should stop. I'm with you," he responded.

"Are you really?"

"Of course. I didn't say anything because I knew it wouldn't help. I know I needed to protect you from them. All you need to focus on is finding Gordon and Hunter."

"What the hell are you looking at?" Samantha yelled at Sandy, Mike, and the others.

"Samantha, please calm down," said Nelson. "We need to set out today. We're losing daylight," he went on, attempting to encourage her.

Samantha turned away from him and walked to the edge of the camp. She looked north toward the desert.

"My dad has volunteered to go with you," Nelson suggested.

"Where are you going?" she asked, still looking toward the desert.

"I think we need to split up. We can cover more ground. I'll head to the mountains, there," said Nelson. He had stepped up beside her and was pointing to a range of mountains to the northeast.

"What am I supposed to do?"

"I'm not going to answer that question; you know I'm with you on this. If they want to go, fuck 'em. My dad and I are here, and we'll help you and Haley."

"Thank you."

"I'm going to get geared up. I'll see you later," said Nelson, touching her arm.

She grabbed his hand and squeezed it. "Thank you again."

"No problem. That's what friends do, right?" Nelson walked away, leaving Samantha at the edge of the camp.

"Where are you? I can't do this without you. Please, God, let me find them, please," Samantha said, looking out toward the mountains.

Tijuana, Mexico

"Where have you been?" asked Alfredo angrily.

"I was taking care of issues on the northern route! So now you're keeping tabs on me?" Pablo challenged.

"I have to. Ever since you've been playing around up north, you've been shirking your responsibilities to your family. I thought we'd had this conversation. Did I not impress it on you then? If not, let me tell you again but more clearly. Stop fucking around. Stop these games. We are running a business and we need to take advantage of the changes to our marketplace. I need your help. Does that make it clearer?" said Alfredo. He rarely yelled, but his son's behavior and absence were frustrating him.

Pablo stood and walked to the bookshelf. He picked up a Waterford crystal vase and looked at it closely, admiring the rainbows it cast when the sunlight hit it. Placing it back down, he turned and finally addressed Alfredo. "Father, I'm sorry that you're upset with me. I want nothing more than for you to be proud of me. However, this is not working for me."

Alfredo asked, "What's not working for you?"

"This, here, our relationship. I'm done taking orders from you. You see, Father, you're a dinosaur. You're incapable of seeing the future. You think that we can turn what has happened into a business. You're wrong, Father. You don't have a true grasp on what has happened. You're thinking you can sell things. But where is your marketplace? Tell me. Our currency has collapsed. The American dollar is destroyed. Who's going to buy your generators? With what money? You're an old fool."

"How dare you talk to me that way?" Alfredo screamed. His temper was building. No one talked to him that way, and if they did, they never left his office alive.

"I'm doing something that will truly change the world. I wanted you to be a part of it, but that's not going to happen," Pablo retorted.

"What are you talking about? You were always such a dreamer. Always gazing into the stars with fantasies. Wake up, Son," said Alfredo, his tone softer now. He approached Pablo and stopped a foot in front of him. "Pablo, my boy. What are you doing? Oh, such a dreamer you are." Alfredo reached out and tapped his cheek.

"Don't patronize me," snapped Pablo, slapping his hand away.

"My son, you're so naïve. You can't do anything without me."

"Not true, Father. I've been planning this day for a while," said Pablo, who then reached in his jacket and pulled out a handheld radio. "Andre, you can proceed."

"What is this? Who are you talking to?" asked Alfredo, throwing his arms up in the air, frustrated.

Moments later the sound of automatic gunfire erupted throughout the house and outside.

Alfredo raced to his security cameras and adjusted them to see what was happening. On the monitors he saw in beautiful high definition his men being killed or executed by men he had never seen before.

"Pablo, what are you doing? My son, what are you doing?" asked Alfredo desperately. He reached into the top drawer and pulled out a small handgun. As he began to turn around, he felt the hard tip of Pablo's gun against the back of his head.

"Put the gun down, Father. I don't want to hurt you."

His hands shaking, Alfredo dropped the pistol on the floor and turned to face his son.

"I'm sorry it had to be this way," Pablo said.

Gunfire now rang out just outside the doors that led to his office. Alfredo jumped each time he heard a shot. "What have you done? What have you done?"

"Not to sound cliché, I've done what I had to. You made your decision. I presented to you numerous times the biggest opportunity the Juarez family would ever get and you scoffed at me. Your thinking is outdated. Now, please stand up. This meeting is over. I'm sorry, Father, but you're now retired."

Cheyenne Mountain, Colorado

Cruz was having a difficult time thinking with so much cross talk going on at the conference table. The communications coming in from the midwestern states were bad.

The governors of Nebraska, South Dakota, and Kansas were reporting hundreds of thousands of survivors entering their states. What tent cities they could muster weren't enough. All the governors were requesting immediate assistance from the federal government.

"Everybody, be quiet," Cruz loudly said to his assembled staff.

Around the table sat Baxter and Dylan, along with a few new to his advisory team.

Bethanny Wilbur, his new secretary of state, was a communications officer at Cheyenne Mountain. She had recently been assigned to the base after being promoted to major. Wilbur was a smart and savvy woman. Given her educational achievements, she could have gone anywhere to work. Upon graduating from Brown University with a master's in global and transcultural communications, she chose a life as an Air Force officer. Her relationship with her father, a retired general, was the biggest influence for this decision. She was a steadfast believer in the government and the military as a force for good.

The other three people in the room were lower deputy secretaries for Baxter and Wilbur.

Like Conner, Cruz had not grown his cabinet to pre-attack size. Logic and need had won over. Conner had appointed only the secretary of defense, who now dealt with everything from domestic to foreign relations and defense. He had below him dozens working to handle physical defense, recovery, and rebuilding.

When Baxter replaced him, his first request was to separate out the foreign relations. Especially with the responses from many global leaders following the nuclear strikes, Cruz needed someone who could negotiate with them to provide aid.

Cruz had proven to be an effective politician while governor of Florida, but what he lacked was the presence that Conner had. Conner could command a room.

"Everyone, quiet!" yelled a flustered Cruz, after his first request failed.

The room fell silent, and all eyes turned to him.

"Now we have a major problem back east. I called this meeting to discuss our options. Obviously we don't have a consensus. What I need are clear options. So, I will start with Baxter and go to each person. I want you to tell me what you think we should do, how you propose it be done, and why. No interrupting the speaker. Now, General, please start," said Cruz, taking a seat at the head of the table.

"Thank you, Mr. Vice President. I will be blunt as you all already know my position. What I want to delve into is why," said Baxter, walking to the map of the United States hanging on the wall behind Cruz. "A week ago we were receiving initial reports of large migrations. Obviously, those reports were accurate, but they did not really shed light on the human tragedy that is happening. The East is a total loss. We all agree on that.

"We all agreed that we would focus on providing aid to the midwestern states because they weren't heavily affected by radioactive contamination. But here's the reality. We cannot feed the numbers we are hearing about. In fact we can't provide support to half. Many of you just found out about the government stockpiles of food, water, and other provisions we had positioned at strategic locations around the country. We hardened these underground bunkers against an EMP. Some of you want us to open those locations to the people. I disagree, and here's why. We don't have enough food. The sheer numbers coming into these states are just too overwhelming.

"I am not cruel. I know some of you think my proposal is inhumane. But we're now at a place where we need to make a tough decision. Do we open these stores and deplete them? Without aid coming in from our allies, we won't be able to replenish them. We have enough food to feed each one of these people for a couple days. Then what? It doesn't do anything. We need to keep that food so we have a functioning government. This includes us, our military, and those governors and their staffs," said Baxter, standing like a grounded statue at the head of the room. When he talked he used his hands to gesture.

"I promised to be blunt, and I will conclude with this. Mr. Vice President, we have to face the facts that we cannot do anything for these people. Using what resources we have left will only leave us unable to proceed with Conner's plan. I say we contact all the governors and tell them we can only provide enough provisions to take care of them, their staffs, and their families. We can do this by transporting them to these bunker locations. In a nutshell, I think we need to take everyone underground until the bulk of the deaths have ended. We need to keep our forces off the coast. Bringing them ashore risks them."

"Mr. Vice President, this is insane!" bellowed Dylan.

"Quiet, Mr. McLatchy."

"But, this is unspeakable!"

Cruz shot back, "Enough, Dylan. Be quiet and let the general speak. None of this is easy. I haven't made my decision, but we can't act immature and emotional. Now, please keep your opinions to yourself till you're called upon."

Dylan sat quietly, but the rage inside him would have been deafening. His face was contorted and his posture stiff. Dylan was stressed, but most of his stress stemmed from not having done a thing to help find Conner. He had promised Julia, but since then he had only offered advice. Deep down he felt he needed to go out and help, but the fear of the outside world prevented him. Shame filled the reservoirs of his heart, but he masked it with anger.

"General, please proceed," Cruz directed Baxter.

"Again, I promised to be blunt, so I will finish with this: What we must do is protect this government and our surrogates so that whoever survives the months ahead will have a system in place from which to rebuild."

The weight of Baxter's words was enough to keep everyone, including Dylan, silent. Many in the room didn't even look up; they just stared at the papers laid before them. The others' eyes were fixed on the general. Deep down, all knew that he was right. What he'd said struck at their deepest survival instincts.

Wilbur kept staring at the map. Not wanting to wait her turn, she chimed in. "Mr. Vice President. I disagree with Baxter, but not on the merits that Mr. McLatchy mentioned. If we are to have any success in getting our allies to come back to the table, we can't be perceived to have abandoned our people. While I understand General Baxter's reasoning, and I would add that it's reasonable, I am making inroads with the Australians. However, it would be a one-two punch if we go forward with this plan. I suggest we determine what we have and divide up a percentage of it, leaving us and other government entities enough to live off for six months. I believe by then I will have secured an arrangement for aid."

Cruz rocked in his chair, his face firmly planted in his hand. He stared at the secretary of state and didn't respond right away. The silence was unsettling, as Cruz deliberated between the two different plans.

Dylan attempted to say something, but Cruz held up his index finger and shook his head.

"General Baxter, your plan has many merits, but I have to agree with Major Wilbur. We need the aid from Australia and others. We can't do something that will isolate us any more. I realize it's a risk, but we must try. General, please proceed with her plan. I want it implemented immediately. Please contact the ARG heading toward Portland and have it pull into the Gulf of Mexico. There we can use their aircraft for support.

"Major Wilbur, contact the governors of Hawaii and Alaska. Ask them what they can provide in the way of ships. Have those ships head to Portland to support our rebuilding. I know they are both seeking independence, but remind them that the equipment they have is the property of the United States. Strike a deal with them. We will officially recognize them as independent nations, but they need to support us," said Cruz, speaking quickly.

He looked around the room and finished by saying, "People,

this country is depending on us. We can't let them down. Soon, some of us will be in Portland setting up a new capital and a new beginning for our country. I want to thank you all for everything that you have done to this point. No one knows how this all will end, but I am honored to be here beside you, as we set out to get the United States back on its feet."

JANUARY 15, 2014

· · ·

Vision without action is a daydream. Action without vision is a nightmare.

—Japanese Proverb

40 miles east of Barstow, California

"Right here. There's a base of some kind. It's very small and there are people there. But get this, they don't look military," said Nelson excitedly as he pointed on the map to an area that showed only desert.

"You sure it's not Fort Irwin?" asked Samantha.

"Hey, I'm not a Rhodes scholar, but you and I have seen Fort Irwin. This ain't it. This place is very small. I saw about two dozen different buildings. There's a runway. It's like a small forward operating base."

"How many people are there?"

"A lot."

"A lot, like, how many?"

"I counted more than fifty. But you know what's odd? Some were working, but each small group had at least one or two people watching over them with guns. Plus, the entire perimeter was being guarded."

"Why didn't you tell me about this last night?" asked Samantha.

"I came back late because I stayed as long as I could. I was able to get close, but not close enough to identify faces. When I got back to camp, my dad said you were in your trailer. I thought to knock, but I knew there wasn't anything we could do about it then," said Nelson. He was now concerned she might get upset.

"It's okay, you're right. I was tired last night. I snuggled up with Haley and went to bed early. So what do you recommend?" Samantha sensed he was being defensive, and after yesterday's argument with Sandy, she didn't want to upset one of the few close friends she had.

"Hey!" said Seneca loudly as she walked up on them both.

Samantha and Nelson greeted her. They carried on some small talk before Samantha subtly gave hints that they were busy.

"Um, listen. Sam, I appreciate you helping us out the other night. Thanks for smoothly things over. I, ah, also want to apologize again for Mack. You could say he's a bit rough around the edges," Seneca said.

"Rough is an understatement," quipped Nelson.

Seneca shot him a slight flirtatious smile.

Samantha noticed the way they looked at each other. She could see the attraction they still had. She'd never understood why Seneca broke up with him. When Seneca left Nelson, she left all of their lives. It had been years since Samantha had seen her. At one time they were inseparable friends. They had done everything together, and if it hadn't been for Seneca, Samantha wouldn't have met Gordon. Then, without warning one day, Seneca broke up with Nelson and disappeared. Samantha once grilled Nelson over what had happened and even accused him of causing her to leave. But she finally just had to let her go. Now, out of nowhere and to everyone's surprise, Seneca had shown up. On the outside she looked different, and Samantha wondered if that change was as pronounced on the inside. Maybe, after they settled down in Idaho, she'd be able to get to know her friend all over again.

"Sweetie, Nelson and I need to go soon. So can . . ."

"Sorry, but I'm not here to chitchat. I want to know if Mack and I can help. We have our car, so we can . . ."

"Yes, of course. Sorry to assume."

"It's fine. I can't imagine what you must be going through. Just let me know what we can do."

Samantha smiled at her old friend. Having her on board to help made her feel better.

The plan they agreed upon took all four of them to a spot closer to the small base Nelson had spotted. He wanted to try to get himself into a position where he'd be close enough to identify who was there.

"So that seems easy," said Seneca smugly.

"We will see. Like I mentioned before, the place is heavily guarded. Let's keep our heads down, be quiet, and whatever we do, don't let them see you."

Cheyenne Mountain, Colorado

Baxter briskly walked through the dimly lit halls, a piece of white paper clinging to his fingertips. As he came upon personnel, they immediately stood at attention and against the wall. When he reached Cruz's door, he hesitated before knocking; what he was about to say was heart-wrenching. The few seconds he bought himself didn't change the fact that he had to be the one to break this news.

He knocked loudly. Then he looked down at the paper and read it again to himself. Maybe he had read it wrong the first five times. Did he miss something? As he slowly scanned each word, he made sure that it said what it said.

The door opened, and there stood Cruz. "General? Is everything okay?"

"Sir, may I come in?" insisted Baxter.

"Sure, sure. Come on in," said Cruz, opening the door more. "Please ignore the mess. We were so used to housekeepers that we forgot how to housekeep ourselves," he said, acknowledging the state of his quarters.

"Thank you," said Baxter, stepping inside.

Cruz closed the door behind him and asked, "So what's this about?"

"Here," said Baxter, handing him the paper. "I thought it best I hand-deliver this."

Cruz took the paper and read it. The concerned look on his face melted to sadness as the words sank in.

"When did they find it?"

"Just thirty minutes ago."

"Call everyone to the command center ASAP. I'll be there in five minutes."

"Yes, sir."

• • •

Cruz was the first to reach the command center. He immediately went into the large briefing room and picked up the phone. "Get me the Colorado governor," he said into the handset, then put it down.

Baxter was the next to arrive, followed by the rest of the team.

Just as everyone was sitting down, the phone rang.

Cruz grabbed the handset before the second ring. "This is Vice President Cruz. Yes, Governor, we have been informed. When can you get your people here? I understand, but you need to evacuate everyone now. I don't understand what you mean. Slow down. Who?" Cruz asked, then began clicking the receiver. "Governor, are you there? Hello, Governor?" Cruz clicked the receiver again. Nothing but silence. He turned to Baxter and ordered, "Get the governor back on the line immediately!"

Baxter turned to leave, but the door burst open before he could reach it.

A young tech sergeant came in, his eyes wide and face flushed. "Sir, excuse me for interrupting, but we have a major situation!"

Cruz dropped the handset and followed as everyone rushed out of the room. The main command center had four rows of glowing monitors, which all faced a much larger LED screen on the wall, showing a computer image of the continental United States. On a smaller screen to the right was an aerial view from an orbiting satellite.

"Sergeant, what is it?" Baxter barked.

"Sir, we just registered a detonation," the tech sergeant said, sitting back down at his computer. "Here, let me put it on the screen."

All eyes turned to the main screen.

The tech sergeant maneuvered a cursor and zoomed in on the Denver metro area. East of the city was a red dot that pulsated. He took the cursor there and zoomed in again. The pulsating red dot now enveloped the Denver International Airport.

"Sergeant, what are we looking at here?" Cruz asked.

"Sir, that large red dot signified a nuclear detonation," the tech sergeant answered soberly.

"Shit!" Cruz blurted out.

"What can you tell about the blast from here?" Baxter asked.

"It's tough, but the blast seems limited or contained. Like it was a subsurface explosion."

"Subsurface?" Dylan asked, not knowing what that meant.

"Dylan, it means an explosion underground," Cruz answered.

"It means the DIA bunker facility is gone and so is the governor and all those people," Baxter then added.

"We have another," an airman bellowed from behind his monitor.

"What?" Cruz asked, confused.

"Yes, we are getting data that there has been an event at Offutt Air Force Base in Nebraska. It looks like another subsurface detonation."

"How is this happening? I don't understand!" Cruz exclaimed.

"Wait, hold on. Sir, we are picking up another one!" the airman yelled.

"Where?" Baxter asked.

Everyone in the room was on pins and needles.

"Raven Rock, Pennsylvania!"

"Mr. Vice President, these are all secure bunker locations, like Cheyenne Mountain," Baxter told him.

"What do we do? Evacuate the base?"

"Sir, I don't think there's much we can do. These all seem to be coordinated. If this base has been targeted, then it's only a matter of time. Somehow these locations have been compromised. They store most of our long-term self-storage foods and other needed resources . . ."

"How is this happening? How can this be happening? Why are we so inept?" Cruz shouted.

"I don't know why, but right now there isn't much we can do from here," Baxter said in an attempt to answer the vice president's repetitive questions.

"There has to be something we can do!" Cruz yelled.

On the big screen a fourth, then a fifth red dot appeared. Dulce Base, New Mexico, followed by Mount Weather, Virginia.

"Sir, those locations held the bulk of our underground stores of food, water, and equipment. We are the last large facility," Baxter said somberly.

"Then we are a target. We need to evacuate immediately!" Cruz exclaimed, clearly frightened.

"Like I mentioned before, we can attempt to evacuate the entire base, but these attacks look coordinated. If it's going to happen, it will happen any minute," Baxter said as he walked to a chair and sat down. He placed his face in his hands.

Everyone looked around nervously. The room was quiet except for the slight hum of equipment and the five low-toned pings that showed the locations of the nuclear detonations.

Cruz also felt the weight of defeat. He walked back into the briefing room and slammed the door behind him.

Tijuana, Mexico

"Is it done?" Pablo asked. "Good, glad to hear it. Really, that's ahead of schedule. How did . . . Never mind, doesn't matter. I'll be there, thank you. Yes, of course I'll have the payment," Pablo said, then hung up the satellite phone. He placed it on his father's desk and twirled it. As he watched it spin, visions of his new role in the world were sinking in. Not since Hitler had someone tried something so bold. Feeling cocky, he stood up and walked to the cabinet behind him. He opened the top door and reached in for a bottle of cognac and a snifter. He poured himself a glass and sat back down. Just as he was about to taste the cognac, a loud knock at the door disturbed his moment.

"What? Who is it?"

The door opened, and in came his mother. Her clothes, hair, and makeup showed the signs of distress.

"Mother! Please sit down. Can I pour you a glass of water?"

She marched over and slapped him across the face.

A look of anger came over him, but it melted away quickly and was replaced with a smile. "Mother, please sit down."

She went to slap him again, but he grabbed her wrist.

"Mother, stop! Now, you can go sit down or I will have one of my men restrain you."

She resisted him, but his grip was tight.

"Do you understand me? Either you behave yourself or I'll have you locked up like Father."

"You insolent, spoiled brat!" she said, then spat on him.

The spit clung to his cheek like thick plaster.

He wiped his cheek with his sleeve and stood up. Still holding on to her wrist with his left hand, he brought her close. "Mother, my patience is not infinite. If you don't behave I will have you locked up."

"I don't care! Lock me up! How dare you tear down everything your father worked so hard to get for you and our family!" she yelled, her face flushed with anger.

"I haven't torn down anything. I will take this family to a higher place than he ever could. You will see, Mother. In three days, I'll show you and Father. I will show you the future of the Juarez family."

Outside unknown military installation

The prospect of knowing where Gordon and Hunter might be filled Samantha with hope. The reality of where and what it was filled her with dread. What Nelson had described sounded like a prison to her. Armed guards not only guarding the gate and perimeter but guarding others who were working sounded bad. She hoped that today's trip would provide them enough information, and proof that Gordon and Hunter were alive, so that they could coordinate a rescue.

They had stashed Nelson's truck behind several large boulders on the opposite side of the mountains that overlooked the camp to the west. The hike to get into a good spotting position took them almost two hours. The steep climb and rough terrain made for an ankle-twisting experience.

Seneca and Mack set up farther south, closer to the vehicle. Nelson was concerned about leaving the truck, so part of their responsibility was to watch the east-west road that led to the camp and make sure no one came up behind them.

Once settled into their hiding position, Samantha pulled out a pair of binoculars. When she first looked through them, the image of the camp was blurry, but as she adjusted the optics, a crystal-clear image appeared. Below her was exactly what Nelson had described. Approximately a dozen armed guards walked the perimeter and stood post at the gate. A group of about twenty men were working on the far east side, too far for her to identify any of them. Throughout the camp she saw others coming in and going out of buildings, but again it was impossible to identify anyone. Frustrated that she couldn't see Gordon or Hunter, she put the binoculars down and grunted, "Damn."

"Let me guess. It's too difficult to make out anyone?" Nelson quipped. He too had a pair of binoculars and was scanning the base; however, he was looking for weaknesses in their defenses.

"Yes, that, and do you see how many armed men are there? Even if we spotted Gordon and Hunter, how would we get them out?" Samantha said. Knowing she needed to get past this feeling, she picked up her binoculars and began to look again. She strained her eyes to see the men on the far east side. She looked for children but couldn't see any. As the men worked on the far side, coming and going, she attempted to spot any of Gordon's obvious traits.

"Hey, do you hear that?" Nelson asked. He lowered his binoculars and cocked his head as if that would improve his hearing.

"Yeah, I do. What is—"

"Over there!" Nelson exclaimed, pointing to the north of the base.

Six Humvees with mounted guns were heading toward the camp at high speed.

Samantha turned and looked. "Who's that?"

"I don't know," Nelson answered.

Shouting erupted from the camp as they too saw the incoming vehicles.

The Humvees soon opened fire with .50-caliber machine guns. The distinct deep thumping sound from the .50s engulfed the valley.

Both Nelson and Samantha watched in amazement as the Humvees drew closer, guns blazing, and the personnel in the camp ran like cockroaches when the lights come on.

Soon, though, the guards recovered and began to return fire. Their collective effort quickly destroyed one of the Humvees.

The berm provided the camp guards adequate protection, and soon they were able to stop two more advancing Humvees.

Samantha peered down on the surreal events. People were running everywhere, but she took notice of the several people running toward the south berm, which was now left unattended. One was a woman dressed in what appeared to be a nightgown. Samantha thought her attire was odd. She watched her run straight across the runway and helicopter pads. Seeing this woman and two men make a break for it gave Samantha hope that if Gordon and Hunter were there, they too might take advantage of the distraction.

Her hopes soon were dashed as she saw someone with a rifle take aim and fire several shots. Immediately following the shots one of the men fell hard. To Samantha it looked as if he was dead before he hit the ground.

The shooting of this man caused the woman to make a hard right and start to head west. Bullets hit the ground behind her as the guard who had shot the man targeted her.

Samantha found herself cheering for the woman—*come on.*

More bullets came flying toward the woman, this time hitting the ground just before her. She darted left, then right, and kept erratically moving until she reached the berm. The woman lunged and rolled to the opposite side. On the far side of the berm and safe from bullets, she plotted her next move. She looked toward the mountain in front of her; the rough terrain and rock outcroppings made it an attractive place to hide.

Samantha was so nervous for this poor woman. Then a thought came to mind—*this woman could know about Gordon and Hunter.*

"We have to help her!" Samantha said loudly to Nelson.

"What? How?" he asked.

"She could know about Gordon and Hunter. We have to help her!"

"Okay, what do you have in mind?"

Inside unknown military installation

The instant the attack came Gordon knew this was his time to act.

He grabbed Derek by the shoulder and said, "Now's the time, let's go!"

"Now?"

"Yes!" Gordon exclaimed as he pulled out the knife Hunter had given him.

The guard who was in charge of watching them was still there, but his attention was focused on the action happening at the north end of the base.

Gordon flipped open the blade and walked briskly over to the guard, whose back was toward him. Not hesitating one more second, he grabbed the man by the face, covering his mouth with his left hand, and slit his throat. Blood squirted out of the open artery; then the large volume of blood just cascaded down from the open wound and covered his body. The guard went limp in Gordon's arm. Knowing he was dead, Gordon let him fall to the ground.

"Let's get my boy!" Gordon said loudly as he picked up the guard's semiauto rifle and what extra magazines he could carry.

Pandemonium was gripping the base. People were running all over the place. Some of Rahab's people ran for the cover of the buildings, while most of his henchmen were assembling at the northern berm and engaging the soldiers. His captives were also reacting in various ways. Some huddled together, scared and unsure of what to do. Others ran toward the perimeter of the base. The other men Gordon was with took off for the eastern berm; beyond them was an open expanse of desert.

Automatic gunfire, screams, and cries made for a symphony of chaos.

"Here!" Gordon said as he handed Derek the blood-covered knife.

Derek reacted with revulsion.

"Take it, goddamn it!" Gordon ordered.

Derek jumped. He took the knife and held it in his shaking hands. The warm blood ran between his fingers and dripped onto his shoes. At first he cringed and tried to wipe off the blood. Then he convinced himself that this bloody knife was the key to his escape. His grip tightened, and he took his first step toward what he hoped was his freedom.

Outside unknown military installation

The woman had made the lower part of the mountain and began to climb.

One of Rahab's guards was still attempting to shoot her. He had been successful in killing the other two who had attempted to escape over the berm, but the woman was proving to be difficult.

The bullets continued to rain down on her position, but she kept her head down. Each time there was a pause, she assumed he was reloading and climbed higher. Her only trouble was that she couldn't see any large rock outcroppings for another two hundred feet. She knew she couldn't stay there, and soon the guard might get help; she would have to make a run for it. Closing her weary eyes she prayed to herself—*you can do this girl, now, one, two . . .* When she opened her eyes to look at the path she would take, she saw a shimmer in the rocks above. She squinted and saw a woman waving to her. A nervous and unsure feeling crept through her.

"Who the fuck are you?" she said out loud.

"She saw me, she saw me!" Samantha said excitedly.

"Now what? She has to clear two hundred–plus feet to get to the nearest cover, then another fifty to get to us," Nelson said.

"We shoot the man shooting at her!" Samantha said confidently.

"That will draw their attention to us. No, no, no!" Nelson insisted.

"We have to help her. We don't know if Gordon or Hunter are even in there. This woman might be able to help us answer that. Now shoot the man!" she snapped at him.

Nelson raised his eyebrows in astonishment at Samantha's bravado. He grinned, popped up over the rock, took aim with his rifle, and squeezed the trigger. When the shot cracked, he almost instantly saw the man's head snap back.

"Good shot!" Samantha squealed in excitement.

"I have to thank Gordon for that," he said, winking at her.

• • •

Seeing the rifle appear, Lexi became nervous. Her back was pressed so hard against the rock she swore she was a part of it.

When the shot rang out, she took a breath and peered around the side of the rock.

The man who had been shooting at her fell to the ground.

She looked back toward where she had seen Samantha waving. No one was there. She peeked again around the rock to make sure it was clear. Seeing it was, she was about to move when she saw Samantha again waving.

"Up here, you're safe with us, I promise!"

Lexi's instincts were crying out that this woman looked safe, but her experiences over the past seven and half weeks yelled, *Don't trust anyone.* She didn't know them. She thought that she could be going from the boiling pot into the fire. But the woman looked sweet, she looked safe. *Where else am I going to go?* Lexi thought. She looked around. Nothing. She was surrounded by nothing. Wide-open desert everywhere. She then thought, *Should I have run toward the soldiers?*

"Fuck!" she yelled out.

Behind her the sound of gunfire was still fierce, but it had diminished.

She looked back up.

Samantha was still there waving for her to come.

Peeking one last time around the rock to see if all was clear, Lexi finally took that step toward Samantha.

"Fuck it!" she said.

Inside unknown military installation

Gordon's deliberate and ruthless nature was in full force. He had shot two of Rahab's men outside the main building.

Derek jumped over the two bodies and opened the door for Gordon.

Gordon came right up behind him. He popped his head in and looked in either direction. No one was there, so he entered the building with the rifle at the ready. The main entrance opened into a small lobby. To either side were long hallways that wrapped around the entire building. On the insides of the hallways were numerous rooms and offices.

Gordon had only been in the building once, but he knew Rahab lived upstairs.

"Now where do we go?" Derek asked with a labored voice. The run from across the base had exhausted him.

"Sshh! Listen! Upstairs!" Gordon said, looking for the closest stairwell.

"There!" Derek shouted out and pointed to a sign on a wall down the main hall.

Gordon, with the rifle firmly in the pocket of his shoulder, tactically walked down the hall.

Derek stayed close behind. He had retired the knife and taken a rifle from one of the guards Gordon had killed at the entrance.

The gunfire was now faint behind the walls of the building.

When Gordon reached the end of the hallway, he slowly reconnoitered the area. When the door to the stairwell entered his field of view, he saw another guard standing there at the ready. Gordon squeezed a shot off, hitting the man squarely in the chest. He then came fully around the corner and put two more rounds in the man. Stepping up to the guard, he grabbed a pistol from him, tucked it into his waistband, and took all the magazines from him and tucked them into his pocket.

Upstairs both he and Derek could hear people running around and the children crying.

A loud voice then bellowed out.

Gordon couldn't tell who it was, but he would soon find out. He entered the stairwell and looked up quickly. No one was in his field of view. He slung the rifle and pulled out the pistol, a Glock

9-mm. He dropped the magazine to inspect the rounds and checked it to see if a round was chambered. The magazine was full and a bullet was loaded. He slapped the magazine back in and proceeded up the stairs.

Reaching the top, he stood with his back against the wall next to the door.

He placed his finger to his mouth, signaling Derek to be quiet.

Derek confirmed with a nod. Sweat was pouring off of him, and his eyes showed a deep-felt determination.

Gordon turned the knob and slowly opened the door.

The second the door opened, the sounds he had heard earlier became amplified.

He let the door close quietly and said to Derek, "When I open the door, I'm going left; you need to come right behind me and go right. Be careful what you shoot."

"Okay," Derek answered nervously.

"On three. One, two, three," Gordon ordered, then opened the door and entered the hallway.

Derek followed right behind him.

Three men stood only ten feet from Gordon.

The men were stunned to see him and began to bring their guns up.

Gordon started to shoot while slowly walking to the right; he wanted to make it harder for them to hit a moving target. He hit the first two before they could fire a single shot.

The third man fired but missed.

Gordon could see the fear on his face, and he squeezed a shot, hitting the guard in the face. The back of the man's head exploded and he dropped to the ground.

Just behind him, Gordon heard Derek fall.

Not seeing anyone else in the hall, he looked over his shoulder to see Derek kneeling on the floor. Blood poured out of his right shoulder.

"Damn!" Gordon barked. He took a few steps back to check on him. "How bad is it?"

"Aah, if this was eight weeks ago and this happened to me on Fifth in Hillcrest, I'd say it's a bad day. But because it's not and I'm not dead, I'll have to say I'll be okay."

"Good man, just stay here and watch the door. I'm going to finish this and get my boy," Gordon said.

The crying of the children echoed off the walls and covered up the fact that the gunfire from outside had stopped.

Gordon tucked the pistol away and brought the rifle back into action. He loaded a fresh magazine and proceeded down the hall. At the corner he scanned and saw some children standing in the hall, but no adults. He paused for a moment to see if one of Rahab's men would make an appearance. None did.

He committed himself and walked fully into the hallway. With the rifle at the ready, he entered a large open room. About fourteen children were there, many crying. No Hunter. Gordon walked up to the oldest child and asked, "Where's Hunter?"

The child pointed to the door next to the room.

"Is anyone in there with him?"

"Brother Jeremy?" the boy answered in a trembling voice.

"Anyone else, any other bad men?"

The boy shook his head no.

Gordon approached the door with ease. His next actions would determine a lot. Scenarios raced through his mind. He didn't know how the room was laid out. Where was Hunter in there? He couldn't just open up and blast, he had to be careful and diligent. Putting all the thoughts out of his mind, he grabbed the handle and opened the door.

Outside unknown military installation

"Who are you?" Samantha asked Lexi.

"Who the fuck are you?" she shot back. Her piercing blue eyes darted from Samantha to Nelson. She was looking for anything that seemed out of place.

"I'm Samantha, and this is Nelson. We're not here to hurt you," Samantha said softly.

"How do I know that?"

"You don't, but why else would we shoot that man down there? You needed our help so we helped," Samantha said flatly.

Lexi stared at Samantha. Her nerves were shot and she was terribly hungry.

Samantha felt bad for this woman before her. She could see the signs of abuse. Bruises covered her face, neck, and arms. She could tell that before the lights went out, Lexi had been an attractive young woman. Samantha guessed that she wasn't older than thirty. Her hair had been dyed blond, but she now had grown-out brown roots, similar to Samantha's. It appeared as if her hair had been cut hastily, due to it being extremely uneven.

"Why help me?" Lexi asked, curious about why they would put themselves at risk.

"I'll be honest—because we think my husband and son might be in there."

"Those people down there are fucked up. They are fucking evil!" Lexi spewed in anger.

"Do you know a Gordon or a Hunter?" Samantha asked urgently.

"Aah, no. Doesn't sound familiar."

"Are you sure? We need to know, *I* need to know," Samantha pressed. She touched Lexi's arm, causing her to flinch.

"I told you, no!"

"Please, did you see a man, tall, over six feet—"

"Yeah, about half the men there. Listen, I told you I don't know a fucking Gordon or Hunter. If they're down there, they're fucked. That Rahab is an evil son of bitch," Lexi interrupted her.

"We have a problem," Nelson said urgently, looking at the base below.

The Fort Irwin soldiers' small attack on the base had been a failure. The Humvees that had been part of the attack now sat smoldering.

"How do you think they got those running?" Nelson asked. "And why would they come with only a handful of Hummers? Doesn't make sense."

Samantha jumped up and looked at the base below through her binoculars. The chaos and disruption had settled down. Random gunshots could be heard from inside the base.

"Nice meeting you all, but I'm outta here," Lexi said, attempting to get up.

"Hey, just stay with us, we won't hurt you. I promise. I need to talk to you more about this place. Please," Samantha pleaded.

Lexi looked at Samantha squarely. She could see the desperation in her eyes and could sense she was a good woman. "Okay."

Inside unknown military installation

The scene before Gordon was taken right out of a nightmare.

Jeremy had Hunter in front of him with a large knife under his throat.

Hunter stood silent, but his eyes screamed with terror.

With the typical words from any Hollywood movie, Jeremy shouted, "Stay right there or I'll kill him."

Never having been in this situation but always having been a critic of those scenes from movies, Gordon did exactly what he'd always said he would do. He immediately shot Jeremy in the mouth with the rifle. No response to his inane and clichéd command. Gordon placed one 5.56-mm round where he knew it would drop the man like a sack of potatoes.

The round traveled the short distance to Jeremy's spinal cord, and blew out the lower part of his skull. Bloody brain matter splattered the wall behind him. His eyes rolled up inside his head, and he went directly down. The knife fell from his lifeless hand and hit the floor with a clang.

Frozen in fear, Hunter stood unsure what to do.

Gordon slung the rifle and went to him. He knelt and embraced his trembling son. "I'm here, I'm here. Everything will be fine. Let's go home. Let's go see Mommy."

Hunter started to cry intensely. The warm tears fell from his eyes and ran down Gordon's neck.

"I've got you now, it'll be okay. I promise. Now let's go."

San Diego, California

Bishop Sorenson's funeral had been over for two hours, but Annaliese still sat staring at the pile of dirt that covered his body. Her gaze had been unfettered and focused. Sebastian attempted to talk with her, but she didn't respond, she just sat staring.

"She's a fucking mess," Brandon quipped.

Sebastian shot him a look and barked, "Shut up! Her father is dead. Show some respect!"

"Whatever, whose parents aren't dead!" Brandon retorted.

Sebastian just glared at him. He knew Brandon had a lot of pain and was unable to channel it in a constructive manner. Not wanting to get into a back-and-forth, he chose to ignore him.

Brandon matched Sebastian's stare but after a few moments chose to leave well enough alone. He walked away mumbling something unintelligible.

"I'm worried about him," Luke said.

"Yeah, I would agree. That kid needs to stop being so fucking angry," Sebastian responded, clearly irritated by Brandon's disrespectful comments.

"So are we leaving?"

Sebastian didn't hear Luke. His attention was completely on Annaliese. He found her incredibly beautiful. Her deep pain at the loss of her father made her so fragile and vulnerable. He had to resist the urge to go over and just hold her. He looked away and asked Luke, "What? What did you say?"

"Ha, I asked if we're leaving."

"Yes, we are. Ask me when, though."

"Okay, I'll play along. When?"

"When she's ready to go. Not a moment before. Got that? I go where she goes," Sebastian said, pointing at Annaliese.

Luke looked at her, then back to Sebastian. He was a bit confused but started to see that Sebastian was making it his responsibility to protect her now that her father was dead.

"Well, I go wherever you go, so I hope you don't mind I tag along?"

"Of course not. Now stop bugging me about when we're leaving."

Willis walked up to the two of them. "Sebastian, Mrs. Sorenson wants to talk with you."

"Sure, where is she?"

"She's in the living room," Willis answered, pointing toward the main house.

• • •

Mrs. Sorenson was rocking back and forth in a rocker recliner next to the large bay window. In her hands she clenched a handkerchief, damp from her tears.

Sebastian knocked on the wall just outside of the room. "Excuse me, Mrs. Sorenson. You wanted to see me?"

"Yes, yes. Come in, please." She motioned to a love seat across from her.

Sebastian walked over and sat. "How can I help?"

"I see how you look at my daughter."

"I, aaah, sorry, but . . . ," Sebastian stuttered.

"Listen, my husband liked you and I like you. You seem like a good man. I also know that Annaliese has feelings for you."

"Aah, please don't." Sebastian continued to stutter. He was put on the spot by her direct comments.

"Please be quiet and let me finish," she softly but firmly commanded him. "Sebastian, you seem like a good man. You also seem like a very smart and capable man. The other men around here, while smart and nice, are not up to the task of protecting my Annaliese and her siblings. You, Sebastian, are that man. I see it and my husband saw it. I brought you in here to ask you to do something for me."

"Anything."

"I have a brother who lives in Sandy, Utah. He has a large piece of land, and like many other Mormons, he's prepared. I know that he's not going to Zion. You see, there's always been a lot of debate about the holy land. He for one thinks it's hogwash. I talked to him today."

"You talked to him?" Sebastian asked, interrupting her.

Mrs. Sorenson stopped rocking and looked at Sebastian with a slightly irritated expression. "We have ham radios. We kept a lot of our equipment in Faraday boxes."

"Okay, sorry to interrupt."

"Our life here is over. Most of the group here wants to go to Zion. We're not going. I have you here to ask if you'd escort me and my family to Sandy."

Sebastian didn't have to think about it. He answered quickly, "I'm your man, but can I ask something too?"

"Sure."

"The two boys I found. I want to bring them with us."

"That Luke seems like a fine boy, but please keep your eye on the other one. He worries me."

"I'll do that. So when do you want to leave?"

"Tomorrow, let's leave tomorrow."

Cheyenne Mountain, Colorado

"Either we're alive because we're lucky or we're alive because it was planned. I don't know. In fact, I'm coming to realize we don't know shit about anything!" Cruz yelled as he slammed his fist down on the table.

Around the table sat his team. No one said a word. They all just looked at the table or the walls.

There wasn't much to say. Either they had somehow averted death or they weren't on the list.

"With the loss of these underground facilities, we have lost a considerable amount of food, water, and other precious resources," Baxter informed the team.

"So what do we do? We don't have enough now to help those in the Midwest. I'm at a loss here, I need some good counsel. Somebody give me something?" Cruz asked.

They all just looked at each other.

Wilbur broke the team's silence. "Mr. Vice President, what happened today might give us a boost with Australia and our South American friends. Knowing that we have lost a large portion of our backup supplies, they might now come to our aid out of sympathy. So, I would also suggest we don't undertake any type of retaliation unless we have solid intel and we run it by them."

Frustrated and tired, Cruz stood up. He started to pace around the large rectangular table.

"So we exploit today's attacks?" Baxter asked.

"I wouldn't use the word *exploit*. We can't change what happened today. We have to use what happened to our advantage. Do you have an alternative?" Wilbur fired back.

"As a matter of fact, I do!" Baxter responded.

"Enough, enough! Stop! There are two things we need to know. Who did this and how? Any thoughts?" Cruz asked. He continued to pace the room.

"These attacks all had similarities outside of the obvious. They were directly targeted at our underground facilities. Whoever did this knew what they were doing and wanted to disrupt our COG plan," Baxter stated before being interrupted by Dylan.

"COG?"

"Continuity of government. Seriously, Dylan, why are you in here? You don't seem to know anything," Baxter said mockingly. His even temper and patience were gone.

"I'm here because . . ."

"Dylan, stop," Cruz ordered him.

"Mr. Vice President, this attack was designed with the sole purpose of preventing our government from reorganizing."

"But why now? Why not do this before? It's so strange," Cruz muttered.

"Does it matter to know why?" Baxter answered.

"Yes, it does matter. Why not here? If we ask these questions, we gain some control and eventually find out who did this," Cruz said.

"Sir, I think whoever did this might have left us alone because they are showing us that we aren't in control; they are."

Inside unknown military installation

Knowing that his window of opportunity was shrinking, Gordon didn't stop to reload or gather more ammunition from the dead guards. He hurried past their bodies down the hall with Hunter in his arms.

When he turned the corner, he saw Derek leaning against the wall holding his shoulder.

"How are you?" Gordon asked.

"I'm good."

"You okay to move?"

"Yeah, I'll be fine," Derek said, slowly getting up. The shoulder wound was painful and would need treatment, but escaping Rahab's grasp took precedence over the pain.

They raced down the stairwell and exited into the hallway.

"Take the lead," Gordon ordered.

Obliging, Derek walked in front of him and began to make his way toward the main entrance.

In their haste, they hadn't noticed that the gunfire outside had stopped.

Carefully looking around the corner, Derek didn't see anyone.

"Seems clear."

"Good, from here, let's get to the hangar where the cars are," Gordon said.

Sticking his pistol straight out in front of him, Derek led them down to the main double doors.

Gordon watched Derek closely; he knew how much pain the other man was in. Only weeks before he had suffered from several gunshots. The respect you have for people comes not from who they say they are but from what they do. Derek had proven himself to be a good man. How strange, Gordon thought, that all these events would lead him and Derek to work side by side. They may not have agreed on everything politically in the pre-attack world, but they were kindred spirits in this new world. Gordon looked forward to having Derek be a part of his group once they escaped this hell they were in.

Derek stopped just outside the doors and took a deep breath. The pain in his shoulder was immense. All he had to do was make it another four hundred feet to the hangar. He knew they weren't out of the woods, but they were closer.

"Hey, thank you so much for helping me get my son. I can never thank you enough," Gordon said.

"Well, you can thank me with a drink when we get outta here. Let's go," Derek said, grimacing from the pain.

He pushed the doors open, exposing the bright light from the outside.

The loud crack of several gunshots rang out.

Gordon saw the bullets rip through Derek's torso.

Derek fell to his knees; he tried to shoot the pistol, but it was more of an involuntary reaction than a deliberate action.

Gordon stepped back from the door. He slouched down, still holding Hunter.

Hunter tightened his grip on Gordon's neck. His whimpering grew louder.

"Sshh, it will be okay," Gordon softly said, but doubt filled his mind.

The double doors closed, leaving Derek out front.

Gordon saw his shadow cast on the doors.

More shots cracked. Two of the bullets went through the glass doors and hit the far wall of the lobby.

Gordon stood and looked at the doors; he saw Derek's shadow disappear as he fell down.

"Hunter, hold on as tight as you can."

Gordon started to run back toward the elevator. He remembered seeing another exit. He turned the corner, jumped over the dead guard near the elevator, and stopped just outside the exit door.

The main doors burst open, and voices echoed down the hallway.

Gordon placed Hunter on his feet and said, "Honey, I can't carry you. When I open the door, come out behind me. I'm going to be shooting and running. Just follow behind me. If something happens to me, you keep running, okay? Don't stop, just run and run."

"No, Daddy, I'm scared."

"I know you are, but I need you to be that big man I know you are. Here, take this. Shoot anyone who comes near you," Gordon said, giving Hunter the pistol.

Hunter perked up a bit and wiped the tears from his cheeks and eyes.

Gordon kissed him on the forehead and said, "I love you." He then stood, kicked the door open, and ran out.

Outside unknown military installation

Nelson observed the guards shooting random people and gathering others up. The Army's feeble attempt to secure the base had been a total failure. Nelson still could not explain why so few troops were utilized.

"So who are those people down there?" Nelson asked.

"Some religious guy named Rahab and his fucking wacko followers," Lexi answered with disdain. Looking bored, she kept picking up small rocks and throwing them.

"How did you come to be captured?" Samantha asked.

"My sister and I ran out of gas out on the 15. Next thing we know a truck shows up, these fuckers jump out and take us. That simple."

"So what happens down there?" Samantha asked.

"What doesn't? Rape, murder, you name it. It's horrific. They murdered my baby sister," Lexi said loudly as she threw a rock.

Samantha could feel her eyes tear up.

"So you never heard of a man named Gordon or a boy named Hunter?"

"Listen, I told you no! They kept us, they kept the women separate. We would see the men but never interacted with them."

Nelson kept scanning, hoping to see something glaring that would help him identify Gordon or Hunter.

More gunfire sounds came from the base.

Moments later Nelson saw a man and child run out of the back of a building. He only caught a glimpse because a large hangar stood in the way. He waited to see them pop out the other side, but they didn't.

More gunfire erupted, then silence.

Nelson was straining his eyes to see. *Was that Gordon and Hunter?* he asked himself. He kept waiting for them to reappear on the other side of the hangar, but nothing. It was like they just vanished. He contemplated telling Samantha, but he hadn't gotten a good look. Not wanting to give her false hope or now, with their disappearance, a sense that something bad had happened to them, he kept quiet.

Samantha looked at her watch, then the sun, as it was already on its slow march toward the horizon.

"Let's get you back to our camp and get you cleaned up," she said to Lexi.

"Sam, I'll stay here till the sun sets," Nelson said.

"No, you need to come with us."

"Please, let me stay. One of us needs to be watching this place. This place. I don't know. This place might be where they are. I need to study it to figure out how we can find out if they're in there."

"Okay, we'll leave Mack's car," Samantha said, reaching over and rubbing his arm.

He looked at her and smiled.

"Come on, Lexi, let's go meet the crew."

Cheyenne Mountain, Colorado

Julia was happy to be back in her room with her things. The only thing she couldn't stand was how boring it was. She had always kept herself busy before. Being locked underground for weeks now was starting to wear on her.

As she paced her room, she thought of some of the activities and groups she could form. She imagined there were so many other women who could use support. She had the influence and needed to have a purpose.

All over her residence were signs of Brad. His clothes still had his smell. On the counter was a pen he'd used to take notes the last time he was there. It hadn't been moved since he placed it there.

She walked into the bedroom and saw on the chest of drawers a comb he'd used. She picked it up and looked at it carefully. Some of his fine black hairs were stuck in the teeth. She put it back down. Next to it was a pile of loose change he'd had in his pocket from when they arrived at Cheyenne Mountain. It still sat there where he'd laid it. The last person to touch those pennies, dimes, and quarters was him.

The same questions popped into her head: *Where are you? Why can't we find you?* Cruz and Baxter had kept the special ops teams out in the field looking for him. Every day they would report—*Nothing found.* She knew they couldn't keep up the search forever; eventually she too would have to say good-bye to him.

She started to feel emotional for the hundredth time. As the sadness filled her up, she sat on the bed. Even sitting up took effort, so she fell back and lay there. She then thought about how much they had reconnected just before he left. She hadn't had those schoolgirl feelings for him since college. Attempting to be positive and mature, she thanked God that if Brad was never coming back she at least had those final moments with him.

"Argh!" she said out loud. She sat up and again blurted out, "Argh!" Her feelings were like a seesaw. One minute there was hope, the next despair. "Pull yourself together, Julia."

Sitting on the edge of the bed, she began to fidget with her wedding band. She twirled it round and round her finger.

Then like a lightbulb going off, she had an idea. She walked out of the room to an internal phone. She picked up the handset and dialed the four-digit number to Cruz's room.

It rang and rang but no answer. She hung up. She picked up the handset again and dialed a different number. A voice suddenly answered.

"Hi, this is Julia Conner. I need to speak with Andrew Cruz; sorry, I need to speak with the vice president. It's urgent."

• • •

"Mr. Vice President, I have the first lady on the phone, line two," the lieutenant said to Cruz, who was meeting with his secretary of state.

"Tell her I'll call her back," he answered, not looking up from a stack of papers before him.

"Sir, she says it's urgent."

Cruz looked at Wilbur and rolled his eyes. "Do you mind?"

"Go ahead, I'll take the break to go get something to drink. I'll be back in five."

"Thanks," Cruz said, then picked up the receiver and touched the line 2 button. "Hi, Julia?"

Cruz relaxed in his chair and listened to her explain how they could help identify one of those bodies found in that abandoned house. She knew there was a chance that Brad's ring would be gone, but if it hadn't been removed it could be an identifying factor. She explained that it would help all if they knew for sure that was his body. While she acknowledged that it would be hard, she needed to know.

Cruz agreed and told her he would order the teams back to that location ASAP. He hung up and dialed Baxter.

He explained to the general everything she had told him. With this new information, they had a chance to move past the unknown. Cruz didn't want the shadow of Conner over him anymore. He missed his friend, but if this could provide closure, then so be it.

Inside unknown military installation

The bucket of water tossed in Gordon's face woke him up. He shook his head and spat out the tainted water that had gone into his mouth. His vision was blurry and his head hurt. Being knocked out is an odd experience. It's similar to a deep sleep. All he remembered was he and Hunter were running away from the main building. When he heard Hunter scream, he turned and saw that he had fallen and one of Rahab's men was on top of him. Gordon remembered shooting the man, but others came at him from the hangar. He remembered being tackled to the ground, and the last thing he saw was his son screaming and reaching for him. Then the darkness came when Gordon was hit over the head. He looked at his arms and legs; he was bound on the cross. They had him tied to the cleansing cross.

"Fuck," he said to himself, feeling defeated.

Looking around, he didn't see anyone. They had placed him on the cross that faced toward the south foothills. The base was behind him. He heard people talking and some commotion, but he couldn't tell what was happening. The heat of the sun beat down on him. He cursed to himself that he was so close. He'd almost made it. Now, he would die.

"Gordon." The voice of Rahab was behind him.

"Rahab? Where's Hunter? Where's my boy?"

Gordon heard the sound of Rahab's shoes on the gravel. He moved his head back and forth to see from which side his nemesis would come.

"Rahab? Where's Hunter?"

Rahab was still silent except for the sounds of his footsteps.

In the distance Gordon could hear more footsteps. They were loud and accompanied by the sound of something being dragged. Fear gripped him as he thought of Hunter. *Are they dragging his poor, fragile little body?*

Soon Gordon knew; two men brought Derek around and placed him against the cross.

"Derek. You're alive?"

Not a word fell from his mouth. Derek was alive but barely. Blood covered his entire body.

Gordon looked at his friend. His chest had three more wounds, from which the blood poured freely.

His limp body just hung. He didn't have an ounce of strength to hold himself up.

An additional person had to support his body so they could tie him to the cross.

Once they'd affixed him to the X, Rahab came into view.

He walked in front of Derek and looked; then he turned his attention to Gordon.

"Gordon, I had a sense about you, but I fought this urge. You have committed a crime against God's messenger, and today you will pay a dear price. But before, I will send your friend here to hell. He will burn in the fiery depths with Lucifer himself."

Gordon had witnessed only one of these executions, but this was different. When Rahab had killed before, he had looked at it as a way to send people to God. This was not what was about to happen to Derek.

"Derek? Derek? Thank you. If you can hear me, thank you!" Gordon shouted.

Derek's head moved slightly.

Seeing that was enough for Gordon; he felt that Derek had heard him.

Rahab faced Derek, removed his large knife, and plunged it into Derek's chest.

Derek let out a slight groan, but that was it.

Not satisfied with knifing him, Rahab then cut off his head. He turned to Gordon and said, "This is what happens to those who defy God. You see, Gordon!" He held Derek's severed head in his face.

"Fuck you! You're a fucking coward! Show me that you're God's instrument and fight me. Come on. If you have God on your side, you can't lose!" Gordon screamed, disgusted by the evil man who stood before him. Gordon didn't care what he said. He knew there was nothing he could do now; he was dead.

Rahab tossed Derek's head and ordered his men over. "Take this man's body and dispose of it. Toss it where we empty the latrines," Rahab said with a grin.

"Come on, big man. Cut me down and fight me. Show your followers you are God's instrument! Come on! If God is on your side he won't let you die!" Gordon taunted.

"Brother Rahab!" a man said from behind Gordon.

"Come," Rahab ordered.

The man walked up to Rahab and whispered, "The cars are

assembled. We have taken care of the others. We can leave when you wish."

"Very good, my brother. Oh, bring the boy," Rahab said, touching the man on his shoulder.

Gordon knew who they were talking about.

Soon he heard more footsteps behind him. He could tell one was lighter and smaller. Shortly he saw that it was Hunter.

"Hunter! Hunter! Are you okay?" Gordon called out.

"Tie him to the cross," Rahab ordered.

"Don't do this! He's just a boy. Don't do this, Rahab! Rahab! He is a boy, he had nothing to do with this!"

Rahab watched as they tied Hunter to the cross. After the boy was secure, he turned and walked up to Gordon.

"Gordon. You made one big mistake when you thought you could challenge me. You are a man of this earth and you follow earthly rules and laws. You see, I'm a man rooted in the spirit, not this world. I have different rules, and those are of our messiah."

"Rahab, he's a boy. He has done nothing! Don't do this!" Gordon said, then turned his attention to Hunter, desperately trying to reassure his son. "Son, you'll be okay. He's just trying to scare you. Nothing will happen to you."

Hunter didn't answer him. He just looked at Gordon with youthful and brilliant blue eyes.

"You killed many of my men today, but now you ask me to forgive or forget that?" Rahab challenged. "Your boy here is of this world too, like you. His body might be young, but his soul is no different from yours. Were you aware that of all the men you killed one was my son?"

"He was going to kill Hunter. I had no choice!"

"Yes, you did. You could have submitted to our rule and followed us, but you made a choice. There are consequences for our actions. You made a choice many years ago to be the man you are. No one forced you to be that way. Something brought you to where you are now. God placed you in my hands to cleanse you. You are a sinner, Gordon, and today you will pay a dear price for your actions. Today you will know the pain that comes from making a decision that is the wrong one," Rahab said, then turned. He pulled out his long knife and stepped toward Hunter.

"No, no, no! Please don't! Stop! No, don't! Please, God no! No, no!" Gordon was screaming. Spit spewed from his mouth as he continued to beg Rahab. "Hunter, I love you! I'm sorry. I'm so sorry I failed you!"

As Rahab stepped to within a foot of Hunter, the boy spoke. "Daddy, I'm scared!"

"Close your eyes!" Gordon cried out.

"Daddy, I love you. You never failed me, because you loved me!"

"No, God! Please, don't do this!" Gordon cried louder. Tears were bursting from his eyes. Thick saliva was building in his throat as nausea washed over him. "Rahab, stop! Please!"

Rahab now stood directly in front of Hunter. He raised the knife high above his head.

"No, no, no!" Gordon continued to cry out. Tears kept pouring forth. He looked at Hunter. He could see his son's beautiful face, his deep blue eyes and light brown, wispy hair. Quick flashes of his little face when he was born came to Gordon's mind. He remembered the first time he saw those blue eyes. How they looked at him with all the trust in the world.

"No, please, God, no!"

Rahab paused for a second, then committed himself and drove the knife deep into Hunter's chest.

Hunter screamed out for a few seconds, then fell silent.

"God no! No, not my baby boy! No! You fucking monster! You're a fucking monster! Aaaw, noooo, my baby boy. Nooooo!" Gordon was sobbing intensely. He was in a state of shock as he looked at his son, the large knife sticking out of his chest. The deep, dark blood rushed from Hunter's chest and ran down his small body. Gordon screamed.

Rahab pulled the knife free and turned toward Gordon. "You killed my son today, so I killed yours. This was not a spiritual rule, this was an earthly rule. Now you have paid the price!" He took a step closer and stood only a foot away from Gordon.

Gordon couldn't stop looking at his son's lifeless body.

Rahab moved so that he blocked Hunter's body from Gordon's view and said again, "You have paid the price. Now you will live with this," Rahab said as he took the knife and sliced Gordon's right cheek open. "Every time you look in a mirror you will remember this day."

The deep cut bled heavily. The tears from his sobbing were mixing with the blood as they both ran down his face.

"Good-bye, Gordon Van Zandt!"

Outside unknown military installation

The image of the man and boy running kept plaguing Nelson. He was determined to find a better spot to view, but he had to figure out how to do so without being seen. To avoid silhouetting himself, he pulled back and headed toward the car. He would navigate along the backside of the mountain, down toward the road, and cut across the open desert that connected the western range and the southern range. He was hoping the southern mountains would give him a better view.

"Damn it," he yelled out in pain as he twisted his ankle.

Sitting down on a large rock, he rubbed his ankle. The terrain was covered with small rocks lying atop loose soil. He calculated that it would take him a bit over an hour to get to the south mountains. Determining his ankle was fine, he pressed on.

Gunfire coming from the base over the mountains stopped him in his tracks. Screams were mixed in the rattle of the gunshots, but then all fell silent. Nelson started to run as best he could. Seconds later, he heard a few more shots. Then silence again.

Halfway through his migration to the south mountains, Nelson expressed to himself regret for being so cautious. He wished he had just taken the chance and gone down to recon the base near the berm. The conflicting internal dialogue consumed him. He thought of Samantha and Haley. If they couldn't find Gordon and something happened to him, that would leave both of them alone. While Nelson trusted Eric, he'd promised Gordon he'd watch over them. To put his regret at ease, he ran harder.

His timing was close; an hour and half later he reached a safe hide position in the south mountains from which to observe.

The base was alive with activity. He saw cars and other vehicles lining up near the main buildings. People were moving back and forth.

A smaller group was gathered near two large X structures on the runway. Nelson found this curious.

Pulling out his binoculars, he took a look. What came into focus shocked him.

On the X that faced him he saw Gordon. His face hung low, and blood covered the entire front of his body.

"Shit!" Nelson cried out. All he could think was that Gordon was dead.

More noise came from the base as the convoy started up and began a slow procession out.

Nelson frantically scanned the base from top to bottom, left to right. He saw no one; it appeared empty.

Once the last vehicle had cleared the gate, Nelson stood up and began his trek down the mountain.

He felt like his heart was going to burst. He ran as hard as he could. He kept his eye on the base for movement, but it now seemed like a ghost town. Clearing the berm with ease, he was almost to Gordon. With each step he took he was hoping he'd see Gordon lift his head, but nothing happened. His body hung strapped to the large wood beams.

Nelson was running so fast and he was so focused on Gordon that he didn't see Hunter on the other cross.

"Gordon? Gordon?" he cried out as he reached his friend. Grabbing his face, he lifted his head.

Gordon moaned a bit and opened his eyes. He peered at Nelson through slits because he didn't have the strength to open his eyes fully.

"Oh my God, you're alive. Shit, man, you had me scared there!" Nelson said, quickly examining his friend. Nelson took notice of the large cut on Gordon's face. "You hurt anywhere else?"

"Hunter," Gordon said above a whisper.

"What's that?"

"Hunterrrr," Gordon said louder.

"Hunter, yes. Where is he?" Nelson asked as he was cutting away the restraint on his friend's left arm.

Gordon pointed with his right hand, which was still bound to the cross.

Nelson saw him point and stopped what he was doing. He just stared at Gordon's right hand.

"Hunter," Gordon said again.

Nelson didn't want to turn around. He hesitated as long as possible; the fear of seeing Hunter dead was too much for him.

"Hunterrrr," Gordon said with a raised voice.

Knowing he couldn't wait any longer, Nelson turned around. His eyes widened when he saw the boy's obviously dead form hanging from the cross. Hunter's face and hands were a pale color. The volume of blood on and around his corpse told Nelson the death must have been horrible. "Oh fuck, no! No, God, no!" Nelson felt his throat tighten, and tears began to collect in his eyes. He walked over to the boy and placed his fingers against his throat to check for a pulse that he already knew wasn't there. Nelson ran his hand up to Hunter's cold face in a gentle motion. Placing his hand then on the boy's head, he leaned in and kissed the top of his head. Not wanting Hunter to remain this way, he took out his knife and cut him down.

Hunter's cold and stiffening body fell into Nelson's arms. With all the gentleness and grace he could muster, Nelson laid him on the ground softly.

"Nelson, cut me down," Gordon said, his voice hoarse from the yelling earlier.

Nelson jumped up and took his friend down.

Gordon too fell into Nelson's arms, but the weight was too much for Nelson to hold him. Gravity continued to play its part, and Gordon fell to his knees. With no desire or strength to try to get to his feet, Gordon crawled over to Hunter's body.

"Aaaaw, nooooo. My baby boy. Noooooo," he cried out.

Nelson just stood, feeling like he wasn't even in his body. Everything just felt so strange. All they had wanted was to find them.

If they had found them sooner, this might not have been Hunter's fate. Then the question came to him: *How would he tell Samantha?*

40 miles east of Barstow, California

"Mommy! You're back!" Haley squealed with excitement seeing Samantha step out of the truck.

Ignoring her daughter, Samantha asked Beth Holloway, "What's happened? Where is everybody?"

"They took off," Beth said flatly.

"What do you mean they took off?"

"She means just that," Eric said, walking up.

"Eric, what happened?"

"The Thompsons and Behrens pulled guns on us. They tied me up and hit Nelson's father over the head," Eric said.

"What did they take?" Samantha asked, concerned that they might have taken some of their stuff.

"They took what they said was theirs and just left. They didn't want to sit around anymore," Beth said.

"So where do they think they're going? Idaho? They're not welcome at our place," Samantha stated boldly. She picked up Haley and asked, "You okay, sweetie?"

Haley nodded and hugged Samantha.

"So no one was hurt but Nelson's father?"

"I'm fine. It'll take more than a hit to the ol' noggin to stop me," Frank joked, from behind Beth.

"Whatever, good riddance," Samantha said.

Lexi stepped up to the others and said, "Hi, I'm Lexi."

"Hi, Lexi," Beth said, holding her child. She looked over at Samantha quizzically.

"Lexi, this is Beth Holloway and this is Eric; his wife, Melissa; and Frank Williams, Nelson's father. You of course already met Seneca and Mack," Samantha said, introducing everyone still there. "Oh, and this is Haley."

The little girl waved shyly, then tucked her head back into Samantha's shoulder.

"Hi," Lexi said with a hand extended in the air. "Hi, Haley," she then said in a softer tone.

Haley reminded her of her little sister, the sister Rahab had killed a few days before.

"I don't want to bore you with the details of what happened to her, but this is our group," Samantha said, looking around, unsure of what else to talk about.

"Where can I get cleaned up?" Lexi asked.

"Come with me," Beth said.

Lexi walked with Beth toward their trailer.

"So how much stuff did we lose?" Samantha asked Eric.

"None of our stuff. They took only their stuff and left. I don't know why they thought they had to hit Frank and tie me up."

"Like I said, good riddance, but I better not see them in Idaho," Samantha shot back. She then looked at her watch. The night would be upon them soon. She was concerned for Nelson but felt confident he'd be careful.

"Where's my son?" Frank asked.

"He stayed back to see if he could find out more about that place," Samantha answered.

"Will he be okay?"

"He insisted," Samantha said. Now that Frank was worried, she started to feel that leaving Nelson there might not have been the best thing to do.

Both turned and looked toward the north as if they just might see him pulling up.

"You're right. He'll be okay," Frank said.

Trying to reassure herself, Samantha said, "Yeah, he's probably just heading back now."

"Hopefully, he'll have some more info on that place."

"Yeah, I hope so, I really do," Samantha answered.

Haley had fallen asleep, and her warm breath on Samantha's neck contrasted with the cool breeze blowing in from the north.

JANUARY 16, 2014

• • •

None love the messenger who brings bad news.

—Sophocles

Cheyenne Mountain, Colorado

Cruz was becoming accustomed to the early morning banging on his door. While he appreciated that they didn't call because they didn't want to wake his family, banging on his door was no less disturbing, he thought.

Wiping the sleep from his eyes, he opened the door to see Baxter.

"General, we really have to stop meeting like this," Cruz said groggily as he leaned against the open door.

"They found the ring and . . . ," Baxter said firmly.

"Shit, okay. Umm, what time is it?" Cruz asked, interrupting him.

"Zero four-thirty-four, sir."

"I don't want to wake her. Let's plan on . . ."

"Sir, she already knows."

"Huh? How?" Cruz asked, standing straight up.

"She's been near the command post most of the night. As soon as the team came in, she went directly down to them . . ."

"I get the picture. How is she?"

"They told me she was blunt and seemed almost emotionless about it. She thanked them then left. No one's seen her since then."

"When was that?" Cruz asked; he was concerned for Julia.

"Not more than fifteen minutes ago."

"Did she ID the ring?"

"Yes, sir, she looked at it. Asked a few questions, then left."

"Let's go see her. I want to make sure she's okay," Cruz said, grabbing his keys and closing the door.

"You're not going to change?" Baxter asked, looking down at Cruz's striped pajamas.

Cruz shrugged off his question.

Both men proceeded with haste to Julia's room. On the way they discussed how they would address the situation.

Baxter said flatly, "We need to get you sworn in immediately."

"That can wait. But I do need to find a new VP."

"Don't look at me, sir," Baxter said, gazing at him from the corner of his eye.

"You have nothing to worry about, General. I have someone else in mind."

"Who would that be?"

"No one you'd know, but sort of a former colleague of mine when I was governor of Florida."

"And?"

"Governor Sheila Morgan. I worked closely with her on the Governors Association and she used to be the governor of Texas. If I can get her, she would prove to be important in our negotiations with the Texas Republic."

"Should I try to contact her today?"

"No need, I already did. She's thinking about it," Cruz said while cracking a smile. He was proud that he was thinking ahead. "I know you're probably thinking, What was I doing calling her before we received any conclusive info on the president? Well, if I'm leaving tomorrow, I better have something in place. It's all about COG, right?"

"What does she need to think about?" Baxter asked, curious as to why someone would turn down such an honor.

"She's been asked to serve in a similar capacity in Texas. She's obviously torn."

"Can I be candid?"

They had reached Julia's door and stopped.

Cruz looked at Baxter and answered, "Sure."

"Besides moving up the date for your departure, you haven't made any plans or decisions in relation to what happened yesterday."

"You said there wasn't anything we could do," Cruz responded, taken aback by Baxter's accusatory tone.

"It was good to start thinking about your replacement, but you need to have third and fourth people in place. You also need to make a decision about what we plan on doing with the millions of refugees entering the midwestern states."

"General, I'll ask you. What would you do?"

"Sir, that's not my call. You're the one in charge."

Cruz was getting pissed by this unexpected confrontation. "After we're done here, let's meet," he said. "This isn't the place to have this conversation."

"Yes, sir."

Cruz took a moment to study Baxter's face. Then, as he was getting ready to knock, Julia's door opened.

She stood there looking unfazed by the recent news about her husband. "Gentlemen, come in," she said.

The men took a quick glance at each other and then entered.

"Please sit down." Julia pointed to the sofa. The same sofa where she had learned of Brad's disappearance.

Cruz and Baxter sat down, both looking sheepish because Julia was definitely in control.

"I know why you're here. I'm okay. I needed this closure. I can now plan my life knowing he's gone," she said, looking down quickly to fight back any emotion. Regaining her composure, she continued. "Andrew, you have been Brad's friend for a long time. I know how this works. Take the oath and do what you need to do. Don't worry about me. Go to Portland. Lead this country out of this."

"Are you sure you're okay?" Cruz asked.

"Yes, now go. I overheard your conversation outside my door. Go, sit down with the general and get your differences worked out."

Cruz looked at Baxter.

Julia was confident and acting as if nothing had happened.

"Please call me if you need anything," Cruz said, then stood.

Baxter followed his lead. Keeping quiet seemed like the thing to do. There wasn't anything he could add.

"Thank you for coming down," Julia said. "I'll be fine. If I don't see you before you leave, be safe." She walked over and hugged Cruz.

Cruz embraced her and whispered, "I'm so sorry, Julia."

"No, it's okay. Thank you," she replied softly.

"Take care, Julia. I hope I'll see you in Portland soon."

"I will. Thank you again for everything. Now, you be safe out there, okay?"

Baxter opened the door for Cruz. Both men left and walked toward the briefing room, not saying a word about the odd meeting with the first lady.

Julia closed the door and locked it behind them. She went into the bedroom and lay back down. Beside her on the bed were a shirt and jacket of Brad's. She brought them to her nose and breathed in deeply. Holding the breath, she hugged the shirt and rolled onto her side. She looked at the prescription bottle on the nightstand. Tears formed in her eyes and dripped onto the bedspread. Reaching out, she grabbed the bottle and opened it.

Salem, Oregon

Barone loved his Marines. They were adaptive and courageous. But today they made him happy with the hot coffee. He stood overlooking the large courtyard where his men had had a confrontation with some civilians the day before. The early morning sun's rays were just penetrating through the thick clouds, illuminating the congealed pools of blood left on the concrete sidewalks. He was also pleased by the way his plan was coming together. He had ordered his XO to begin training civilians in Coos Bay. The local leadership was more than helpful in supporting their needs, and to reward them for their loyalty and obedience, Barone started to give more and more responsibility to them. He knew they'd eventually find out about his mutiny, but if he had made them dependent enough on him, they'd have no choice but to deepen their relationship.

Governor Pelsom had proven to be very helpful. With the threat of his own people suffering any consequences for not supporting Barone locally with information, Pelsom answered every question the colonel asked.

The Salem population had created some problems, but the Marines had been able to quell the one riot that had formed outside the Capitol.

Not one to play games, Barone gave a single warning to the group of two-hundred-plus civilians. He first offered them positions within his army. Some took advantage of this offer; the majority didn't. When they refused to comply, Barone had his Marines shoot the leaders. The clash was bloody but lasted only a few minutes before the rebellious civilians dispersed, leaderless.

Barone didn't want to have clashes; he actually hated having to be harsh. The reality was that he didn't have the resources to help these people. He was willing to incorporate them into his new army and give them jobs, but he wasn't about to feed millions. There wasn't enough food. It saddened him to watch those people, many hungry and desperate. He could have been one of them. He didn't blame them for not having the tools and food to keep themselves alive, but at the same time he didn't have sympathy for them. For too many years local or regional incidents had given warnings that something could happen. Most people, he thought, just lived in a state of denial, thinking it would never happen to them and that their government would protect them. It was true that their government had plans to help, but not on this magnitude. This was why he did what he did. When he heard that it had been a super-EMP and that D.C. had been nuked, he knew it was over. He had been in the military long enough to know that the government's only strategy for such an event was government continuity. Hunker down and come out after the bloodletting.

Those people who had rioted today were innocent, but they

were also culpable in their demise. To trust their government was their first mistake; to trust him was their second.

Barone was proud of his Marines and his civilian allies in Coos Bay. Soon he'd have a much larger army to deal with what the United States was about to throw at him.

One thing he now thought he needed was a rallying cry. Survival was one element to motivate people, but if they knew they were fighting for a greater cause, then he could recruit a dedicated army.

He knew the day was coming when he'd have to face his new civilian friends and tell them that the United States was gone and was not coming back. He needed to make the national government the bad guy and himself the savior, these people's liberator.

He didn't know how to do that just yet. One thing he did know was that he had the upper hand against the United States because he knew their moves. What he needed next was leverage.

Putting out his cigar on the railing, the colonel walked back into the Capitol. He proceeded to the room where the governor was being held.

Not wanting Pelsom to coordinate any escape, Barone kept him sequestered from his staff.

Pelsom looked disheveled. His hair was greasy and unkempt. His face had grown a thick stubble. The dark circles under his eyes indicated sleep deprivation.

Barone had been making sure he was being provided food, but Pelsom wasn't eating.

Opening the door, Barone found the governor sitting on the edge of the cot with his head in his hands.

"Senator! How are you today?" Barone asked. He kept hearkening back to their congressional days so that Pelsom was constantly reminded of the clash they'd had.

Pelsom didn't look up.

Barone grabbed a chair in the small room and sat down.

"Senator, I'm here to see if you have anything else you'd like to tell me before I let you go."

Pelsom lifted his head and looked at the colonel. "You're going to let me go?"

"Senator, I don't need you anymore. The president is coming to bless us with his arrival early, so we will need to depart. You've given me everything but . . ."

"You're letting me go?" Pelsom repeated and looked at him strangely.

Barone leaned in closer. "Is there anything else you'd like to tell me? Anything at all?"

"I've told you everything; I'm not withholding anything. I promise," Pelsom said, his eyes begging Barone.

Barone returned the governor's stare, but his gaze was to see if he was lying.

"So you have told me everything you want to tell me? There is nothing else you'd like to say before I say good-bye to you?"

"Aaah, no. I've been very open. You know everything."

Barone stood, grabbed his chair by the top, and moved it back to the spot he had found it.

"Corporal!" Barone yelled.

The door opened and two Marines came in.

"Take the senator to the main entrance. Hold him there. Then go get his staff and the entire legislature. I want them all there. I'll be with you shortly."

The two Marines walked in and grabbed Pelsom, whose face showed his uncertainty and anxiety about what would happen next.

Barone watched from a distance as his captives were assembled. He found a mirror and looked at himself. He straightened his cover and ensured his uniform looked good. Once he was ready he marched over to Pelsom, who stood at the top of the marble stairs that led into the rotunda.

"Colonel Barone, what is this?" Pelsom demanded.

"Senator . . ."

"I'm the governor. I'm not a senator anymore!"

"Senator Pelsom, I asked you one simple question and you didn't answer it. You could say I'm being petty, but weren't you being petty years ago?" Barone said loudly.

All in attendance were staring in amazement at the spectacle they were witnessing.

"I have been forthright with you. I've given you everything! What do you want?" Pelsom screamed. He could sense that his life was in the balance.

"A fucking apology! Something! You know what you did years ago to that young Marine in my command. He was doing his job when he shot that terrorist in the mosque. But what did you and your political allies do? You persecuted him. You had your friends in the media drag him through the mud. Then, when that wasn't enough, you came after me because I was his commanding officer!"

"We were conducting an investigation! We were doing our job!" Pelsom fired back.

"So what the fuck is your job? What was your job then? You didn't like the war, so you found a useful incident to politicize it.

I don't know where that Marine is today, but he left the Corps after that. Then you set your sights on me. You wanted to make political points. Have you ever been in combat? No! But you can judge those who have been from your comfortable and protected world. Well, Senator, that protection is gone! The rough men who stood ready and gave you your cushy life are here now asking for a fucking apology!" Barone screamed.

"I represented a constituency that was against that war. I did my job!" Pelsom responded with equal vigor.

Barone looked at everyone and yelled, "We loved this country, but you took it all for granted. Now it's gone. Even in its collapse you expect us to protect you while you look down on us. Well, the sheepdogs are tired of being kicked."

"Colonel Barone, if you want an apology—"

"Shut up!" Barone yelled, then pulled out his pistol. The rage built in him. His speech had brought out years of repressed anger.

Many in the group gasped upon seeing Barone brandish the pistol.

"Colonel Barone, I'm sorry. We must now come together as a country. We can't look to the injustices of the past. I made a mistake back then. I'm sorry, I was wrong," Pelsom begged.

"Senator, now realizing your life is truly near its end, you beg like a bitch. You don't even have the fortitude to stand by your beliefs. You are pathetic, and your kind is not welcome in this new frontier," Barone said as he walked up to the governor and placed the pistol against his head.

"Please, Colonel, I'm so sorry. I was wrong then. It was all political. We just wanted to embarrass the president. We didn't mean to harm you. I swear. I'm so sorry, I'm so sorry."

"Fucking typical politician. You're pathetic," Barone said, then squeezed the trigger.

40 miles east of Barstow, California

"Do you know how to handle that?" Samantha asked Eric, who stood behind the .50-caliber.

"You bet. I'm good," Eric answered, rubbing his hand across the feed tray cover, almost caressing it.

"Frank! Let's go!" Samantha yelled.

Frank was saying good-bye to his wife, Gretchen. Shaken by Nelson not having returned, she feared for her son's life.

The group had waited until first light to search for Nelson. Not wanting to walk into an ambush in the darkness, they chose to wait.

They knew he must have been taken by those people. Lexi had been very open about her experiences with Rahab's group.

Insisting on helping out, Lexi had armed herself with two pistols holstered in shoulder harnesses and was carrying a Ruger Mini-14 rifle. She hadn't ever been around guns before, but she insisted on taking the rifle, so Mack quickly explained how to use it. He was impressed with her eagerness to go into the fight. He also didn't mind looking at her.

Samantha was going and taking Frank, Lexi, and Eric. Mack, Seneca, Melissa, and Beth would stay behind with the kids. Samantha was ready to face the people in the base and to see if Gordon and Hunter were there.

They started the jeep and Nelson's truck and were pulling away when to the north they spotted a dust trail coming toward them.

Frank called out, "It's Mack's car! It's Nelson!"

Samantha felt like a weight had been removed from her shoulders. She turned off the truck and got out.

The little Gremlin was traveling at high speed; the dust trail followed it for a hundred yards, drifting slowly in the air.

"Thank God he's okay," Frank said.

Nelson pulled the small Gremlin beside the jeep and got out of the car.

He had a blank expression on his face.

"What happened? Where were you?" Samantha asked as she walked up to him and touched his shoulder.

Nelson didn't answer. He looked around the much smaller group but didn't ask about the others. He then turned and faced Samantha.

"Nelson, what's wrong?" she asked, seeing how strangely he was acting.

Not saying anything to her, he looked at each person in the group.

All had their eyes locked on him.

"Son, what is it?" Frank asked, walking up to Nelson.

"Sam," Nelson said, now looking at her again.

The uneasy way Nelson was conducting himself finally sank in for her. The pit of her stomach tightened, and she knew he was about to disclose something horrible.

"Sam, I, uh, I found them."

"Where are they? What do you mean?" Samantha asked, her voice trembling. She turned and looked in the car.

She placed her hand on her mouth when she saw what looked like a body wrapped in sheets in the backseat.

"Oh no. No. Please. No," she said quietly and almost unintelligibly.

Nelson stepped forward and embraced her.

"No. No. Who is that?" she asked.

"Sam, let's go sit down and I'll explain."

Pushing him away angrily, she yelled, "Who is that, Nelson?"

Choking back tears, he answered, "It's Hunter."

"Noooo! Oh my God, noooo!" she cried out as her legs failed her. Her breathing became labored as her cries ebbed and flowed.

Nelson didn't know what to do. He, like the others, just stood and watched her grief.

She reached over and opened the car door. Fumbling with the seat adjustment, she screamed again, "Nooo!" She brought the front seat forward and crawled into the car.

Her cries paralyzed the group. No one knew what to do.

She cradled Hunter's body in her lap and unwrapped the top of the sheets to expose his face. Her tears splashed onto his cold, pale face. She gently wiped the tears away and petted his head.

The group watched Samantha hug, talk to, and kiss Hunter.

This went on for an uncomfortably long time, until Haley's sweet voice shattered the paralysis.

"Momma? Where are you, Momma?"

Samantha snapped out of her state and hastily crawled out of the car and closed the door.

"Here, honey. Mommy's over here," she said, wiping her cheeks. But not having wiped her hands off, she inadvertently smeared Hunter's blood on her face.

Haley ran up but stopped just short of hugging Samantha. "Mommy, what's on your face?"

Samantha quickly wiped, but her wet hands only made it worse.

"Mommy, is that blood?"

Beth Holloway ran over to Haley and directed her away from Samantha.

Samantha didn't know how to talk to her daughter right now. She looked at her reflection in the window and wiped the blood off her face.

Nelson walked up and said, "Samantha, it's about Gordon."

She stopped wiping her face and braced herself against the car.

Nelson handed her a dirty, crumpled white envelope.

"What's this?" she said, lifting herself up.

"Gordon gave it to me."

"What?" she asked, snatching it out of his hands.

"He's not coming back, he . . ."

"What do you mean, he's not coming back?" she asked, looking at the envelope, then put her attention on Nelson. "He gives you an envelope? That's it?" she asked, again looking at the envelope.

"He told me to tell you to go. Go to Idaho. He will catch up with us there."

"I don't understand. What do you mean? Why? Why is he not coming back?" Concern was quickly replaced by anger. She took the crumpled envelope and shoved it in her pocket. "What could he possibly be doing that's more important than being here taking care of his family?"

"He's going to go find the man who killed Hunter."

Salton Sea, California

Sebastian waved good-bye to the bulk of Bishop Sorenson's group. He and his group had driven with them as far as they could. Their route took them along smaller highways and through small towns.

All had agreed, the more they could stay away from heavily populated areas, the better.

Sebastian and his small band of survivors would head north now and eventually get on Interstate 15. They'd take it directly into Sandy, Utah. He estimated that driving with only stops to refuel, they could be there in twenty-four hours.

Sebastian was an optimist but also a realist, so he had communicated with Annaliese's uncle. They would link up near St. George. From there they would follow him to the compound.

As the last glimmer from the last car died over the horizon, Sebastian felt loneliness grip him. Yes, he had eight others with him, but not being part of the larger group made him feel more vulnerable.

He walked back to his car and sat on the hood. Ahead of them was the expansive Salton Sea.

"It's beautiful," Luke said, walking up next to him.

"It reeks. What the fuck!" Brandon followed up.

"I swear you two are yin and yang," Sebastian said, pointing at each boy.

"Sebastian, we should go," Annaliese said. She walked up to him and put one arm around his shoulder.

"One sec, I'm taking in this view. I don't know why this is mesmerizing me. Heck, I've never seen it up close. I always remember flying over it. Plus, my old man told me about a trip he had out here years ago. It reminded me of him."

"You haven't mentioned your parents before. Where are they?" she asked, looking at him closely.

Sebastian just kept gazing out across the flat sea.

"They're dead."

"I'm sorry," she quickly said as she tightened her embrace.

"Nothing to be sorry about; it happened years ago. My older brother, Gordon, kinda took on the job of being my parent and brother."

"Where do you think he is?"

"I don't know. Out there somewhere," he said, pointing north. "He's out there somewhere."

40 miles east of Barstow, California

"Hey, psst, Nelson?" Lexi was trying to get his attention.

Nelson was busy tying down gear on the top of the Gremlin. Talking was not something he wanted to do, especially to someone he didn't know.

"Nelson, you got a minute?" she asked.

"What? What do you want?" he snapped back.

"Chill out."

"Hey, my best friend's son is dead and he just up and took off on me, on us!"

"I'm sorry, but this is not the last death you're going to experience. I lost my sister recently. That's why I want to ask you a couple of questions."

Nelson stopped what he was doing and looked at her scornfully. Catching movement over her shoulder, he then saw Samantha sitting in the open desert next to Hunter's grave.

The group had buried him over an hour ago. Once they finished with the ceremony, everyone had begun preparations for the continued trip to Idaho. All of them had heard what Gordon was doing, but no one said anything about it. After Hunter's death, no one dared bring up Gordon.

Samantha sat next to her son's grave singing old nursery rhymes and songs while the desert winds kicked up dirt and whipped her hair.

Refocusing on Lexi, Nelson asked, "What do you want?"

"You're a dick, you know that," she shot back.

"Are you going to ask me what you want or not?"

"Your friend, Gordon. Did I hear correctly, is he going after Rahab?"

"I don't know who Rahab is, but if he's the guy who murdered Hunter, then, yes. He's going after him."

"Do you know where Rahab and his people went?"

"All I know is I saw them head north. Beyond that, I have no idea."

"Anything else?"

"Why? What does it matter?" Nelson asked, now curious about her questions.

"Because."

"Because, what?"

"I want to hunt that fucker down and kill him too!" Lexi said with a determined look on her face.

"You do whatever you want. You can stay or you can go. But don't think you're taking any of our shit. Do you understand me?"

Laughing, Lexi walked away from Nelson.

He watched her as she left. He didn't know her, but there was something alluring about her.

Shaking his head to clear the inappropriate thoughts he was having about her, he went back to packing. If they could get on the road in an hour, they'd have a good three or four hours of drive time.

So much had happened in the eleven days they'd been camped out there. Their group was now broken. His best friend's son was murdered, and that best friend had abandoned them in search of vengeance. Ahead of them were still days and days of rough, dangerous road.

He was now the leader of this group and, more important, the guardian of Haley while Samantha dealt with her grief.

JANUARY 17, 2014

• • •

A person often meets his destiny on the road
he took to avoid it.

—Jean de La Fontaine

West of Tijuana, Mexico

Pablo coughed out some of the thick dust that was floating in
the cab of his SUV. For him it was important that his father got
the best perspective on what their future looked like.

Today was the day he'd be able to prove to his father that he
now was the true leader of the Juarez family. Years of planning
would finally be revealed, and he hoped his father would respect
him for it.

"The view of the ocean from where we're going is superb. You
can see for miles up and down the coast!" Pablo said excitedly.

Alfredo sat unresponsive in the backseat. His gaze out the side
window hadn't changed since they'd left the compound over an
hour ago.

Finally Pablo gave up trying to talk to his father. "Forget it," he
said. "You're just a grumpy old man."

He turned back around and watched the road as it changed
from highway to surface street to isolated paved road to remote
dirt road.

Pablo's takeover of the cartel had gone very smoothly. The last remnants of his father's old guard had been swept away in what many were calling the Night of the Bambino.

"Right there!" Pablo pointed to a spot high on the hill. "Park right there."

The large Yukon came to a stop near the crest of the hill.

"Okay, Father. Let's go," Pablo said.

Pablo, Alfredo, and two guards got out of the SUV. Pablo led them the final distance to the crest of the large hill.

When Pablo reached the top, he threw his arms in the air and shouted, "Aha, they're here!" He spun and took a few steps to bring his father all the way to the top.

At first Alfredo resisted his touch, but he gave in when Pablo grabbed him forcefully.

"Come on, Pops! Aha, should I call you that from now on? It's a gringo term. Would you like it better if I referred to you as that instead of the old stuffy *Father* bit?"

Alfredo still remained silent.

Dragging him the last distance to the top, Pablo said, "There! Feast your eyes! That there is one piece of my puzzle to conquer parts of the United States and Mexico."

"Mexico?" Alfredo now spoke.

"Yes, I couldn't be completely honest about what I was up to. You see, the new dawn happened the day those beautiful bombs blew up there," Pablo said, pointing up in the air. "The sun has been rising in our favor since then, until I saw that my small, amateur army wouldn't be able to complete the task. You know something, Father? You bringing me back here was the break I needed. I was able to clear my head and see what I had to do."

"My son, do you really think you can be successful?"

Shooting him a hurt look, Pablo answered, "Yes, I do, Father. Everything is going the way I wanted it to; there were just a few corrections needed. Some fine-tuning. Today marks another step toward my new empire." Pablo finished, then spread his arms out in front of his father.

"I never thought I'd say this, but you're crazy."

"People who didn't have the depth of understanding said the same thing about all the great leaders. From Alexander to Caesar and Napoleon; now me, Pablo Juarez."

Alfredo shook his head. Disappointment was etched along every deep wrinkle on his face.

"Father, I brought you out here so that you could see with your own eyes. Today is the first day of my new empire," Pablo said and again held out his arms. "Tomorrow, along with the Villistas, my guerrilla army, we will begin the invasion of the United States!"

Lifting his weary head, Alfredo looked over his son's outstretched arms. What he saw did amaze him. In his entire life he had never seen an armada as large. Stretching for over two miles, naval warships numbering in the dozens were sailing up the coast. As his gaze followed them toward the Friendship Park along the U.S.-Mexican border, some ships were off-loading hundreds of ground troops.

"Father, I present to you the army of the Pan-American Empire!" Pablo declared.

Portland, Oregon

Cruz looked with awe through the small window of the plane at the skyline of the city. Decay had already begun to take hold of the area. Abandoned cars had riddled every road and highway he saw on his approach to the airport. Now on the ground, he could see the decay in closer detail. Weeds were already growing out of cracks in the runway. Garbage lay discarded. Luggage sat on conveyor belts just outside planes, not touched for weeks. Some of the windows of the main terminal were smashed. Reports from his advance team were that most of the damage was cosmetic. Still, it would take a long time to get all electrical equipment back online.

So much to do, he thought.

The door to the command center opened, and Bethanny Wilbur stepped in.

"Mr. Vice President. Sorry. Mr. President."

"It's all right. What is it? You have that look," Cruz said, swiveling away from the window to face Wilbur, who stood there holding a piece of paper.

She walked over and fell into a chair.

"Really, more bad news?" Cruz asked.

"Your pick for VP has declined. She's staying in Texas," Wilbur said, tossing the sheet of paper on the table.

"Shit. Well, back to square one."

"When I talked to her, she told me it's really no better there than here. They are dealing with starvation, murder, and rioting en masse. These are her words, mind you, but she said *large herds* of people were coming into Texas from the East."

"Large herds, huh? Well, that's not surprising. People thought that since they went independent they must be surviving okay, when all along this breaking away from us was more bravado politics than anything else."

"Maybe so, but it doesn't look like we'll get much from them since they're knee-deep in it. Have you thought about the former governor of Alaska?"

"Yes, I have. I need someone who's willing to work hard. He just seems, I don't know, lazy. I mean, he's a good guy. I just don't know if he'd be a good part of our team."

"The only reason I mention him is that he was a successful governor, popular. We could use Alaska's support. I think they'll come on board, but if one of their own were in the administration, then that would kinda marry them to us."

"Ha, we sound like some medieval chancellor whose job it is to find the appropriate bride for the king."

"We sorta are now. The days of politics are gone; it's about getting things accomplished."

"I wish things were that easy; politics is such a pervasive thing. It would find a way to penetrate and pollute anything. That's why it's important to find the right match," Cruz stated. He swung his chair around, stood, and began to stretch.

"Where the hell is the advance team to take us to the secure location?" he asked, bending down and looking at the window.

As if fate had heard him, a small parade of Humvees appeared from around one of the Jetways at the end of the taxiway.

"Good, finally," Cruz said. He began to gather his belongings and pack them up.

The Humvees pulled up next to the plane. Moments later gunshots ring out.

"Get down!" Cruz yelled as he ducked under the table, his preferred hiding spot for instances such as these.

The sound of gunfire moved like a snake from outside to inside.

Loud voices and yelling reverberated off the thin interior walls of the plane and made their way to just outside his door.

Wilbur pulled out a pistol and held it to defend herself. She had taken up a position behind a chair.

A loud banging on the door was followed by a gruff voice. "President Conner, come on out. We won't hurt you."

Cruz looked puzzled.

Wilbur shot the door several times.

Cruz jumped, not expecting her gunfire, and covered his ears with anticipation of more shooting.

Wilbur was terrified. She held the pistol straight out with her shaking arm.

Nothing happened after her shooting. Then voices began to talk. But it was too difficult to understand them.

Cruz didn't know what to do. It was a mistake for Wilbur to think that she could defend them. Whoever had come in those Humvees had men and arms, enough to take out his security team.

"Wilbur, put it down," he ordered.

"What? No, sir," she replied defiantly.

"Wilbur, we can't win this!" he yelled at her.

Just then automatic gunfire ripped through the door. Papers, pieces of wood, plastic, metal all were flying through the air as the bullets tore in, hitting the table, chairs, and cabinets in the small room.

Cruz flinched again and ducked his head.

Wilbur fell to the floor and held her hands over her head. Her desire to resist now gone, she dropped the gun.

The gunfire stopped as quickly as it had started, and a voice filled the empty air. "President Conner, we're coming in. Don't shoot. We don't wish to harm you."

"Then stop shooting!" Cruz yelled back.

A moment passed before the door was kicked open.

Cruz saw three men in camouflage uniforms enter and take up

positions on either side of the table. One walked over to Wilbur, kicked the gun away from her, and commanded her to stay put.

"I'm coming out!" Cruz said as he began to crawl out from under the table.

He heard someone else enter the room as he was getting up. He looked and saw a tall, burly man wearing a desert camouflage uniform.

"You're not Conner?" the man said.

"No. He's dead. I'm President Cruz, his replacement."

The man looked at Cruz with his head cocked in curiosity, then said, "President Cruz, I'm Colonel Barone. Welcome to the Pacific States of America. You're now my prisoner."

Cheyenne Mountain, Colorado

"General Baxter, we have a situation," a tech sergeant reported.

"What do you have, Sergeant?" he asked.

"Here," the tech sergeant, said, then pointed to the main screen. He had been monitoring the outside perimeter cameras when something caught his attention.

"Looks like we have visitors. Nothing new," Baxter replied, shrugging off the people on camera.

At least once a week since the attacks, people would gather at the base entrance. Baxter and his team would ignore them, and eventually they'd leave.

"No, sir, look here," the tech sergeant said, zooming in the camera on a tall bald man holding a sign that read, OPEN UP OR WE KILL HIM.

"Okay, so what?" Baxter asked. He looked at the video feed, and all he saw was a man holding a sign above a hooded person.

"Just that we've never had this happen. It's strange."

"Sergeant, everything is strange now. Get used to it."

Baxter returned his attention to the logbook and walked off.

Moments later the tech sergeant yelled out, "General Baxter, look!"

Startled, Baxter turned, and what he saw on the screen shocked him. "Send a tac team topside with me ASAP!"

• • •

Baxter followed closely behind his six-man tactical team as they stepped beyond the large blast doors of Cheyenne Mountain.

The bright sun and brilliant blue sky seemed more intense, since they had not seen the literal light of day for weeks.

His tactical team members spread out and waited at the ready.

Baxter walked past them and stopped a few feet short of the bald man.

"We want to make a deal," the bald man said with a deep baritone voice. "This man for food, water, and a vehicle."

"I don't know who you are, but we don't make deals with people like you. Now, just hand over our man and we will let you go without any trouble," the general replied.

"Hmm. You don't seem to know who we have here. This isn't one of your soldiers who you keep sending in on a regular basis." The bald man chuckled. "Why don't I have him tell you himself who he is?" The man ripped off the hood.

Baxter's eyes widened, and the blood drained out of his face when he saw who was kneeling just feet away from him.

The bald man roughly tore off the duct tape that sealed the man's mouth shut. He then smacked him in the back of the head and said, "Tell him."

The man squinted and blinked rapidly, trying to adjust his eyes to the bright sunlight. He looked around at everyone in front of him, focused his attention on Baxter, and said, "General, I'm Brad Conner, the President of the United States. Please do whatever this man says."

East of Austin, Nevada

Nelson was tired after a long drive. They had covered more than four hundred miles since yesterday. He was happy, but he wouldn't feel secure until they reached Idaho.

He wondered what was in the envelope Gordon had had him give to Samantha. He assumed it was a letter, but what did it say? What could it possibly say to ease her mind? He just didn't understand his friend. He knew the loss of Hunter was weighing heavy on both of them, but Samantha didn't quit.

She hadn't left her trailer since they departed yesterday.

Haley was the only proof of life to have come from the trailer when they had stopped during the long drive.

Nelson knew time healed all things, but how long would it take for Samantha to heal from this?

He would never forget the look in Gordon's eyes as he told him what he was doing. Different scenarios ran through his mind now that it had all passed. Each one resulted in the same outcome.

Samantha hadn't asked him further questions about Gordon since he gave her the news. He was afraid that one day he'd have to answer those questions. But until then he would save those moments. That last night with Gordon was between him and his old friend, wherever he was now.

The tap on his truck window startled him. He sat up and tried to see who it was, but the darkness outside made it impossible.

"Yeah," he called out.

"It's Lexi, you awake?"

Exhaling deeply, he opened his truck door.

"What's up?"

"Do you have a minute?"

Remembering how short he'd been with her the day before, he decided he wouldn't be now. "Sure. You want to sit in here?"

"If you don't mind; it's chilly out," she said and stepped inside the truck, closing the door behind her.

Nelson took out his lighter and lit a small candle he had in a tin can on the dash. The soft light illuminated both of them.

"So what's—" he tried to ask before she interrupted him.

Lexi looked at the tin can and the orange glow that emanated from it. Next to it sat the key she'd seen him use yesterday to unlock the supply trailer.

Making a mental note, she said, "Hey, I never really got a chance to thank you. I now realize how bitchy I was. You guys have helped me a lot, and I can never repay you for that."

"Of course. No worries."

"That's why I think I owe it to ya'll to tell you." She paused for a moment, then continued. "To tell you that I'm gonna take off in the morning."

"What? Where? Why would you do that?" Nelson asked. He was truly concerned for her.

"You don't know me. The thing is, I have something to do."

"What could you possibly have to do?" he asked as he watched her nervously scratching her arms.

"Where you found me wasn't just a labor camp; it was more like a concentration camp. The man who ran it is a cruel, sadistic fuck. He murdered my sister in cold blood. My baby sister, who did nothing wrong but fight back after refusing to be raped for the hundredth time by them. They beat her, took her out to a cross, and stabbed her in the heart. He's a sick fuck, and I'm going to hunt him down. I'm gonna kill him."

"I'm sorry for your loss, but how are you going to find him, and even if you do, how will you kill him? This all sounds like suicide. Look, you have a chance with us. A new chance at life in Idaho."

"Really?"

"Yes, really."

"No, really? Do you think you can hide from these types of people? They're probably everywhere now, feeding off the anarchy. If you think you'll go to Idaho and live this peaceful life with unicorns and rainbows, you're kidding yourself." Lexi paused to catch her breath. "I may not survive this whole thing, but I will kill as many of those types as I can along my way."

"I see you've thought about this."

"Before all of this craziness, I was just a young, stupid girl who was living in a small apartment. I worked as a human resources assistant. Spent my weekends partying with my friends and just not caring about much. My sister, Carey, had come out to see me when all of this shit happened."

"Just give it a day or so before you leave."

"No. I thought I owed it to you to let you know. I also wanted to ask you something. I know it's a lot, but, hey, you don't get what you don't ask for."

"And what's that?"

"Can I take a pack, food, water, and a couple of guns?"

"Is there anything you forgot on that à la carte menu?" he asked sarcastically, accompanied by the old Nelson grin.

Lexi looked at him, then turned away when she saw he was grinning. "So that's a yes?"

"I think we can do that, but on one condition."

"And that is?" she asked, cracking a slight grin herself.

Nelson sensed she was flirting with him now.

The candlelight cast wavering shadows over her effervescent, champagne-brown eyes and olive-toned skin.

"You have to wait until we get to Idaho. I want you to see where we're going. Then if Idaho doesn't offer you the hope we think it will, you can take what you want."

Lexi sat unresponsive for a minute, then answered him. "Deal." She leaned over and gave him a full kiss on the lips.

"Aaah, I wasn't expecting that," he said, then continued. "Good. I'm glad you agree. Umm, tell me more about . . . you."

"I'm sorry, but I'm pooped. Thanks for talking and for our deal," she said, quickly opening the door and shutting it behind her. She walked away grinning ear to ear.

"You're slick, girl. Let's go shopping," she said out loud as she tossed the key that had been on the dash in the air and caught it.

Nelson was in shock at how fast she had split. He laughed to himself and blew out the candle, not noticing that the key was missing. He turned and lay down on the truck's bench seat. He replayed their conversation in his mind.

Lexi had a point: What if there wasn't a safe place to call home? What if there wasn't a sanctuary from this cruel new world?

JANUARY 18, 2014

• • •

It is a most mortifying reflection for a man to consider what he has done, compared to what he might have done.

—Samuel Johnson

Ridgecrest, California

Gordon's entire body hurt. From his feet to the throbbing wound on his face, he ached. Only his will to find Rahab and avenge his son kept him going .

He was walking through the desert, parallel to the highway. Being alone, he felt it safer to keep his distance from the roads.

He saw the small community as he cleared a low rise. He wasn't exactly sure where he was, but from the map he'd found at Rahab's camp, he was assuming he was in Rivercrest.

Walking into a neighborhood was not what he wanted to do, so he squatted and took off his pack.

In one of the side pockets was a bottle of water. Grabbing it, he took a long drink. His aching legs finally convinced him it was time to sit down.

So many thoughts were flashing before him. Hunter for the most part consumed him. He had to fight the visions of his son's death. The one thing that distracted him was focusing on finding Rahab.

He opened the pack and pulled out a large piece of paper. When he unfolded it, a map of Oregon and Washington State appeared. There was some writing scratched in the right column—*Rajneeshpuram.* He had no idea what that meant. Maybe it was a place, maybe it was a person.

After Nelson had left him, two days ago, he had spent the entire day tearing the base apart, looking for any clues about where they might have gone. In Rahab's quarters he'd found this map among scattered papers on the floor. It was all he had going for him.

His plan was to track Rahab down, kill him, then carry on to Idaho. The one thing he needed was a car, but that would not be easy to come by.

Thoughts of Samantha and Haley came into his mind. He was so conflicted about his mission, but he had to avenge Hunter. He had to make sure no one else suffered at the hands of this butcher.

Rahab had been right: He would look in the mirror and see the scar, but the wound only reminded him of his need to kill Rahab.

A scream from the community over the rise made him look up from the map. He quickly folded it and put it back in his pack.

He grabbed the binoculars that Nelson had left with him and low-crawled to the crest of the hill.

Another scream echoed out.

It was hard to see through the thick creosote plants and fencing around the houses.

The screams were those of a woman.

Now a child's scream was added.

He kept looking, but he could not tell where it was coming from; he saw no movement at all.

Again more screams.

Gordon's first instinct was not to get involved. *Don't deviate from the plan,* he told himself.

Again the screams erupted; now they weren't just screams but calls for help.

"Just stay put, this isn't your business," he told himself out loud.

He kept scanning the houses as best he could, but he saw nothing.

The cries for help now sounded different. At first they had sounded muffled, like the people were inside; now he could tell they were outside.

The child screamed out, "Mommyyyyy!"

"Goddamn it!" he bellowed. Gordon rolled over, tucked the binoculars away, put on the pack, and grabbed the AR-15 rifle that Nelson had given him. He stood up and began to run toward where he heard the screaming.

He got to the fence that bordered the community in about a minute. Fortunately, part of the fence was down. He made his way through and ran up to the side of the first house.

All the homes in this neighborhood were single-level ranch-style houses. Many looked similar on the outside but for the colors of the stucco siding and the composite roofs.

The house he was next to was at the end of a cul-de-sac. He walked toward the front to get a view of what or who he was dealing with.

Reaching the corner, he peered around and saw about five men but no woman or child.

The screams and cries had stopped. He wasn't sure why.

Again he thought, *Gordon, just leave, there's too many of them.*

The screams he had heard from the child were what had prompted him to get this far. He imagined the child shaking in fear, crying, scared.

"Fuck it, let's get some," he said to himself as he headed back toward the rear of the house. He wanted to move down the back-yards until he got to the home the men were standing in front of.

He cleared the rear corner and headed quickly, rifle at the ready, to the second home. He stopped briefly and listened.

Nothing.

As he walked he made sure to look inside each home. No one, empty.

He was about to move toward the third home when around the corner came a woman and a boy of about five. Her protective at-titude told Gordon he was her son.

The woman was about to scream when Gordon grabbed her and covered her mouth. "Sshhh. I'm not here to hurt you."

She struggled to break free.

Gordon grabbed her tighter and repeated, "Please, be quiet. I won't hurt you. I'm here to help. I heard you screaming, so I came to help."

Her resistance ebbed as she heard the other men coming closer. They were inside the third house, and the sounds of them crashing furniture confirmed that they were looking for her and her son.

"If you want me to help you and your son, stop."

She finally stopped struggling and went limp.

Her son looked terrified and had a white-knuckle grip on her hand.

"I'm going to uncover your mouth. Screaming would be stupid.

There's no one but me here to help. Tell me how many men there are," he whispered into her ear.

"I don't know, maybe six or seven."

"Okay. What we're going to do is walk back that way," he whispered, nodding toward the first house he'd come to. "From there we'll make for the desert."

She acknowledged his command with a slight nod.

They all turned, but someone came up behind them and grabbed the boy.

Gordon reacted quickly by punching the man in the face, causing him to fall backward with the boy in his grip. Gordon pulled Nelson's sheath knife and jumped on top of the man, plunging the knife through his throat into his head.

The man coughed up thick, dark blood and died instantly.

Gordon pulled the knife and resheathed it without cleaning it off. He grabbed the boy and motioned for them to go.

They ran down to the first house and stopped near the corner. Gordon didn't want to just make a run for it without knowing if anyone was there.

He peered around the corner but saw no one; however, his ears picked up sounds near the front of the house they were using for cover.

"Damn, I think someone is there," he whispered.

The boy and woman clung to each other, both shaking.

"I wish we had a car; this on-foot stuff is bullshit."

"We have a car," the boy said quietly.

Gordon's eyes lit up. "You do? Does it work?"

The woman answered, "Yeah, that's what they first came for."

Excited by this news, Gordon said, "Our plans have changed. Do you know how to shoot a gun?" he asked the woman.

She shook her head no.

"It's easy. Just keep pulling the trigger at anyone trying to kill you," he said as he handed her a Glock 9mm. "Where's the car?"

"Our garage," the woman said as she stared at the pistol in her hand.

"Let's go," Gordon said, moving to a crouch position. "Stay right behind me. And whatever you do, don't shoot me," he said to her.

She gave no response. Her eyes were wide open with fear.

With his rifle back at the ready, they turned back toward where he had killed the man who'd grabbed the boy.

Sounds of breaking glass, voices, and more tossed furniture came from the second house.

"Stay here," Gordon commanded, then went to look inside. He saw one man walking through the house grumbling to himself.

Seeing only the one inside, he made his plan.

He entered the house through the unlocked back sliding door that opened to the kitchen. He slung his rifle and took his knife back out. Tiptoeing, he made it to the edge of the kitchen and hallway.

The man was walking back toward him from one of the bedrooms.

When the man cleared the corner, Gordon jumped him. He slit his throat and gently laid him on the floor.

Gordon walked in the direction the man had been going, the front of the house. The hallway opened up into a living room with a large bay window that looked out onto the edge of the cul-de-sac. From there, he had a view of most of the street and the three men out front.

With two dead and a guess of six or seven total, that left Gordon four or five.

He needed a way to draw them out, and he now thought he had the plan.

Making it back to the woman and the boy, he explained his idea.

She at first refused. But with a lot of pressure she agreed.

Gordon went back into the house and set up a sniper's position at the bay window.

"C'mon," he whispered loudly. He had the rifle firmly against his shoulder, but he kept peering out of the corner of his eye to see her.

Suddenly one of the men in front of the third home yelled out, "Her and the boy are here!"

The three men made their way toward her but stopped when she brandished the pistol.

"That's a girl," Gordon said to himself.

"Stop right there. I have the keys, but after I give them to you, you have to leave!"

"Hey, boss, she has the keys!" one of the men called out.

"Toss the keys to us now, bitch!" another man yelled at her.

"C'mon," Gordon said again. The situation was tense, but it escalated when one of the men drew his pistol and pointed it at her son.

"I'll kill your fucking boy, now toss me the keys!"

"C'mon!" Gordon said louder.

Like God had answered his prayer, two other men came onto the street with guns drawn. They were walking quickly toward the woman.

Gordon didn't know if this was all of them, but he couldn't wait any longer. He aimed and squeezed off the first round, hitting the first man with the gun in the head. The man instantly dropped to the ground. Gordon slightly turned and took another shot, hit;

another, hit. The last two men didn't know where the shots were coming from, but that didn't stop them from shooting in all directions.

Gordon took aim on the fourth man and shot him in the chest; the force of the round pushed him back, and he fell down dead. Gordon had taken aim on the last man when a shot rang out, this time from the woman.

She shot at the man, missed him at first, but kept shooting. The second and third rounds hit him squarely.

He turned to face her, but she kept pulling the trigger. Three more rounds burst forth from the pistol and hit him in the torso.

He dropped to his knees and fell facefirst into the pavement.

The woman stopped firing after he fell. Her son was standing behind her with his hands covering his face.

Gordon's ears were ringing after the shoot-out. He shook his head, thinking that would clear his ears, but like every time before, it didn't. He stood and left the house.

The woman looked at him, still standing in the exact spot from which she had fired.

Gordon walked over, took the pistol out of her hand, and said, "Good job, very good."

The boy came around to the front of his mother, and she held him close. His long, brown, curly hair was tucked into a black beanie.

Gordon looked at her; she was a young woman. He guessed she couldn't have been older than twenty-eight. Her copper hair was partially hanging out of a scrunchie that was holding the rest back. Dirt, grime, and dried tears were smeared across her freckled face.

"You two are all alone, right?" he asked.

"Yeah, my husband died a couple weeks ago. These guys had been his friends."

"I'll make you a deal. Let me borrow your car and I'll take you both with me to Idaho. I have a safe place to stay up there."

"Okay, but what's your name?"

"I'm Gordon, Gordon Van Zandt. Come on, let's go to Idaho."

OCTOBER 15, 2066

. . .

Olympia, Washington, Republic of Cascadia

"That's it? You're ending there. What happened?" John exclaimed. Her stories were so dramatic and intriguing he didn't want them to end.

Haley exhaled heavily, then said, "I'm tired, John. It's been a long day. Remembering and talking about all of these things takes a lot out of me. Let's resume tomorrow."

"But tomorrow is a holiday!" he barked out.

"So it is. Let's resume Monday, then," she said, standing up and walking toward the kitchen.

The other two men began to tear down the equipment and pack it away.

John wasn't satisfied with that answer, so he followed her into the kitchen.

Haley stood at the sink. A window gave her a view of a large green park. She was bracing herself against the counter. Physical and emotional fatigue were weighing her down.

"Haley, I'm sorry, but I can't wait to know. What happened? Did they make it to Idaho safely? You never mentioned what was in the letter from Gordon. What about Gordon—I'm sorry, your father? I've heard these stories before," John said desperately.

She again exhaled deeply and turned to face him. "John, these aren't stories like you read in a book. These things happened. People died. My brother died. So, please don't treat them like *stories*."

"I'm sorry, I meant no disrespect. I promise you. Please don't take what I said in any way—"

"They made it to Idaho safely, without my father. But when they arrived, well, let's just say that Lexi was right. First off, they couldn't reach McCall. The mountain roads were snowed in. With no equipment operational, there was no way to clear the roads. They were stuck in Eagle for the rest of the winter."

The two photographers walked past the kitchen, said their farewells, and left.

John was standing like a dog waiting for a treat.

"That's it? They were stuck? What happened?"

"I can talk about that on Monday. Okay?"

"Did that girl Lexi go to Idaho with your group?"

"No, she left," Haley said. She had moved away from the counter and was walking toward him.

"You never heard from her again?"

"No." Haley paused, then continued. "Technically, yes, but I can tell you about her later."

"What about your father?"

"Monday, John. That's it. No more. I'm tired, and we will reconvene on Monday," Haley said as she walked past him and opened the front door. Her eyes seemed weary, and her face looked almost gaunt.

"I'm sorry. So Monday it is. I'll be here at nine a.m. sharp," he said, walking through the open front door.

"Good, have a nice weekend," she said, closing the door and walking back toward the den.

She opened the small box on the shelf where the compass was and took it out. She reached back in and removed a yellowed, crumpled, and dirty envelope.

She walked to her lounge chair and sat down. The compass again soothed her troubled thoughts as she rubbed it. She stared at the envelope. It had been years since she'd read the paper inside, but today seemed like an appropriate day. She placed the compass down on the small table and opened the back flap. Inside was a thin piece of paper. It too was now yellowed and stained.

As she read the words on the page, tears fell. She grabbed a tissue from the box next to the compass and dabbed her eyes.

The letter contained so much love for her mother, but also pain, when she had read it.

All they were looking for as they traveled the long road was a safe place to call home. But that safe place, that sanctuary from the horrors of the world, would not be realized for some time. What was coming their way was something that none of them could ever imagine.

Don't miss the other books in the New World series by
G. Michael Hopf

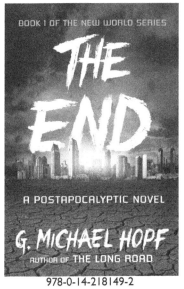

978-0-14-218149-2

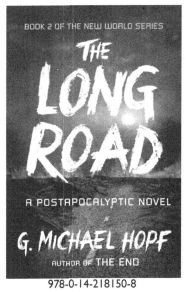

978-0-14-218150-8

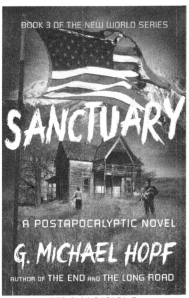

978-0-14-218151-5

Available wherever books are sold

www.gmichaelhopf.com

Printed in the United States
by Baker & Taylor Publisher Services